Trans Mission

Evan Baldock

SRL Publishing Ltd

SRL Publishing Ltd
London
www.srlpublishing.co.uk

First published worldwide by SRL Publishing in 2022

ISBN: 9781838279882

1 3 5 7 9 10 8 6 4 2

A CIP catalogue record for this book is available from the
British Library

SRL Publishing is a Climate Positive publisher, removing more
carbon emissions than it emits.

For Transgender people everywhere
who have suffered unfairly

ONE

November 1993

Standing 6'4" tall, strongly built, with an immaculately made-up face and wearing an electric blue flared trouser-suit, Petra attracted attention and admiring glances from several men as she stepped out of Our Pink Life, a nightclub in Old Compton Street, into the bracing November air.

She was arm-in-arm with a tall, strikingly handsome man she'd just met. His name was Robert, and he was blessed with an athletic physique, short, dark-brown hair, deep, emerald green eyes and a dazzling white smile. She thought he looked stunning in his torn jeans, blue and white striped shirt and light blue casual jacket.

The road was, as usual for Soho at 2.30 on a Saturday morning, heaving with hundreds of late-night revellers, some moving in time to *The Pet Shop Boys*, blaring out from the doorway of another club. The spectre of Aids still haunted the minds of the ignorant and the bigoted, turning them vehemently against gay and trans people whom they saw as perverted and dangerous to so-called normal people. But their prejudices had failed to prevent the gay community going out to enjoy themselves and there was nowhere they felt more at home, nowhere they felt more safe and secure, than in Soho, where they enjoyed the company of hundreds of like-minded souls.

Petra and her new friend turned left, intending to

make their way up Greek Street to Bateman Street, where Petra rented a basement studio flat. As they picked their way through the crowds, she felt waves of excitement and anticipation, the potential of enjoying a night of sex with this delicious man thrilled her. Like the rest, Petra felt at home on these streets, she felt alive; for once, her life was going well, and she intended to thoroughly enjoy it while it lasted. She threw back her head and sang along with the music.

Turning left into Greek Street, Petra spotted a man with buzz-cut light-brown hair and a designer beard making his way through the crowds towards them and her heart sank. He was smartly dressed, in sharply creased dark-blue trousers, light-blue shirt with no tie, shiny black shoes and an expensive looking three-quarter length navy-blue overcoat; he looked distinctly out of place on the Soho street. She was about to turn away and attempt to conceal her identity, when he looked directly at her and their eyes locked. It was Tony Waters, her supervisor at Duke's Garage, where she worked as a mechanic in Sevenoaks, Kent.

Tony knew Petra as Peter Hardy, a 21-year-old man who had been employed by the firm for just three months. It was his first job as a fully qualified mechanic, having successfully completed his apprenticeship with a different garage the previous July. Tony stopped in his tracks and stared at Petra in disbelief. He couldn't fully take in what he was seeing, then slowly but surely, a cruel smile swept across his face and he swerved to block their path, preventing Robert and Petra from walking any further. Tony wasn't a big man and the couple dwarfed him, but he looked up at Petra with a mixture of disgust and disbelief.

'Evening Pete, aren't you going to introduce me to your fella?'

Petra was horrified; she really didn't need this on a night out. She'd been tormented by people like Tony Waters her whole life but hadn't expected to encounter him in the very place where she felt safe, felt at home. Ignoring his request, she towered over him, glaring down at him with contempt.

Robert turned to face her. 'Who is this Petra? What's going on?'

Looking back at Robert, Petra remained stubbornly silent. She slowly shook her head then returned her gaze to Tony who had patently been drinking; his breath smelt of whisky and his words were slurred.

'Well fuck me, Petra is it? I'd worked out that you were a shirt-lifter Pete, but I'd never have guessed you were a tranny too!'

On hearing this, Robert released Petra's grip from his arm.

'Who is this, Petra? Look, I'm sorry darling, but I don't want any trouble, I'm going home.'

Petra held on to his arm.

'Please don't go Rob, he's just being a dick.'

Tony laughed and jabbed a finger into Robert's face.

'Tell you what mate, a dick's exactly what you'd have got once Pete got you home, right up your arse.'

Shaking his head in disgust, Robert yanked his arm from Petra's grasp, walked swiftly away through the crowds and was soon lost to her sight. She turned on Tony, a familiar anger burning through her, an anger she'd experienced again and again throughout her life; but until now she hadn't done anything about it.

Tony and the company boss, Des Thayer, had continually ribbed and bullied Peter at work from the day he arrived, calling him vile names like shit-stabber, cock-sucker, fudge packer. Peter had bitten his lip and taken the abuse for weeks, his hatred for them slowly building, to the point where he found himself imagining scenarios where he had them at his mercy, torturing them and making them suffer, just as he was suffering now. Years of pent up hurt and anger simmered just below the surface; he'd always managed to keep his feelings under control, but now he was like a volcano about to explode. Whenever he tried moving forward to the next section of his life, bigotry, hatred, and prejudice were following not far behind and right now, he'd had enough.

Glaring with fury, Petra said, 'Thanks for fucking up my night. Why do you hate me Tony, what have I ever done to you?'

Tony threw back his head and laughed. 'You've not done anything, doesn't mean I shouldn't take the piss though. We work together and that's fine... but you're a poof and I don't like poofs; I've just saved that poor fucker from a fate worse than death.'

'What do you mean?'

'You don't get it, do you? You're not normal, you're a fucking pervert. What you do, it's... disgusting!' He practically spat the words at her.

'Why am *I* disgusting? Because you don't like the way I look, or the way I choose to live my life? Sorry Tony, if you don't like it, that's tough.'

'I'll tell you why it's disgusting. How do you think he'd have felt once he discovered you're a bloke?'

Shrieking with laughter, Petra said, 'You really are a dinosaur, aren't you? For fuck's sake Tony, he likes men... he fancies men... he's gay! He knew exactly what he was getting himself into and you've just ruined a good shag for both of us.'

Tony looked momentarily confused, then shrugged, and pouted mockingly.

'Oh boo-hoo, I'm really upset.'

'It's not funny, you moron.'

4

Suddenly Tony's voice took on an angry edge.

'Serves you fucking right. You disgust me! I can't wait to tell the lads in the garage on Monday that I've seen you dressed like a tart, they'll make your life hell.'

A lifetime of abuse and mickey-taking had risen like scum to the surface; Petra was in danger of losing control right there and then. Ever since childhood, Peter Hardy had felt uncomfortable in his own body, sensing that inside his increasingly obvious masculine skin lived a girl, so on reaching adulthood Peter created a female alter-ego and gave her the name Petra, an alter-ego which nobody knew about where she lived in Kent.

But now Petra had been exposed; one of her work colleagues had seen her enjoying life as a woman, the cat was out of the bag, and was bound to cause her untold misery. She had to find a way to persuade Tony that, although she was transgender, she was a decent person, just living a different life to his. If she didn't manage to convince him, he could ruin her life yet again, just like so many others had before.

Her voice shook. 'Please don't tell anyone Tony, I'm begging you.'

'Fuck off! I'll be dining out on this for weeks. They'll love it at the club.'

'What club?'

He jabbed a finger in her face.

'A club that would never let in people like you.'

'Please… please don't tell anyone.'

Tony was a poseur and owned a 'Simon' mobile phone, something only very few people possessed. Pulling it from a coat pocket he said, 'I've got to tell the boys at work. It'll whet their appetite for Monday morning.'

Snatching Tony's phone before he could make the call, Petra pushed the sizeable object down the front of her dress. Her anger boiling over, she hissed, 'You're not telling anyone about me you nasty fucker.'

'Give me my fucking phone, Pete!' He reached towards her chest to retrieve it.

Grabbing his hand, she almost crushed it in her powerful grip, causing him to groan in pain, before easily pushing him away. Tony knew she was far stronger than he was.

'For fuck's sake Pete, don't be a twat!'

An idea was forming in Petra's head. She'd taken enough of this shit from the likes of Tony Waters and it was time to stand up for herself. She recalled that a leaflet had been pushed through the door of her flat from the local council; CCTV was being upgraded and would not be operating from midday on Friday until midday on Saturday in the streets between Old Compton Street and the top end of Soho Square, which almost certainly meant their meeting wasn't being recorded on the system. There was a chance that private cameras might catch glimpses of them, but that was a risk she had to take.

She stepped forward and looked down into Tony's eyes from only a couple of inches away.

'Just give me a few minutes to explain why I'm like I am, then I'll return your phone, I promise.'

'Don't be a prick Pete, I need to go home.' He sounded a lot less confident now and Petra shook her head.

'The first trains don't leave until after five, so you've got at least a couple of hours to fill before heading for Victoria.'

Indignation at having lost possession of his phone registered plainly on Tony's face.

'Look,' he said, 'I won't call anyone and I promise I'll listen to whatever you've got to say, just give me my fucking phone back.'

Petra was silent for a few moments, considering her options, then removed the phone from her cleavage, switching it off before handing it back. She glowered menacingly.

'Put it in your coat and leave it there. If you so much as touch it before you've let me explain things, I'll smash it.'

Tony was shaken by the naked aggression in her voice and slipped the phone into his coat pocket. Then, relieved that his precious mobile was safe, some of his cocky arrogance returned.

'You're not going to convince me that lady-boys are normal, but as you say, I've got a couple of hours to kill, so knock yourself out. This might even be amusing.'

Petra felt a mixture of revulsion for the pathetic little man standing in front of her, and relief that he seemed to be willing to fall in with her plan.

'Right, follow me.'

A troubled expression appeared on Tony's face.

'Hang on a minute. I'm not being seen out drinking with you, people will think I'm bent!'

Petra rolled her eyes and said, 'Stop worrying, I've got a studio flat just around the corner.'

'You've got what?'

'A studio flat. I'll make you a coffee. You smell like a brewery so you could probably do with something to sober you up. Don't worry, your precious heterosexual reputation is safe. We'll be well away from prying eyes.'

Tony looked astounded.

'How the fuck can a young knob jockey like you afford a flat in Soho?'

She ignored the insult, needing to keep her powder dry.

'I don't own it, I rent it.'

'It must cost a fortune.'

7

Petra shrugged.

'My gran left me some money in her will and I decided to spend it on renting a place where I spend most of my weekends. Come on, it's just around the corner.'

She could see he still had doubts but her loathing of him was almost choking her; she simply had to persuade him against speaking out.

'Oh for fuck's sake! Look, I'll walk on this side of the road, you walk on the other. We'll be yards apart with dozens of people and a line of vehicles between us. That okay?'

Pulling the collar of his coat around his neck against the cold, Tony nodded and followed Petra's lead, his head lowered to avoid anyone's gaze. Greek Street is one-way and a queue of vehicles were heading down towards Old Compton Street and Shaftesbury Avenue. Dozens of people were in the street, on the pavements, spilling onto the roadway and dodging between the cars. It was noisy, vibrant, alive; it was a multi-cultural, multi-racial and multi-sexual place; it was the place Petra loved.

They walked in parallel but yards apart on opposite sides of the street. She lost sight of him once through the crowds, but he reappeared, keeping his side of the bargain. Petra reached Bateman Street a few seconds before Tony, and waited outside the tattoo shop which sat above her flat.

Twenty seconds later she was leading him down a flight of black painted iron steps to her basement flat front door. She removed a key from her leopard-print handbag, inserted it into the lock and swung open the door. After reaching inside to turn the light on, she held out her arm, allowing Tony to enter first, before following him inside and closing the door softly behind her.

TWO

Tony quickly checked out the inside of the flat. There was a tiny, recessed kitchenette containing grey units with gold handles to the left wall; a king-sized bed with a pillar-box red duvet and pillows against the right wall; a small matching two-seater settee to the left of the kitchenette with a tiny, glass coffee table in front of it and a large flat-screened television attached to the wall directly above the settee. His eye was caught by a red velvet curtain at the far end of the room, which stretched from wall-to-wall and floor-to-ceiling.

'What's behind the curtain?'

'A shower room, a toilet, and my favourite part of the flat, but I'll show you all that in a minute.'

Moving to the kitchenette, she picked up the kettle and filled it with water.

'Fancy a tea or coffee? I know I do.'

Flopping down onto the settee, Tony shook his head.

'I can't believe this is happening. It's weird sitting here with you dressed as a tart. You're one of the lads at work for fuck's sake.'

'I still am one of the lads at work. We'll still be working together come Monday, nothing's changed.'

Tony sat forward with his hands together and his elbows resting on his thighs. Looking up at Petra he raised his eyebrows in disbelief at her words.

'I've always known you were a bit odd, but this shit is off the fucking scale.'

He looked up at the TV.

'What's the point of having a TV in the one place you can't see it from the settee?'

As the kettle began to heat up and gurgle into life, Petra laughed.

'I had it put there deliberately. I prefer watching telly in bed.'

'I bet you do,' said Tony. 'I think I'll have that coffee.'

'How do you like it?'

'Black, no sugar.'

The kettle boiled and Petra poured the drinks, adding a little cold water from the tap to cool them. She handed Tony his cup.

'You see? I'm making a work colleague a nice cup of coffee, an ordinary person, living a normal life, just like you.'

Sipping his drink, Tony leaned forward, looked up at Petra and grimaced.

'Sorry, Pete, this might seem normal to you, but a strapping great bloke dressing as a bird in his spare time and taking other blokes back to his flat for… for fuck knows what, is not normal.'

'It is around here. There were hundreds of others out there tonight just like me. That's why I like spending my weekends here.'

Shaking his head firmly, Tony fixed her with an icy stare.

'It's disgusting, it's perverted, and it should be illegal.'

He could see by the reaction on Petra's face that his words had hurt her. He shrugged.

'Sorry mate, but that's how I feel.'

Petra ran her finger around the rim of her coffee cup.

'You do know it's 1993, don't you, Tony? You understand that attitudes are changing?'

He snorted.

'My attitude's not changing and nor is the attitude of most blokes in this country. They support my point of view, not yours. People are pissed off with all this 'be kind to queers' bollocks. I'd have thought you'd learned a lesson when your chums started dying of Aids.'

Petra fought the urge to throw her drink over him and punch him in the face, simply sipping her coffee instead to calm herself.

'In a minute, I'll explain everything that's happened in my life and turned me into the person I am now.'

'Okay, fire away, I'm listening.'

"Before I do that, would you like to see what's behind the curtain? I can see you're curious.'

Tony cautiously sat up straight and nodded. Petra's air of confidence and almost teasing smile were slightly unnerving but curiosity got the better of him.

'Go on then.'

Grinning, Petra placed her cup down, moved over to the curtain and pulled it halfway across the room, revealing two full size doors and what looked like a cupboard door. One door led into the toilet, another into the shower, and Petra opened the cupboard door to reveal a small wardrobe. She smiled enigmatically at him.

'Now for the best bit, what do you think of this?'

With a theatrical gesture, she swept the curtain across the remainder of the room, revealing a mini-gym that was only about eight feet wide, complete with wall-bars, kettle-bells and free-weights resting on rails. There was also a parallel bar high up the wall close to the ceiling, jutting a foot out from the wall. This allowed her to carry out chin-ups and leg-raising exercises. Finally, a padded gym bench was bolted to the floor; it was about four feet long and ten inches wide, with foot straps on the floor either side of one end of the bench, set about eighteen inches apart.

Tony crossed his arms and sat back; it was the first time he'd seen a home gymnasium, but it certainly didn't impress him and he didn't understand why Pete was making such a performance of showing it. He laughed out loud to himself at the absurdity of it all. When he'd set out that evening for his Friday night at the club with his mates, he'd never imagined being in the situation he was in right now: sitting in the flat of a well-built man dressed in women's clothing, showing off his home gym.

'Why the big reveal? Am I supposed to be impressed?'

Taking one of the lighter free weights from its place, Petra made bicep curls as she replied.

'I thought you might think a little more of me if you knew how fit I kept myself, how hard I work at keeping strong and in shape. Yes, I enjoy dressing as a woman. Yes, I enjoy having sex with men. Yes, I enjoy a different lifestyle to most men, but I'm still a strong, fit bloke, and more importantly, I'm decent human being.'

'Decent?' Tony laughed. 'Don't bother trying to explain, Pete, it won't make me change my mind. People like you make me feel fucking sick.'

Still raising and lowering the free weight, Petra watched his every move like a predator eyeing up its prey. Her anger had reached boiling point but she would not be goaded into a reaction.

Tony stood up and placed his cup on the draining board.

'Thanks for the coffee, but I'm not staying here a minute longer.'

Taking a step towards Petra, his eyes betrayed his contempt. He pointed a finger at her face.

12

'I'll fucking destroy you at work on Monday. That'll be fun.'

Turning his back on her, he moved towards the front door.

It took just a couple of seconds for Petra to catch up with him and smash him around the back of his head with the free weight in her hand. With a groan, Tony fell face first onto the shiny wooden floor, between the coffee table and the bed. His vision was hazy and it took an immense effort to raise himself onto his hands and knees. Then he felt another crushing blow to the back of his head… and his world went black.

THREE

Tony had been thoroughly enjoying himself inside the Concord Rooms Nightclub in Rathbone Place, no more than 400 yards from where he was now lying unconscious. He went there every Friday night and had done so for the previous twelve months. As usual, he was with his three friends, Duncan, James, and Stan, his Friday night drinking pals. They would trawl various clubs, pubs, and bars in the West End, trying somewhere different each week, but always ended the night at their favourite venue, the Concord Rooms.

This night had been better than most, because the monthly meeting of their club was being held in an upstairs function room. They would normally not bother entering the Concord Rooms until around eleven, but the club's meeting started at nine, so unusually, they'd spent most of the night drinking there.

The club's full name was Keep Britain Straight (KBS for short) and its purpose, as they saw it, was to fight back against society's growing acceptance of people wishing to live alternative (or as they put it, perverted) lifestyles. Their venom was mostly targeted at those who were openly gay and those in the trans community, whom most of them blamed for the Aids epidemic which had swept Britain. All the members present at the meeting were prepared to stand up for the cause when required.

The numbers attending the meeting on this particular Friday night were slightly larger than normal, with around fifty in attendance rather than the usual thirty. At 9.30, Tony had been pleased to see that two of the new faces walking through the door and being stopped by security, were his boss from work, Des Thayer, and one of the mechanics, Andy Clark. Tony knew they both shared the group's views about gays and had told them many times about the club's meetings, urging them to attend. He made his way over and shook their hands, eager to welcome them into the KBS fold.

'Great to see you lads, it's been a long time coming! So, you've finally decided to take the plunge, eh?'

Des smiled. 'Wanted to see what all the fuss was about.'

'You'll love it, boss. A good drink, bit of grub, a natter with people who talk sense and later on there'll be a couple of guest speakers.'

Andy nodded and smiled. 'Sounds good.'

After vouching for them to security and signing them in, Tony pointed towards the bar.

'Come over here and meet the boys.'

Introductions were made and the group stayed together chatting, laughing, and drinking.

The first guest speaker was Heinricht Mitten, a member of a far-right minority party in Austria. His strong accent made understanding him tricky for most of the audience and although they politely tolerated him, most of them were glad when he finished, seeing him off with a half-hearted round of applause.

The second speaker was much better: Billy Stephens, an ex-army private who had been dismissed from the service because of his outspoken views on homosexuals in the armed forces. He was both charismatic and a good orator, berating the gay culture thriving in Soho and Brighton. He successfully whipped up his audience into what was approaching a frenzy of homophobia. His final rallying cry to "fight back and return Britain to the decent land it once was" gained him an enormous cheer and standing ovation.

'That was fucking brilliant,' said Andy.

'Couldn't agree more,' said Des, 'but if we don't get a move on, we're going to miss the last Sevenoaks train. See you on Monday, Tony, and thanks again for the intro!'

The remainder of the evening had been largely uneventful, but when the Concord Rooms closed at two, Tony wasn't ready to go home. Billy Stephens' rant had ignited the fire of hatred in him and this was further fuelled by several large whiskies. Why not take a stroll down Old Compton Street, the gay heart of Soho, and tell all the queers and queens down there exactly what he thought of them? He realised he was likely to receive abuse in return and that someone might even take a swing at him, but the drink had filled him with Dutch courage. He was determined to do his bit for the KBS cause, whatever the consequences.

His mates tried to talk him out of it, especially James, a Detective Sergeant at Sevenoaks Police Station. As such, he shouldn't really have been attending meetings held by KBS in the first place, but he shared Tony's loathing of gays and loved KBS meetings, loved being in the presence of like-minded people. He always wore a baseball cap and a pair of thick, black-rimmed glasses on their Friday nights out, ensuring he wouldn't be recognised on CCTV if anything were to kick off.

James knew there was a good chance Tony might get himself in trouble by shouting his mouth off in Soho and although he strongly believed in the group's aims, he loved his career as a police officer more and didn't want to be linked to anything involving direct action. However, despite all their best efforts, Tony's mind was made up.

He set off towards Soho fired up with hatred and with a spring in his slightly unsteady step.

He'd been walking down Greek Street ten minutes later, when he saw an unusually tall, strikingly dressed woman arm-in-arm with a man. He thought she looked strangely familiar, then, after a couple of seconds he was certain. He recognised her as his work colleague, Peter Hardy; someone he'd been certain was a poofter, and now it was confirmed. Not only was Peter heavily made-up and dressed outrageously as a tart, but he was with a man and it looked like they meant business! This was simply too good a chance to miss, so he crossed the road and confronted them.

FOUR

The man whose evening he was about to wreck had enjoyed a relatively happy early childhood, living in a standard family unit as the middle of three brothers. Peter Hardy's home life was no different to millions of other children growing up in similar families; there was nothing unusual about him. His father worked shifts as a fireman in London and his mother worked part-time in a bank.

But his early childhood happiness began to slowly dissolve. From the age of eight, for reasons he couldn't possibly comprehend at the time, he started to feel uncomfortable in his own skin. He would cry himself to sleep at night, unable to speak with anyone about his feelings and scared of the reaction he would receive from his parents, his brothers, his friends. Slowly but surely, he began to hate the fact he'd been born a boy.

In the school playground he spent most of his time playing with girls rather than boys. His classmates, pupils who were once his friends, started teasing him while others either ignored or shunned him. Then, the verbal abuse began to get physical; sometimes a group of boys would gang up on him, even though he was bigger than most of them, forming a circle around him and pushing him from person to person until their bullying was eventually broken up by a teacher.

A gentle and kind-hearted boy, he couldn't understand why his friends were being so nasty and he spent many sleepless nights crying into his pillow. Inside his young head, he was only doing what seemed natural, so why was everyone making such a fuss, why were they being so horrible?

Teachers began to notice this change in behaviour, and intervened in the playground games, pulling him away from the girls and encouraging him to play with boys. Over time, some of the teachers became more assertive in their approach, trying to shame him into conforming, into behaving like the rest of the boys. Sometimes they even made fun of him in front of his classmates, leaving Peter humiliated and wretched. It was cruel.

When a particularly spiteful teacher said to him, "If you want us to put you in a dress so you can play with the girls, then we will," something clicked in Peter's mind. There was something more going on inside his head, something more than just wanting to be with the girls and play with the girls; he wanted to dress like the girls, he wanted to look like a girl, he wanted to *be* a girl.

Life at home wasn't much easier. For as long as he could remember, Peter had been bought construction toys and football kits (which he could never see the point of, seeing as he never played the game). He coveted the *Fisher Price* kitchen he once saw in a toy shop but was quickly told that they were for girls. The only "boys' toys" he enjoyed playing with were cars; he wanted to know how they worked and got in trouble for trying to dismantle them in order to repair them.

Then it got worse. For his final three years at primary school, his parents, especially his father, gave up trying the subtle approach and began resorting to vicious comments and insults.

Why can't you be a normal child?

Why can't you be a proper boy like your brothers?

But the most hurtful one was something his father

said in front of a group of his friends.

You realise you're going to grow into a fairy, don't you?

That single comment caused days of bullying and he hated his father for it.

His brothers were just as verbally unpleasant as some of the boys at school, although they never resorted to physical bullying. Life was utterly miserable for a confused young boy and not being able to escape the abuse even in his own home, made life difficult, uncomfortable, and desperate.

Unsurprisingly, Peter failed his 11+ exam and his parents had to decide which school to send him to. In order to lessen his contact with girls, they placed him into an all-boys school on the outskirts of Sevenoaks, somewhere away from the lure of girls for the next five years, where they hoped he would be toughened up before reaching adulthood.

However, being removed from daily contact with girls in classrooms and the playground didn't change his feelings about wanting to be a girl. It did, however, make them much easier to control. In fact, his first couple of years at secondary school were reasonably pleasant; there were no issues with bullying and he made some good friends. For a while, life was tolerable.

Problems resurfaced when he reached puberty, suddenly he felt even more confused. Sexual attraction began rearing its head, with Peter finding himself fancying both boys and girls. He soon identified a couple of other boys in his year who were suffering the same confusion and made a point of befriending them. By the age of fifteen, he had started having relationships with both sexes and finally gave in to the urge to wear women's clothes, trying on his mother's underwear and dresses whenever he was alone in the house and even dipping into her make-up. He thrilled at the experience of seeing himself dressed as a female for the first time, loving the sensation of the soft fabrics on his skin, as he stared at himself in the bedroom mirror.

His unusual behaviour at school was soon spotted by his peers and it caused problems with many of his earlier friends who began to drift away; testosterone-filled teenage boys did not wish to be associated with 'poofs.' The most upsetting thing was when his best friend, Seb, slowly distanced himself from Peter as rumours about him spread, until one day Seb completely disowned him after discovering Peter kissing another boy.

Life became more and more miserable at school, with continual taunting, bullying, and abuse. Several times he received a bloody nose or a black eye. Peter felt a searing anger burn away inside him. He wanted to take revenge on the bullies, to badly hurt those who seemed to take so much pleasure in ridiculing him, but being violent just wasn't him; he hated the thought of it and had always shied away from violence and aggression. No, he would never act on those feelings.

After leaving school at sixteen, he got a job as an apprentice mechanic with a small village garage a few miles away. The relationship with his parents and brothers hadn't improved over the years and family life was becoming unbearable, so at the tender age of seventeen he moved out, renting a bedsit with a separate lock-up as part of the deal in the small town of Edenbridge. The rent wasn't cheap, using up two-thirds of his weekly take-home pay, so he made use of the lock-up and took on private vehicle repair work, which he carried out during evenings and weekends to help make ends meet.

He had found something he liked doing and attended college one day a week under the government's Youth Training Scheme as part of an apprenticeship. At college, he seemed to be accepted and had even begun to make tentative friendships. Unfortunately, life at the garage was going rapidly downhill. It was as if his work mates had a sixth sense which enabled them to tune in to his sexuality and soon the bullying started. The worst thing was that, if he called them out, complained or showed his feelings, it was met with, *Can't you take a joke? It's only a bit of banter*, just as it always was.

Eventually, the owner came to the decision that Peter's presence was having a severe impact on the efficiency of the working environment and sacked him. Peter was devastated, seeing his dismissal as punishment for simply being himself. It was a feeling he would become familiar with.

He decided he wouldn't make that mistake again and when he landed another apprenticeship with a garage in a larger town, he consciously altered his voice, his mannerisms, and stifled his natural character in order to blend in.

On evenings out with college friends, they tended to start the evening as one large group then separated into males and females later on. Peter would soon find the company of the male group grated on him; they were only interested in drinking heavily, acting tough, or talking about football and the girls they'd shagged, so he would usually drift over to the females. However, this behaviour soon created jealousy among the lads, some of whom had girlfriends in the group. Peter started to get involved in arguments and scuffles which eventually resulted in him having to stop attending college nights out. His sense of isolation deepened.

FIVE

Desperate to feel "normal" and longing to be accepted by others, Peter made a deliberate decision to try conforming to what society expected of him, in his social life as well as at work. He'd had no serious boyfriends or girlfriends since leaving school, but at the age of nineteen, he met Suzanna.

The first time a friend took him round to her flat, he was fascinated by her. She opened the door to them wearing black tracksuit bottoms, a loose grey tracksuit top and bare feet. Her long dark brown hair was tied up on her head and, what really impressed him, she was carrying a large club hammer in her left hand.

They followed her through to the bathroom, which had bricks and other rubble strewn over the floor. She simply walked over everything in her bare feet, apparently impervious to pain and continued knocking out a shower unit with the club hammer while talking to them.

Peter had never met anyone like her before; she looked like a woman, a beautiful woman, but conducted herself like a man, the perfect mix of male and female, something he'd never seen in a human being before. He quickly found himself falling in love with her, which he knew was ridiculous, but he was convinced his feelings were real. Luckily, Suzanna seemed to feel the same way and within a few weeks he'd moved in with her.

She was ten years older than him, but the age gap didn't seem to matter. She understood him like nobody had ever done before; they shared everything about themselves and had no secrets. She was fascinated about the feelings he'd experienced throughout his life and wasn't in the slightest bit concerned that he fancied both men and women; she simply accepted him for who he was.

Peter experienced two blissful years with Suzanna, until she developed M.E. and became seriously ill. During her illness, she became more reliant on other friends, opening up to some of them about Peter's sexuality. Many of them had been completely unaware of this and were so worried by her revelations and concerned about Suzanna, that they began the process of poisoning her against him, eventually succeeding in breaking their relationship apart.

After several difficult and often tearful conversations Suzanna moved out, leaving him once again totally alone in the world. He was distraught, broken hearted and for days even began to feel physically ill. Flu-like symptoms and blinding headaches kept him in bed, drained of energy and aching all over. He didn't know which way to turn.

Suzanna had been his confidante, his best friend and, he had believed, his saviour. She had been exactly what he'd been looking for in another human being, the perfect balance between male and female. She'd given him the love he'd so desperately needed and now she was gone. His love for her had suppressed all the turmoil in his head from the moment they'd met until the day she'd moved out, but now that she'd gone, his demons came raging back… worse than before.

Peter knew he had to distance himself from the area where they'd lived, the friends they'd shared and the places they'd go to for meals or nights out. In fact, removing himself from everything about his life with Suzanna would be the only way he could survive. He needed to run away, just like he'd always run away when life got difficult. His only option was to move back home with mum and dad temporarily: not a perfect solution, but at least it allowed him time to search for somewhere else to rent. Life wasn't likely to be comfortable at home, but he had no choice.

As if to compound his misery, he lost his job through no fault of his own, but this time he had completed his apprenticeship and received a great reference, enabling him to find employment at Duke's Garage in Sevenoaks. He didn't realise it at the time, but this would prove to be a pivotal moment in his life, because this was where he first met Tony Waters.

Peter still felt like a woman trapped inside a man's body. Although he liked women and preferred their company, he didn't generally find them sexually attractive; he mainly fancied men. On nights out with old college friends, he began to take an eclectic and dangerous mix of drugs to ease the pain and confusion inside his head. After all this time and all he'd been through, he still wanted to be one of the girls.

Feeling that there must be something badly wrong with him and deeply ashamed of his feelings, he once again found himself getting into arguments. Sometimes the lads would mistrust his familiarity with their girlfriends; and they felt uncomfortable about his possible feelings towards themselves. He couldn't win.

Desperate to find a space where he could belong, Peter drifted increasingly toward London, taking the train up to visit Soho alone on Friday and Saturday evenings; he loved the packed streets, the undercurrent of sexual freedom, the whole vibe of the area. More than anything though, he enjoyed meeting people like himself. It was the 1990's, the Aids problem was still around, but had drifted out of the headlines and gay people were confidently venturing out again.

Peter swiftly made friends at various bars and clubs and gradually, Petra was born. For the first time in her life she'd found somewhere that she could safely dress as a woman, be herself, without receiving the abuse and violence she suffered nearer to home. It was so liberating!

Then came two wonderful pieces of luck. The father of one of the office workers at Duke's Garage owned a farm on the outskirts of a tiny village called Underriver, just outside Sevenoaks. He had a small cottage lying vacant at the end of a bumpy unmade road that none of his farm workers seemed interested in renting. It was rundown and needed some TLC, but it boasted a telephone landline, was furnished and basically habitable. He was happy to offer it to Peter at a ridiculously low rent for as long as he needed it. Peter jumped at it and three days later moved out of his parents' house and into Heidi Lodge.

At last, his life seemed to be moving in the right direction. The pain of losing Suzanna was gradually easing and he was employed doing the work he loved on a decent salary. Then came his second stroke of luck, when his gran left him some money in her will, money he promptly used to rent a flat in his favourite place. So began Petra's secret weekends in Soho where she enjoyed good company, plenty of clubbing and an increasingly adventurous sex-life. The flat was her greatest joy, a quiet and private sanctuary where she felt comfortable and secure.

At work, little had changed. He loved the work but the ribbing and abuse he had met with throughout his life followed him there from his work colleagues, particularly Tony Waters and Des Thayer. He managed to cope easily enough with their taunts, only losing his temper and snapping at Tony a couple of times. They sensed he was different, effeminate, but they didn't know exactly what his preferences were... and that's how he wanted to keep it. He would have to leave Duke's for certain if everyone knew of his other, secret life; his colleagues would have torn into him and made his life unbearable.

So, that night in Soho, she'd come to a decision – she wasn't about to allow Tony Waters to destroy everything, yet again.

SIX

Tony gradually came to with a splitting pain at the back of his head; his vision was fuzzy and he blinked hard several times to clear his sight. As his senses slowly returned to normal, terror quickly overcame him. He found he could only breathe through his nose because some kind of tape had been wrapped several times around his head. It pulled painfully around the sides of his face, sealing his mouth tightly closed. He was on his back somewhere in the home gym looking directly up at the ceiling. It only took a moment for him to realise he was lying on the gym bench, to which he was securely tied, and completely immobilized.

There was a burning pain across his middle, where his waist was secured to the bench by a tightly fastened belt and his hands were bound together underneath the bench, wrenching his shoulder joints back. His lower legs were bound to the supports at one end of the bench and when he tried moving his feet, he found he couldn't; they had been placed into the foot straps on the floor and tightly secured by some method which he was unable to see. Trying to lift his head caused instant pain in his throat, because some form of restraint was fitted around his neck, almost choking him and keeping his head and shoulders firmly in place. He was entirely at the mercy of whatever Petra wanted to do with him.

His socks, trousers, and shirt were still on, but his jacket, overcoat and shoes had been removed. The feelings of helplessness and vulnerability were alien to him and he began shaking, tears forming in his eyes as he looked around for Peter. He couldn't see him anywhere and wondered if he'd tied him up then gone back out clubbing. He tried struggling against his bonds and screaming, but his position was hopeless. Fighting to remain calm and desperate to fend off the rising sense of panic inside, Tony tried to focus his mind; he had to think of a way out of the terrifying situation he found himself in. The knowledge that he was securely tied up, unable to call for help and completely vulnerable in an unhinged tranny's flat filled him with dread and revulsion.

Despite his efforts to fend it off, the panic swept back. He fought his bindings as hard as he could, but they held firm, cutting into his wrists and ankles with every move. He moaned as loudly as he could, but nothing much came out; unsurprising really, given that his mouth was completely sealed shut. He strained his neck in both directions trying to look behind him, but was unable to see any further than his shoulder. His breathing became ragged and he was starting to feel light-headed when suddenly, he heard the toilet flush and heard his colleague's voice.

'Fucking hell, big tough Tony Waters is crying! Don't be such a baby. Robert was really looking forward to his time in my flat until you fucking ruined it for him, so you owe us.'

She walked out of the toilet and moved to stand to one side of Tony's outstretched body. Tony saw that her outrageous clothing of earlier had been replaced with another equally flamboyant outfit. Petra stood with hands on hips proudly showing off her Leopard print onesie.

'Sorry, had to get changed, I feel more comfortable in my onesie once I'm back home after a night out.' She gave a twirl. 'What do you reckon, not too shabby eh?'

29

Tony thrashed his head from side to side, trying to say something, but his words were unintelligible, just a garbled mass of groaning and gurgling. Once again, he tried grunting and moaning as loudly as possible, hoping against hope that someone would hear him.

Petra smiled. 'You're wasting your time, darling. The basements either side of this flat belong to the shops above them. I know for a fact that both of those basements are empty and the tattoo shop directly above my flat won't be opening until nine – that's about five hours from now. So you can scream as much as you want, you're just wasting your energy. But carry on if you want.' He grinned wickedly. 'It gets me hot when my men scream.'

Tony glared furiously through his tears, but knew that further resistance was pointless, so he stopped struggling.

Petra crouched down until her face was within a couple of inches of Tony's right ear.

'Now then, you're going to listen to what I've got to say whether you like it or not.'

She shuffled to get more comfortable, sitting on the floor with her back resting against the wall. Tony turned his head to face her and saw she was staring at him: cold, emotionless.

'The fear and helplessness that you're experiencing right now, is what I've had to endure almost every day since I was a small child. It isn't nice, is it?'

Standing up, she towered over him, looking for all the world like she was about to hit him, causing his eyes to widen in fear.

'Don't look so shocked, you've been treating me exactly like shit ever since I started working at Duke's. This is a small payback for what you've put me through.'

Tony's chin quivered and he tried to shake his head.

'First, you're going to listen to a little bedtime story. I hope it won't give you nightmares.'

Petra sat back down, leaning against the wall, and began to tell him her life story, from the first time she became aware that she should have been born female, through the torments and bullying of school life, the rejection by her parents and loss of close friends simply because of who she was. She told him how she felt, year after year, having to re-start her life each time she was targeted by bigots and homophobes and feeling ever lonelier and more lost. Then she told him how she had thought Duke's Garage might be her final chance of happiness, until Tony and Des had poisoned the well and made her life a misery once more.

Petra wanted to make sure Tony fully understood just how much hurt she'd been through and how much hurt he personally had caused her. The whole process had taken twenty minutes, but instead of being cathartic for Petra, as she had expected, it had merely stoked her anger at having been the victim of so much abuse... so many vile attacks over the past thirteen years of her life. She now had nothing but thoughts of revenge in her mind and found that she had no intention of removing the tape from around Tony's mouth to see if he wanted to apologise for his behaviour. No, she didn't want to hear his lies; instead let him suffer... just like she'd suffered.

Petra climbed to her feet then crouched down on her haunches again to look directly into Tony's eyes.

'This will never make up for the misery I've gone through, but at least I can enjoy these few moments of watching you suffer. That's something, I suppose.'

Tony's expression showed he didn't understand what she meant. Petra leaned in closer.

'Because you're going to suffer, Tony, trust me.'

31

Tony's eyes widened with a mixture of terror and incomprehension.

'Don't worry sweetheart, it won't be half as painful as what you've put me through over the past three months.'

Tony frantically shook his head from side to side, trying in vain to loosen the strap around his neck then suddenly felt Petra punch him hard on the side of his face... and again... and again.

Tony thrashed around as violently as he could, but his binds held firm; his arms were pulled tightly underneath him and he was unable to move sideways because of the neck, waist and leg restraints; he was practically paralysed. His shoulders were almost dislocated and burning with pain. Tears flowed freely down both cheeks and mingled with the blood now oozing from the cuts.

Petra moved around to straddle his body directly over his thighs, facing Tony's head. Then, lifting one leg up high, she stamped down hard on his groin, making his body convulse in pain and forcing a long, muffled groan of agony from underneath the tape sealing his mouth. A flurry of wild punches to his head, ribs, and stomach caused such intense, burning pain that Tony went into a full-blown panic attack. He could barely breathe because his nose was broken, spraying blood around the gym... he was slowly suffocating. After what seemed like a lifetime, but in reality was around thirty seconds, she stopped, leaving him desperate for breath, the cheeks of his face swollen and red with pain and blood.

She walked slowly round his wrecked body twice then crouched down to bring her face close to his once more. He looked nothing like the confident, cocky colleague she had always known. His face was contorted with pain, his nose had snot and blood running from each nostril, his one open eye was full of tears. Suddenly he began jerking violently; Petra realised he couldn't breathe.

She quickly grabbed a tissue and wiped his nostrils, allowing Tony to take in a small amount of air, but it was not enough. She ran to the kitchen and removed a sharp knife from the drawer; returning to Tony, she carefully cut a slit in the tape around his mouth. Tony gasped for air, as if he had just surfaced from a deep dive. She then retrieved more kitchen tissue and held his nostrils tightly with it.

'Blow hard, it will clear your nose.'

The pain of Petra holding his shattered nose was intense, but Tony blew as hard as he could and was relieved to feel the cool flow of air once more.

Petra threw the tissues into the kitchen bin then stood over him again, her expressionless face staring down at him.

'There. I bet you enjoyed that, didn't you?'

Tony's eyes were pleading with her for mercy.

'Getting angry always makes me thirsty. How about you, are you thirsty Tony?'

He quickly nodded his head, desperate for a drink, anything but another beating.

Unable to see what she was doing, he heard Petra pouring something into a glass or cup; he was hopeful that his ordeal might finally be coming to an end. Then she appeared standing over him once again, two glasses of what looked like a soft drink of some sort in her hands.

'Here you go, blackcurrant squash, I hope that's okay.' She placed a glass on the floor. 'Tell you what, I'll gulp mine down then I'll help you with yours.'

She swiftly drank the squash down, placed the glass on the floor then picked up the other glass.

'I'll remove the tape for a few seconds, but if you shout or scream, it goes back on and then I'll stamp on your balls until they're a mulch. Understand?'

Tony's eyes widened; he knew she would carry out her threat, so nodded his head frantically. She pulled hard at the edge of the tape at the back of his head and gently unwound it from around his head, each loop ripping out several hairs. It stung, but he was beyond caring.

She told Tony to turn his head to one side and held the drink up to his mouth with her right hand, smiling and gently stroking his hair as she did so. He found himself revolted by the sensation of her gentle touch, but nevertheless greedily drank the whole glass down.

'There you go, Tony. Sorry about all this, but I needed to make you realise just how much I've been suffering at the hands of people like you.' As he swallowed the final mouthful she asked, 'Do you understand what I'm saying?'

Tony gave a small nod of his head.

'Please let me go Pete... please,' he whispered, hoarsely.

Petra shook her head and put her finger to his lips then she rewound more tape around his head three times, closing his mouth once more. She sat on the floor alongside him and crossed her legs.

'The boys will love hearing about this on Monday morning, won't they?'

He shook his head and looked at her in desperation.

'Tony, if you say anything about seeing me up here, you'll regret it. You see, I've filmed everything on my camcorder.'

His eyes widened.

'I could arrange a film show. They'll see you trussed up like a chicken in my flat and see me beating the shit out of you while you cry like a baby – or a girl! I'll send them each a copy so they can enjoy it with friends.'

Tony whimpered and tears flowed again, his eyes imploring her not to do that. She gave him a reassuring smile.

'You needn't worry Tony, I haven't really filmed it. I wouldn't do that, and do you want to know why I wouldn't?'

She leaned forward to whisper into his left ear, 'Have you ever heard of the drugs Rohypnol and Diazepam?'

Tony's eyes widened again in terror. He nodded frantically.

'Good, because you've just had a good drink of them both. In a few minutes you'll be out like a light, which, believe it or not, is a good thing for you, because you'll be unconscious and won't suffer too much when I kill you.'

He couldn't believe what he was hearing, only able to shake his head and stare at Petra through terrified eyes.

'Normally, the effects don't begin for about fifteen minutes, but I've given you a rather large dose, so it could be sooner. Anyway, I need to know before you die that you truly regret your past behaviour. You do regret it don't you, Tony? Yes, I'm sure you do. Deep down inside there may even be a decent human being trying to get out, but we'll never know now, will we?'

Tony began thrashing as hard as he could, desperately tugging and pulling at his anchors. But his efforts were futile and after several minutes he gradually calmed down, partly through exhaustion, partly because the drugs had started to take effect, partly because he was struggling to breathe again.

Petra moved her face close to his for one last time.

'You're going to hell, you fucking piece of shit. When the time comes for me to finish you off, I hope you're at least coming round a little because I want you to feel the hopelessness, the terror, the pain.'

There was no more fight left in Tony. His breathing had become shallow, his muscles were weak and his eyelids felt heavy. He fought the sensation of drowsiness as hard as he could and tried desperately to keep his eyes open, but he was fighting a losing battle. Eventually, they closed and he drifted into unconsciousness.

SEVEN

Petra flopped down onto her bed, shaking with a mixture of exhilaration, nerves, and blind terror. Something like this had been building inside her for many years and now she'd finally given in to it.

What the fuck have I done?

Then she started to cry. She'd run away from bullies, abuse, and taunts her whole life, having to start her life over again somewhere new each time, but this time she'd refused to run, this time she'd stood her ground, this time she'd fought back and it felt good - so, so good. She was a thoroughly good person, of that she was certain, but from now on, she would punish anyone who attacked her for being different, just like she was punishing Tony.

Five minutes later, she sat up, sucked in a huge lungful of air and rose to her feet. She needed to get her emotions in check and start doing something; she had to move Tony from her flat before the morning. He should be unconscious for around three hours, giving her more than enough time to complete her plan.

Peeling herself out of her onesie, she went to her wardrobe and pulled out a dark grey hooded tracksuit, black socks and black trainers. She quickly wiped off her makeup and washed her face, leaving herself looking nothing like the glamorous woman of an hour ago and more like the burly mechanic who worked at Duke's Garage Monday to Friday.

She pulled on a pair of plastic gloves and got to work. Gradually Petra disappeared, to be replaced by

Peter – and he had a job to do. Over the next thirty minutes he released Tony from his shackles, removed the gag and put his jacket, overcoat and shoes back on which, with Tony as limp as a rag doll, proved unexpectedly difficult.

Rushing from his flat with the tracksuit hood up, Peter collected his Ford Escort from a nearby private car park, where he rented a parking space. The car was an old banger that he'd taken as payment for private work on a high-end BMW. He rarely used it because it wasn't the most comfortable of rides, much preferring his newer Vauxhall Astra, but this weekend he'd decided to give it a run to keep the battery charged, so had driven it up to town.

Peter drove the 250 yards from his parking space to Bateman Street and parked right outside the staircase leading down to his flat. Greek Street and Frith Street at either end of his road were still relatively busy with pedestrians, but Bateman Street itself was quiet.

Once back inside, he used his immense strength to pick his victim up from the floor, then held him by folding Tony's left arm around his own neck, holding Tony's left hand with his own left hand and supporting him under his right armpit. Peter dragged him from the flat and with some difficulty manhandled him up the flight of stairs, heaving him upwards one step at a time, stopping twice on the way up for a few seconds to catch his breath.

Tony occasionally made a small grunting noise as his body fought to regain consciousness, but Peter was confident he would remain incapacitated long enough for his needs.

He was struggling to support Tony and open the passenger door of his car at the same time, when he was horrified to feel a tap on his right shoulder. Looking round he came face to face with a huge black guy whom he recognized as a bouncer at a club on Wardour Street. The bouncer looked decidedly worried.

'Jesus, he looks pissed. Need a hand?'

Peter breathed out a sigh of relief; he could do with some help and luckily the bouncer didn't seem to have noticed the blood on Tony's shirt.

'Yes please, he's rat-arsed. His wife will kill me – and him - when I drop him off.'

The bouncer laughed and between them they poured Tony into the front passenger seat. Peter folded his coat over his shirt, making sure the blood spots were concealed then secured the seat belt.

'Cheers.'

'No problem.' The bouncer nodded at Peter's hands. 'What's with the plastic gloves?'

Fuck it! Think of something!

'I've been clearing up his sick downstairs, it was disgusting. I didn't realise I was still wearing them.'

The bouncer grimaced, an expression that faded and changed to one of concern as Tony's head rolled back against the seat.

'Christ! What's happened to his face?'

Once again, Peter had to think quickly.

'He was pissed as a fart when he left a club earlier, he was easy prey for a couple of queer-bashers who gave him a right kicking. That's why I brought him back here.'

The other man winced, said, 'Good luck, mate!' and made off towards Greek Street with a wave of his hand.

Peter breathed a sigh of relief. Climbing into the driver's seat, he quickly checked on Tony's condition and was pleased to find him still in a stupor.

What the fuck are you doing? You'll never get away with it!

The thought repeated over and over in his head, but he banished it to the deepest recesses of his mind, before starting the engine and driving off.

As he drove over Westminster Bridge, Peter wound down the window and hurled Tony's solid block of a mobile phone over the car's roof, over the side of the bridge and into the River Thames, where he hoped it would never be found. His fingerprints were on it, so he couldn't take any chances.

Coming off the M25, he made his way to the village of Seal, then took the smallest, quietest backroads, quiet country lanes which he knew like the back of his hand, roads where he had little chance of being spotted and no chance of being captured on CCTV.

An hour and ten minutes after leaving the flat, shortly after six, Peter's car arrived in a tiny hamlet, seven miles outside Sevenoaks. He knew that Tony lived nearby and planned to dump him somewhere on his route home from the nearest train station, Borough Green. He pulled into a small lane where he'd played as a child. Tony would have almost certainly returned home this way; the station was only half a mile away and taxis were unlikely to be waiting outside the station that early in the morning, meaning he would have had to walk, so his presence in the area wouldn't raise too many eyebrows.

Pulling up at the roadside, he turned off the car lights and got out. Thankfully, it was still almost completely dark, with thick cloud obscuring the moon. There were no streetlights and only one house nearby, which was in total darkness. It was quiet, remote, and perfect for his purposes.

Peter walked round to the passenger side of the vehicle and opened the front door, producing a faint glow from the car's internal light. Undoing Tony's seat belt, he dragged the top half of his body from the car, allowing him to fall to the ground, hitting the side of his face hard on the dust and gravel at the roadside and causing him to groan. Tony tried unsuccessfully to lift an arm after hitting his head. He was slowly beginning to surface and Peter smiled; he wanted Tony to have some awareness of what was happening, he wanted him to feel fear and be aware of exactly what fate awaited him.

The car was parked next to a tiny stream that ran alongside the road, which was ideal for his plans. Seeing him lying helpless on the ground, Peter felt a warm glow of satisfaction. He grabbed both of Tony's wrists with his gloved hands and pulled him completely free from the car, his legs and feet flopping uselessly onto the ground.

Thirty seconds later, after a huge amount of effort, he'd managed to drag him to the edge of the stream, which was in full flow but only three or four inches deep. Crouching down in the darkness, he could just about make out Tony's features. He seemed to be trying to force his eyes open, but still had no control of his limbs.

He whispered gleefully into his ear, 'Time to go Tony. I'm glad that you're at least a little bit awake, I wouldn't have wanted you to miss this.'

In the near darkness, Peter was certain he could see fear spread across Tony's features, but that could have just been wishful thinking.

Peter forced his right hand under Tony's left shoulder blade and his left hand under his left hip, lifted with all his might and rolled him into the stream, face down. Peter watched with mounting pleasure as Tony appeared to be making pathetically weak efforts to roll himself over, but his arms and legs simply didn't have the strength. He imagined seeing the air bubbles from Tony's mouth surfacing, then becoming fewer and fewer, but in reality, the dark night robbed him of the view.

Two minutes later, he was certain Tony was dead. For almost the first time since they'd met, he enjoyed an incredible feeling of release, release from his jibes and taunting, release from the dread of seeing him when he arrived at work every morning, release from the misery that had been heaped on him.

His problems weren't over by any means; there was still his boss, Des Thayer, who was just as vile. From now on though, he would stand up to him, he would confront and deal with anyone who belittled him for simply being himself, not cower and run away from them. He felt strength and conviction course through his veins. He would battle for both himself and anyone else like him. This would be his mission, his trans-mission! He chuckled at the thought.

That's very apt for a transgender mechanic!

EIGHT

Peter drove back to Soho, his thoughts at first alternating
between a sense of unreality and downright terror.
Gradually he began to calm his nerves and to plan how to
spend the remainder of his weekend. He found he was
suffering remarkably few feelings of guilt at having taken
the life of another human being. Quite the contrary: by
the time he arrived in Bateman Street, he was
experiencing something bordering on euphoria. He'd
actually taken pleasure at abusing, beating, drugging, and
killing Tony Waters. The fact that he was experiencing
such sensations both surprised and alarmed him – was he
turning into some kind of homicidal maniac? He hoped
not.

For many years he'd climbed into bed at night after
yet another day of taunts and bullying, then lain there
imagining taking violent revenge on his abusers. He
would spend hours thinking about punching them,
kicking them, burning them, stabbing them, torturing
them, killing them, always in truly grotesque ways, but he
always believed that he couldn't do it, wouldn't do it.
Instead, he would turn the hatred in on himself,
occasionally self-harming. He was a good person who
abhorred violence and something deep inside had always
prevented him from acting on it… until now.

Now, after all these years, he'd finally done what
he'd wanted to do for so long - followed through on his
desires, leaving himself feeling ecstatic!

When Peter entered his flat and looked around at the

evidence of carnage, he was immediately brought down to earth and set about thoroughly cleaning everything that had been touched by his victim, or where small amounts of blood had spattered, especially around the gym bench. He took everything from the bin and together with the onesie Petra had worn when beating Waters, placed it into carrier bags. He then travelled to the nearest refuse tip and disposed of everything at the bottom of a huge container marked 'Household Waste.'

Then, sitting on the settee, he stared at the home gym, reliving in his mind the events that had taken place, experiencing a thrill each time he recalled certain moments, especially punching Tony's face with all his might, then hearing his groans of pain. That had been the best part – hurting him.

However, his excitement gently subsided as it was replaced by the fear of getting caught, a fear that gradually developed into a full-blown feeling of panic. He'd actually killed someone! As a huge fan of crime investigation programmes, Peter knew that the vast majority of murderers were identified, arrested, and convicted, usually because they'd left an obvious clue somewhere at the crime scene. His work had barely begun.

Just in case the police somehow identified him as a suspect, meaning they would undoubtedly be searching his flat at some stage, he spent the remainder of the weekend regretfully dismantling his home gym, placing everything into a storage unit he'd rented in Tottenham Court Road. He wasn't certain that doing this was necessary, but it felt like the right thing to do. Working as quickly as he could, he continued late into the night and started again early on Sunday morning.

After removing the various hooks, nails, and bar supports attached to the wall, he covered the space by fixing a laminate panel to the area. Placing family photos into picture frames, he fixed them to the new walling then laid down laminate flooring, screwing it to the floor and covering it with a thick, second-hand, brightly patterned rug. The flooring successfully covered up areas where the bench had been fixed to the floor, and where the feet straps were secured. He purchased a small, bright-red, shabby-chic table and two chairs, which fitted nicely into the small space and perfectly suited the outrageous décor in the room.

Once he'd finished, he stood back and admired his handiwork. It had taken all weekend up until Sunday afternoon to complete the work, including two visits to B&Q and one to his favourite second-hand furniture shop, but he couldn't have been more pleased with the result. It was like the gym had never existed and everything he'd replaced it with looked as if it had been there for years.

There was one last thing left to do. On Sunday afternoon, Peter visited a car breakers yard in Kentish Town, where he managed to find another Ford Escort with the same seat upholstery as his. He purchased a front passenger seat, and it was an easy job to remove the one from his Escort and replace it with the new one which would have no fibres or hairs which could connect him to Tony. Then he gave the car a valet standard clean inside, especially around the front passenger side, and parked it back in the usual space in the car park.

Happy with his weekend's work, he drove back to Kent late on Sunday evening, ready for work on Monday morning. His life had changed that weekend and although he didn't know it at that moment, it would never be quite the same again.

NINE

Detective Chief Inspector Natalie Neider paced irritably backwards and forwards across one end of the crowded CID room in Sevenoaks Police Station. She'd called in all CID staff for nine on Sunday morning and it was now five-past, yet only three-quarters of the twenty-odd officers she was expecting had arrived. Latecomers were casually strolling in, chatting and laughing, in no apparent rush.

Unable to control her anger any longer, Natalie exploded.

'For fuck's sake! Get in here! Stop talking, and close the door!'

She stood facing the door with both hands on her hips, the look on her face could have curdled milk.

'This is a murder enquiry in case you've forgotten, and most of you are on double-bubble, so show some professionalism!'

The last few officers hurried sheepishly through the door, the final one closing it quietly. The whole of Sevenoaks Police Station's CID department, plus a few detectives from nearby Tonbridge, settled down wherever they could; the lucky ones had seats on chairs or the edges of tables, the remainder were standing around the sides and back of the room. The room quickly fell silent, all eyes on the irate woman in front of them.

Everyone present was aware of Natalie Neider's reputation: a fearsome DCI with a hot temper, a boss who demanded that every officer worked as hard as she did, which would have been difficult to say the least, because her career was everything to her and she rarely took time off. She could justifiably be called a workaholic.

Natalie studied the officers assembled before her and the officers returned her gaze. She was a short woman, 5 foot 3 tall, 43 years old, with an unremarkable face and neat, mousey, bobbed hair; she was dressed smartly, as always, expecting the same high standards of appearance from every member of her staff.

What they didn't know was that she had recently separated very acrimoniously from Thomas, her husband of just four years, after he admitted having a brief sexual relationship with a man. The only reason for the confession was that she'd come across them one night in a car, parked in a quiet corner of an edge of town car park. The sounds coming from the car and the positions of the two men were hardly ambiguous. The shock was so great that she stood rooted to the spot for several seconds, before yanking the car door open and screaming hysterically at both men. The man with his hand inside Thomas's trousers looked briefly up into her face; he looked barely out of his teens and began to stammer out an apology while struggling to recover items of clothing in the confined space of the car. Natalie was in no mood to listen to his words and replied with a tirade of abuse as he fell from the car and fled from the scene.

No matter how much she loved her husband, she found herself unable to forgive him, or even to look at him or listen to his excuses, and a few days later he moved out of their home. The incident had traumatised her, leaving no way back for their marriage. She felt baffled and deeply ashamed about her husband having an affair with another man, as if she'd somehow been inadequate as a wife. Was she in some way responsible for her husband's actions?

Deciding to keep their dirty little secret quiet, she made up a story, telling colleagues he'd gone off with another woman. She was only too aware how unforgiving the police grapevine could be and worried her name would become a laughing stock among her colleagues if they ever learned the truth.

Hitching up the trousers of her light-blue trouser suit and tucking in her cream blouse, she looked round at the assembled officers before pointing to a set of photographs pinned on the wall.

'This is Tony Waters, a local man. He was 46 years old, divorced from his wife eight years ago, with two teenage daughters. He was popular with everyone who knew and worked with him at Duke's Garage in Sevenoaks, where he was the workshop foreman. His body was found lying in a small stream about 500 yards from his home near Borough Green at 7.15 on Saturday morning by a passing motorist. He normally spent Friday nights drinking in London with friends, before either getting a lift home or sometimes, as on this occasion, catching an early train to Borough Green, then walking the mile or so to his home.'

She took a small sip from a cup of water.

'It was assumed he'd fallen and hit his head, rolled into the stream drunk and lost consciousness, before eventually drowning. However, the initial investigation and the post mortem result have changed all that.'

She drummed her fingers on the table's edge, a stern expression on her face.

'We now have a full-blown murder enquiry on our hands.'

Her flow was interrupted as Chief Superintendent Colin Hayler entered the room in full uniform. Everyone seated quickly stood up to show respect for his rank, then returned to their seats as he said, 'Thank you, please be seated.' He turned to Natalie, who hadn't expected to see him and was more than a little peeved he was gate-crashing her briefing.

'My apologies, DCI Neider, please continue.'

Natalie may have been irritated, but she smiled warmly before picking up a copy of the post mortem report. Slowly turning the cover page, she cast her gaze across the room.

'Because of the state he was in, we thought there might be suspicious circumstances, but we weren't certain… until the pathologist brought some interesting details to our attention.'

She waved the report in the air for everyone to see.

'We know that Tony Waters was alive when he entered the stream, because his lungs were filled with water, showing that the cause of death was drowning. However, prior to drowning, Waters appears to have been struck on the back of the head not once but twice, with some kind of blunt instrument, blows that were made with such force that the pathologist estimates they would almost certainly have been sufficient to render him unconscious. Marks on his wrists, neck, legs, and waist show that he appears to have been forcibly restrained, to the extent that he had bruising to all those areas which suggests he was either tied down very tightly, or he'd tried very hard to free himself - possibly both.'

She turned a page on the report and looked back to the room.

'We think that while he was restrained, he was beaten. There was significant bruising on his face, lower abdomen, and chest. His testicles also showed signs of heavy bruising, indicating that during the beating they received a particularly severe blow. At this stage it is unknown how, or why, the beating took place. It is also unknown whether he was hit by fists, boots, or if an implement or weapon was used.'

Her words had prompted uncomfortable shuffling from many officers, particularly the male ones, some of whom visibly squirmed as the injuries were described.

'Finally, toxicology reports showed he had a large dose of both Rohypnol and Diazepam in his system, something that would have rendered him unconscious and incapable of defending himself.' She waited for her words to take full effect before saying, 'This leaves us with unanswered questions. Why would someone want to torture him like this? Why was he tied up and assaulted?

'Assuming he was incapable of travelling home by train in that condition and with those injuries, the killer must have brought Tony to the scene by car before dumping him in that stream, so are there any CCTV cameras which may have captured this vehicle on the way to, or leaving the scene where his body was discovered? Who were the friends he normally met on his Friday nights out in London and where did they go after splitting up with him? Which leads me to my final question. Where did these assaults happen?'

Colin Hayler walked quickly around the perimeter of the room to join her.

'May I say a few words please, DCI Neider?'

'Certainly, Sir.'

She moved to one side, indicating that the floor was his. Natalie was unimpressed with yet another interruption, but there wasn't much she could say, after all, he *was* the boss.

'Thank you.' Hayler faced his officers. 'This is the first murder in the Sevenoaks area since I've been Station Commander. The local press is all over this and I'm certain that because of the restraint and torture elements, not to mention the victim being drugged, it won't be long before the national press turn up too. I'll be expecting every one of you to perform to the very best of your abilities, anything less and I'll be asking some serious questions. Does everybody understand?'

A chorus of 'Yes, Sir' was the response.

Hayler smiled.

'Good. I'm expected at headquarters in Maidstone to brief the Chief at ten, so I need to get going. I'll leave you all in the capable hands of DCI Neider.'

Nodding his thanks to Natalie, he left the room.

Natalie took up her position in the centre of the room once again, standing directly in front of the grim pictures of Tony Waters' body lying in the stream. She couldn't quite hide her irritation.

'Well, that helped a lot, didn't it?'

There was a gentle ripple of laughter.

'You will be divided into three teams, each comprising one DI, one DS and six DC's.'

She picked up a notebook and checked her notes.

'Team 1 will concentrate on interviewing Waters' family and work colleagues. I want to know his sexual habits, who his closest friends were, whether any of them travelled to London with him on Friday nights, whether they know anyone who would wish him harm, or whether any of them know if he's badly upset anyone in the past few months.' She turned to face one of her Detective Inspectors. 'DI Plant, you will head up team 1.'

Peter Plant nodded, 'Yes Ma'am.'

Natalie selected DS Pincent and six DC's to assist him.

'Team 2 will initially be working with team 1, but once we know who Waters was with on Friday night, and more importantly where they spent the evening, they will concentrate on retrieving and viewing CCTV at every location they visited. Once you've located the victim on

CCTV, I want his movements followed throughout the evening until he leaves the group. After that, I want you to concentrate fully on finding out where the fuck he went after leaving his friends and who, if anyone, was with him. This team could end up with a huge amount of CCTV to review, so I may supplement you at a later date. DI Jameson, you've got team 2.'

Carolyn Jameson smiled, 'Yes Ma'am.'

Once again, Natalie selected a DS and six DC's.

Taking another sip of water, Natalie gave deployment details for the next team.

'Team 3 will concentrate on checking CCTV cameras on roads heading in and out of the area within two miles of where Tony Waters was found. I doubt there will be that many, but once seized, I want you to check images between 3 o'clock and 7.30 on Saturday morning. Any vehicles seen heading towards Borough Green, then shortly afterwards leaving, could well be our suspect. In addition, I want door-to-door enquiries conducted at every premises on the main drags within half a mile of the scene. It's unlikely, but there may just be a small chance that someone was awake and saw something. DI Waterman, you will head up team 3.'

Tim Waterman nodded and was assigned officers to complete his team. Rubbing the palms of her hands together, Natalie paused, a thoughtful but distant look in her eyes.

'This is going to be a very tough nut to crack, ladies and gents. Intensive forensic work is currently taking place on Tony Waters' clothes and belongings, and we already know that there are blood splashes on his shirt. I have also directed that his home address, which is only 500 yards from where his body was found, be thoroughly checked and searched, just in case some of these assaults took place there, although that seems unlikely.'

Natalie was grim faced.

'This appears to be a carefully planned attack that resulted in the torture and murder of a popular and well-respected member of our community. Because of the brutal nature of the assault and the tying up and beating involved, we have to consider the possibility that someone had a serious grudge against him, perhaps someone he owed money to, or someone he'd badly upset. Whatever the reason, he didn't deserve to die like this... nobody does. Any questions?'

Officers looked at each other and there was much shuffling of bottoms on seats, but no questions were forthcoming.

'Good. Let's find his killer and put them away. Thank you all for your attendance.'

TEN

Peter pulled into the staff car park of Duke's Garage at 7.55 on Monday morning with a broad smile on his face. He was wearing his work boiler suit, just like every other morning, ready for action. He was looking forward to a day at work without the constant abuse from his supervisor. As he stepped from his car, Bill Daly, one of his fellow mechanics, pulled up alongside and wound down his window.

'All right, Pete?'

'Yes thanks. Good weekend?'

Bill climbed out of his car, closed the door and pressed his key fob, which locked the car with a high-pitched 'click-click.'

'Brilliant, thanks. Went to watch West Ham on Saturday and we beat Spurs 1-0. How about you?'

Bill moved closer, as if watching him intently. Peter's defence mechanism kicked in, putting his mind on alert but he soon realised this was simply his guilty conscience; Bill wasn't behaving oddly at all, it was just his short-sightedness which sometimes meant he focused on you closely when he spoke. After a moment he relaxed, smiled, and proceeded to lie about his activities.

'I went out with friends in London on Friday and Saturday, then visited Ightham Mote on Sunday.'

Laughing, Bill walked towards the workshop alongside Peter.

'Fuck me, Ightham Mote? That's a National Trust house for pensioners, isn't it?'

'Yep, that's the one.'

'And you went there after being on the piss in the smoke? I wouldn't have thought that would be very high on your wish-list. I s'pose you poofs prefer girly things, don't you?'

Peter ignored the insult.

'I didn't go into the house. I walked there from home, had a drink at the Plough in Ivy Hatch, then walked back.'

'Sounds fucking boring to me.'

'It was rather lovely actually, but I wouldn't expect a Neanderthal like you to understand.'

Bill laughed at Peter's reply and patted him on the shoulder.

'Nice one!'

They walked into the workshop together, where they found fellow mechanics Andy Clark and Vince Groves deep in conversation. Andy and Vince were both in their early 40's and appeared not to notice Peter and Bill coming in. They were standing near the kettle making themselves cups of tea, deeply engrossed in their private exchange. Peter was surprised that Andy wasn't his usual shouty and abusive self. He was normally almost as horrible to him as Tony and Des, always making some snide remark as he arrived at the workshop, but today there was nothing. Instead, both men were speaking in hushed tones, grim expressions on their faces.

'All right lads,' shouted Bill. 'What's up with you two? Looks like someone's just pissed in your tea.'

Andy glared angrily before snarling, 'Tony's dead.'

Bill, who had picked up his mug prior to pouring his own tea was stunned, his smile quickly vanished

'Fuck, but how…? What happened?'

Andy put his cup down and faced them, hands on his hips.

'I went up to The Concord Rooms with Des on Friday night to join Tony and his friends. He'd been wanting us to go to a meeting of his club for months.'

Bill frowned. 'What club?'

'It's called *Keep Britain Straight*,' he glared at Peter. 'It's a group whose members don't like what's happening to this country.'

Peter didn't respond but remembered Tony's comment about 'The Club' and made a mental note of the name for future reference.

'We stayed until about half eleven, then got the train home.' He shook his head. 'He was fine when we left, but yesterday I got a call from his mate, Duncan, who said the police had contacted him about Tony's death and he told me what had happened. Apparently, after we left, the four of them had a few more drinks, until Stan was ready to drive them home at two.'

He removed the teabag from his cup and flicked it in the bin before taking a gulp.

'Go on,' said Bill, eager to learn more.

'Tony was pissed and didn't want to go home. He wanted to tell the poofs what he thought of them.' Once again, he glanced at Peter. 'So, he said goodbye to his mates and headed off towards Soho... alone.'

'Weren't they worried about him?'

Andy shook his head, 'No, Duncan said it was something he often did.'

'And?'

'What do you mean?'

Bill looked exasperated.

'What happened to him? How the fuck did he end up dead?'

'The next time he was seen was lying face down in a stream, a quarter of a mile from his house.'

'Jesus Christ!'

Bill took the place of Vince, who had moved away from the kettle, poured hot water into his cup and shook his head.

'How the fuck did he drown in a stream? Had he fallen in? Was he too pissed to lift himself out?'

'No. According to the detectives, he'd been hit over the head, tied up, drugged and beaten before he was dumped in the stream.'

Peter was alarmed at how fast the news had travelled and thought it would look odd if he didn't join in the conversation.

'How did you find out so much information? Have the detectives spoken to you?'

Once again, Andy stared stonily at him.

'I told you, Duncan called me yesterday. They contacted Des too and he told me those extra details. No-one's spoken to me… yet.'

Bill still had a puzzled expression on his face, unable to fully comprehend what he was being told. Andy rolled his eyes in exasperation.

'For fuck's sake Bill, isn't it obvious? Tony was murdered!'

Andy's account had shaken Peter. He hadn't expected to hear his actions being talked about this quickly or in so much detail and was worried about the effect it was having on him. He thought he'd better join the conversation again.

'That's awful. Have they got any idea who attacked him?'

Andy shook his head.

'No, nothing at the moment.'

'Why did Duncan call you?' asked Bill. 'You'd never met him before Friday night, had you?'

'No, but we got on well in the club and chatted for ages. Funnily enough, we discovered that we'd played in the same football team, although a few years apart. We talked a lot about people we both knew from our time at the club. At the end of the evening, we swapped phone numbers and promised to keep in contact.'

Bill nodded and poured milk into his cup. For a few seconds all four men stood looking at each other in silence, an uneasy atmosphere swiftly developing.

Andy Clark was a short man, slim and wiry. His angular features were countered by dark, sunken eyes, giving him a perpetually aggressive appearance. Since Bill and Peter entered the workshop, Andy had been casting furious looks at Peter, but Peter wasn't going to be intimidated and returned his looks with equal aggression.

'I expect you're over the moon, aren't you, Pete? You hated Tony, didn't you?'

This wasn't good. Peter knew he should try to defuse Andy's anger.

'I didn't hate him. We just didn't see eye to eye on some things - a clash of personalities, that's all.'

Andy's face darkened in fury and he pointed angrily at Peter.

'Bollocks! He picked you out as a shirt-lifter from the day you started here. All he ever did was have a laugh about it but you behaved like a big girl and got all moody.'

The tense atmosphere was suddenly broken by the workshop door sliding open. Everyone turned to see Rosemary, the receptionist from the sales department, who was standing in the doorway, flanked by two men in suits. They stepped in and walked up to the four mechanics, holding out police warrant cards.

'Good morning, gentlemen. We're from Sevenoaks Police Station investigating the murder of one of your colleagues, Tony Waters.'

The officer speaking was the shorter of the two:

slim, about thirty, wearing a dark grey suit, white shirt and grey tie.

'I'm Detective Sergeant Pincent and this is Detective Constable Dawes.'

He indicated his colleague, who was also smartly dressed, and seemed quite young.

'We need to speak with you all individually.'

Andy instantly recognised Detective Sergeant Pincent as James, one of Tony's friends from the club on Friday night. They had been told about James's occupation by Tony, and that his attendance at the meeting was to be kept tightly under wraps, or he might lose his job. Andy played his part to perfection and acted like he'd never met him. He was the first to speak.

'We don't know anything about Tony's death, we just worked with him.'

'Okay, understood, we're just after some background. We've been offered use of an office in your sales department. Perhaps you'd like to volunteer to be interviewed first?'

Shrugging, Andy looked over at his colleagues, swapped a knowing look with James, then nodded and walked with the detectives through the sliding door.

Warming his hands on his mug, Vince turned to Peter.

'Don't worry about Andy, he hates all poofs. It's nothing personal.'

'I know, but it's not great when you're expected to accept piss-taking day after day without saying anything in response, let alone being able to make an official complaint. I've got no chance of that with Des, have I? Now he seems to have me cast in the role of a murderer just because the two of us didn't get on.'

Bill broke in, 'Fucking hell, what a shit start to the day.'

Pulling his shoulders back, he stood up straight.

'Anyway, we're paid to fix cars, so let's get on with it. Tony's gone but the world won't stop turning. He wouldn't have let us stand around chatting and scratching our arses, so let's get on with our work.'

Peter's insides were churning. He hadn't anticipated the police speaking to everyone at work only two days after Tony's death. His smile on arriving at work that morning had quickly faded, his newfound happiness and confidence through ridding the world of Tony Waters had been replaced with fear for his own future. He suddenly felt vulnerable and threatened all over again.

Feeling himself shaking with fear, he knew he needed to regain control of his emotions, quickly, and threw himself into his work, trying hard to concentrate on what he was doing. Ninety minutes later, Bill returned from his interview and told Peter the officers wanted to speak with him next. He was the final one of the four mechanics to be invited into the sales office and his mind was full of questions.

Why am I last? Do they know I met him in Soho? Have they found something incriminating?

Putting on a brave face, he walked from the workshop, ready to face whatever was thrown at him.

ELEVEN

Peter nervously entered the small side room adjoining the sales office. It was normally used by the garage's sales staff, somewhere to speak privately with customers in the hope of clinching a sale, but on this occasion, it had a very different purpose – and atmosphere. Peter saw Pincent and Dawes sitting side-by-side at the small table with two steaming cups in front of them, the mixed aromas of tea and coffee in the air. At the opposite side of the table were two red plastic chairs with soft black fabric seats; Dawes gestured for Peter to sit down. Feeling more than a little nauseous, he did so and forced a smile.

'Good morning. Terrible business this. How can I help?'

Pincent was reading through notes in his pocket book. His mouth smiled at Peter but his eyes failed to follow, his dislike of gays making it difficult for him to produce a genuine greeting. He leaned back on his chair until it was precariously balanced on two legs.

'Good morning Peter, make yourself comfortable.'

'Thank you.'

Peter shuffled the chair forward, so he could rest his forearms on the table, an action that helped him control the nervous quivering.

Dawes indicated his cup with a forefinger.

'Would you like a cup of something before we start?'

'No thanks, I've just finished one.'

His fake smile fading fast, Pincent rocked forward

and fixed Peter with a disconcerting stare.

'How well did you know Tony Waters?'

Peter instinctively shuffled his bottom back in the seat defensively, removing his arms from the table.

'Only as my boss at work.'

Pincent noted down his answer.

'You've never met him outside work?'

Uncomfortable at the directness of the question, images of meeting Waters in Greek Street flashed through his mind. Peter scratched his cheek and shook his head.

'No, we weren't friends outside the garage, just work colleagues.'

Once again Pincent noted down the reply. Dawes apparently had the job of monitoring his mannerisms, he didn't ask questions, but seemed to be studying Peter's every move.

Pincent took a sip from his cup, screwed up his face and scratched the back of his neck.

'Peter, are you keeping something from us? We're well aware you weren't friends. Would it be fair to say you hated him?'

Peter knew where this was going and decided his only option was to continue lying through his teeth.

'That's ridiculous, I didn't hate Tony.'

Pincent knew from conversations with Tony on their Friday nights out that Peter was almost certainly gay. Meeting him in the flesh only confirmed that. He was finding sitting across the table from him almost creepy, repelled by what he perceived as his slightly camp mannerisms and voice. Raising his eyebrows at Peter's reply, Pincent flicked theatrically through several sheets of paper.

'That's not quite true though, is it Peter? Everyone we've spoken to so far, the other three mechanics, the members of office staff we've spoken with, even the owner of the garage - all of them said you detested each other. Are they all lying?'

Peter could feel himself becoming red. He knew they were clutching at straws and hadn't gathered any real evidence, but he still felt under intense pressure.

'Look, we weren't best buddies, I'll admit that, but there's banter wherever you work. That's all it was, just banter, it didn't bother me.'

Pincent nodded at Dawes, who took control of the bundle of papers in front of him and tidied them into a neat pile. He gently rubbed his chin with the forefinger and thumb of his left hand, before posing his first question.

'Where were you between two and eight on Saturday morning?'

'I walked to my flat in Soho at around two.'

A surprised expression appeared on both officers' faces, causing Dawes to ask the obvious question.

'How can you afford a flat in Soho?'

'I was left a decent lump of money by a relative in her will. I like to spend my weekends with friends in London, so I thought I'd rent a place up there.'

'Where were you before two?'

'I visited a café and a couple of bars, before ending up at *My Pink Life*, a gay club in Old Compton Street.'

'A gay club?' The officers exchanged a glance. 'So, you're admitting that you're gay, are you?'

'Yes, and it's not an admission, it's a statement of fact, and I'm proud of it. I'm also trans so I was dressed as a woman all night.'

Pincent closed his eyes, pushed his lips tightly shut and shook his head in barely concealed disgust.

'Can anyone confirm you were there?'

'Yes, loads of people. There's my friends at the club,

the bar staff, the door staff… loads of people.'

'Hmmm,' said Dawes. 'A flat in Soho, eh? Lucky you.' He folded his arms and sat back, 'What's the address?'

'56A Bateman Street. Why?'

'It might be of interest later,' said Pincent, noting down the address.

Peter could feel a tightness across his chest and shoulders as if someone was pulling him back against the chair. He didn't want police visiting his flat. He'd cleared up as best he could, but would that be enough?

'Why should my flat be of interest?'

Pincent didn't reply, just moved onto the next question.

'Are you aware of where Tony Waters went missing?'

'No.'

Pincent fixed him with an icy stare.

'He left the Concord Rooms just north of Oxford Street shortly after two. He was last seen heading towards Soho, which just happens to be where you were.'

Peter shrugged. 'So were thousands of other people.'

'Well?'

'Well what?'

'Did you see him in Soho?'

Peter could sense his whole body begin to shake; the pressure was building and he was beginning to wonder whether they already knew the truth. Could their questions be luring him into a trap? He decided to stay as close to the truth as he dared.

'I left the club with a man called Robert. We turned into Greek Street, kissed goodbye and he left to make his way home.'

'Where did you go?'

'I made my way to the flat.'

'Can anyone confirm that?'

Peter shook his head.

'No, apart from Robert, I was alone.'

The detectives exchanged another glance, before Pincent scraped his chair back across the floor and stood up.

'You do realise we'll be checking CCTV at The Concord Rooms and following Mr Water's movements once he's out on the street? It'll be interesting to see where he went won't it?'

He left the question hanging in the air menacingly as he paced the room, his eyes never leaving Peter for a second.

Peter knew the council's CCTV images would show Tony heading towards Soho, but was confident his meeting with him wouldn't be a problem because of the maintenance being carried out. Pincent was on the right track with his suspicions and he was turning the screws, but Peter had to stay strong and front out the questions.

'I've no idea where he went. I didn't see him, he certainly wasn't with me.'

He felt himself flushing, his face betraying him to the officers. As if to confirm his suspicions, Pincent placed his hands on the table's edge and leaned over.

'You've gone very red, Peter. That suggests to me you're not telling the truth.'

'Sorry, this is making me feel rather uncomfortable. I've never been questioned by the police before.'

Pincent snorted dismissively.

'You see Peter, there are several factors that concern me about you and Tony.'

He lifted his hands from the table and folded his arms.

'Firstly, according to your work colleagues, Tony Waters didn't like you because you were gay. He deliberately made life difficult for you at work, didn't he?'

Peter fought hard to keep his face expressionless.

'No, not really, he just took the mickey.'

'Don't lie Peter, you know he did and that must have grated on you. Secondly, Des Thayer and the other workers from the garage have told us that the relationship between yourself and Mr Waters was abrasive, one person even described it as toxic. Thirdly, and I would suggest most importantly, the last time anyone saw him alive, he was heading towards the area where you were enjoying your evening,' he paused for effect, 'and where you have a flat.'

Peter was now looking down at his hands, unable to hold the officer's gaze. This was becoming unbearable and Pincent wasn't about to ease up.

'Now, all that could be a huge coincidence, but it shows that a chance meeting might well have given you the opportunity to gain revenge for his past treatment of you. Let's face it, you certainly had motive.'

'Hang on a minute, you're asking me questions like I'm a suspect. If you're going to carry on like this, shouldn't I be offered a solicitor or something?'

Pincent rolled his eyes.

'You're not a suspect, Peter… at least not yet. This is just a friendly chat. We're trying to establish a few facts, that's all.'

Peter couldn't believe what was happening. He'd only killed Tony two days ago and wrongly assumed he'd done everything necessary to avoid detection. Yet here he was on his first morning back at work, clearly under suspicion and being grilled mercilessly. He needed to remain calm and stick to his story.

'Like I said, I've no idea where he went. Whatever happened to him was nothing to do with me.'

The detectives continued to interrogate Peter for a

further ten minutes, but the questions had lost their bite. Dawes seemed satisfied but Pincent made it patently obvious that he believed Peter was somehow involved. He leaned back on his chair again.

'Right, Mr Hardy, that's all for now. We'll be checking everything you've told us and we may need to speak with you again.'

Fighting to keep his breathing shallow and regular, Peter shrugged and tilted his head to one side.

'That's fine, I've nothing to hide.'

Pincent rocked his chair forward onto all four legs, leaned across the table and stared intimidatingly at Peter, his tongue moving backwards and forwards under his top lip. His professionalism slipped for a moment as he remembered his murdered friend.

'You're lying. You had something to do with Tony's death… I'm certain of it and I'm going to prove it.'

'Don't be fucking ridiculous! I'm hardly likely to kill someone over workshop banter, am I?'

Pincent leapt on the comment.

'Ah, but it wasn't just banter, was it? He hated queers like you. He was bullying you and it was driving you to distraction, so you decided to do something about it and when the opportunity came along, you killed him.'

Pincent had hit the nail on the head. Peter could feel the whole world closing in around him but forced out a phony laugh.

'You can think what you want, Sergeant, you can't prove anything.'

As soon as the words had left his lips, he bitterly regretted his choice of phrase.

Pincent leapt on it.

'So, I can't prove anything eh?'

He glanced at Dawes.

'Well Matt, what do you reckon? Sounds like a

challenge from someone with something to hide.'

Dawes nodded, then fixed Peter with one eyebrow raised.

'Why did you say that? Up until then, you'd convinced me you were telling the truth.'

Peter inwardly kicked himself; he had no option now but to apologise.

'Sorry... look, it was a bad choice of words. What I meant was you won't be able to prove anything because I haven't done anything.'

Pincent abruptly stood up.

'Thank you for your time, Mr Hardy.'

He held out an arm towards the door.

Peter pushed his chair back causing a horrible grating sound on the floor, like fingernails being dragged down a blackboard, then rose to his feet and made towards the door. As he passed Pincent, in a flash the officer grabbed hold of his arm and walked out into the corridor with him, leaving Dawes in the office tidying up papers, out of earshot. He pulled Peter close to him and spoke into his right ear.

'For the record, I'm in agreement with Tony Waters about people like you.' He lowered his voice to a whisper. 'You hated him and somehow the chance to kill him came your way. I don't know how you did it but I'm certain you're responsible and I'm going to make sure you're punished.'

Unable to believe what he was hearing, Peter angrily shrugged off his grip and glared angrily at him. Once again, the years of taunts, abuse, and bullying came rushing to the surface. He leaned in, his mouth only a couple of inches from the detective's ear.

'You've got fuck all on me.' He checked to make sure that Dawes was still in the room. 'Whatever happened, that nasty prick got what he deserved. It's what everyone with that vile mentality deserves.' Their eyes were locked, as the precise meaning of Peter's words hit home; they were a direct challenge to Pincent's personal views.

'So, you either produce some evidence to show I was responsible, or fuck off back underneath whatever stone you crawled out from and leave me alone.'

Pincent drew back with a startled expression. He was a bully and had verbally abused suspects for years, but rarely received aggression like this in response.

Peter pursed his lips, narrowed his eyes and blew Pincent a kiss, then smiled broadly, before calmly walking away and returning to the workshop.

TWELVE

As he entered the workshop, Peter slammed the sliding door closed, kicked over a waste bin, walked over to the car he was servicing and banged his fist hard on the vehicle's roof. Andy, Vince, and Bill stopped working and exchanged glances.

'What's up with you?' asked Vince innocently.

Picking up a huge monkey wrench, Peter walked over to where Andy was standing with his left thigh resting against the wing of a Ford Mondeo, wiping oil off his hands with a filthy rag. Rage burned through Peter. He had been the victim of Tony's abuse for so long - abuse the other mechanics, in particular Andy - had joined in with. Now that Tony was dead, he'd wrongly assumed things would change. But that hadn't happened; instead, they'd been more than happy to point the finger at him in their interviews with the detectives.

'What's wrong with me?' He spat out the words through clenched teeth. 'You've dropped me right in it. They think I might have killed Tony because of you lot.'

Andy narrowed his eyes, 'Well... did you?'

'Did I what?'

'Did you kill him?'

Despite Andy hitting the nail on the head, Peter smacked the wrench firmly into the palm of his opposite hand, and squared up to him.

'Take that back you little prick, or I'll wrap this around your weasly fucking face.'

Bill quickly ran forward and placed a hand on Peter's

shoulder.

'Calm down Pete, he didn't mean it, did you Andy?'

He looked over at Andy, who didn't reply, but shook his head and looked down at the floor for a couple of seconds, before returning his stare to Peter.

'Prick!' shouted Peter.

Bill gently pulled him away.

'Look, everyone's in shock. People are saying things they don't mean.'

Peter and Andy continued to glower at each other from opposite sides of the workshop without speaking.

Vince said, 'I'll tell you what's fucking unbelievable, we've just lost our boss and instead of backing each other up, we're at each other's throats. And I can't believe Des isn't letting us have the day off.'

'Well, he's not,' said Bill, 'and he's paying us good wages to do a job, so let's stop arguing and get on with our work.'

'Just one more thing,' said Peter.

His colleagues turned to look at him.

'I'm not putting up with any more crap. If anyone insults me again, they'll fucking regret it.'

He threw the wrench onto the floor with a deafening clatter and returned to his work.

THIRTEEN

James Pincent knocked firmly on DCI Neider's office door and waited for the call to come in. Opening the door, he stepped inside and saw his boss sitting behind a desk, working at her computer. She looked up from the screen, pushed her blue-rimmed glasses onto the top of her head and smiled.

'Hi James, what've you got?'

He held up a folder containing notes they'd made of staff interviews at Duke's Garage.

'We've spoken to the owner and most of the members of staff. One of the mechanics stands out, he's a big fucker, well-built and at least 6'3"-6'4", his name's Peter Hardy. He's been identified by the other members of staff as having a serious grudge against Waters. Apparently, Waters constantly ribbed him about being queer.'

She nodded but didn't reply, something he'd said seemed to be troubling her. Confused by her reaction, he took her silence as permission to continue.

'We're returning to speak to the last three members of office staff this afternoon.'

Natalie remained silent for a few moments. Her husband had told her the name of the man he had been seeing, the man who'd made pathetic attempts at apologising for destroying her wonderful marriage and destroying her happiness, his name was Peter and he was a tall, strapping man. Surely it couldn't be the same one?

She looked down at her desk and formed her fingers

into steeples, pressing them so firmly together in her fury that the tips went white. She slowly returned her gaze to him and pointed at the chair opposite.

'Tell me more about Peter Hardy.'

He sat down on the black plastic chair, pulled it closer to the desk and placed the file on the table's edge, considering his words carefully before speaking.

'I might be wrong, boss, but I've got a hunch Hardy might be our man.'

She narrowed her eyes, removed the spectacles from her head and placed them down gently on the table, but she made no response, which Pincent once again took as an indication to continue.

'The other members of staff painted a picture of Hardy being abused about his sexuality by Waters ever since he joined the firm. Apparently, it was relentless. The mechanics said that Waters was extremely homophobic.'

'I'm not exactly a fan myself, James. It doesn't make Tony Waters a bad person.'

A look of mutual understanding and agreement passed between them. In that moment, he knew she felt the same about gays as him and would back him to the hilt.

'I didn't say it did. I'm just saying he used Hardy's leanings in that direction as an excuse for bullying him.'

Natalie was interested, but didn't appear particularly impressed.

'A bit of bullying about his sexuality in a workplace like a garage wouldn't make most people kill. Sorry James, you'll have to do better than that.'

He fidgeted on the chair, crossing his right leg over his left.

'Their relationship was described by everyone we've spoken to so far as abrasive, even toxic. The other mechanics admitted joining in with the piss taking, although two of them said they did it just to keep in Waters' good books as he was the man who dished out overtime and they wanted their slice. They described their comments to Hardy as "mild banter" compared to what Waters dished out.'

He pulled a couple of sheets from the file and quickly scanned them, refreshing his memory about what had been said.

'What's more interesting is that Hardy has a flat in Soho, where he likes to spend his weekends with friends.'

Natalie raised her eyebrows enquiringly.

'By friends, you mean other queers?'

Pincent laughed at her directness.

'Probably, yes.'

She smiled at him.

'Go on.'

'We can place Hardy in Soho on Friday night and we also know that Waters was last seen leaving The Concord Rooms at around two. His route into Soho would almost certainly have taken him down through Soho Square and into either Greek Street or Frith Street,' he leaned forward with a conspiratorial smile, 'and guess what? Hardy's flat is in Bateman Street, which just happens to link those two streets.'

Natalie sat forward in her chair; this revelation suddenly had her very interested.

'Fucking hell, James, good work.'

She stood up and walked across to the window, resting her hands on the sill, looking down at the vehicles parked in the station yard.

'The abuse gives us motive, albeit a weak one, but if we could prove they bumped into each other in Soho, we might also be able to show he had opportunity. But apart from having a flat in the area, did he really have the means?'

Pincent shrugged, 'We don't yet know.'

Now in full flow, Natalie continued her assessment of the evidence.

'Waters had been beaten after being restrained against something which caused bruising to his hands, lower legs, abdomen, and neck. There was no significant bruising anywhere on his back, which means he was tied up either against a wall, or lying down on his back.'

She turned from the window and began to pace the room, walking past Pincent's chair to the door and causing him to turn around as he listened.

'There was bruising across his face, chest, and abdomen, possibly caused by fists, possibly by a weapon, but if there was a weapon, we've no evidence of it. He had suffered very painful injuries, especially to his groin, but there was nothing of note on his body to point forensically towards the identity of the assailant, let alone anything pointing towards Hardy.'

As she spoke, she returned to the window. Pincent had an idea.

'Maybe we could bring him in, ask a few more questions and apply a little pressure? You know, shake him down, like we used to in the old days? It could work, he might buckle.'

She turned around to face him, leaning back against the window sill, her mind made up.

'Yes, bring him in… and while you're at it, apply for a warrant to search his flat.'

He looked enquiringly at her.

'But we don't have anywhere near enough for a search warrant yet.'

Natalie rubbed her nose between forefinger and thumb, before looking up at the ceiling.

'You might have a point. Tell you what, I'll make the

application myself at the court's afternoon sitting. It will add clout to our chances, having a DCI's name on the application. I think the Magistrate sitting today is Andrew Wolfe. He's a disgusting letch but has always had a soft spot for me, I could make use of that.'

Pincent grinned widely and nodded.

'Do you want us to speak to the rest of the office staff, or just pull him in?'

Natalie thought for a moment.

'You'd better speak to the others first. We must show that we've gathered in all the relevant information before making our move. Who knows, we might unearth some more dirt on the guy.'

Pincent returned the papers to the file.

'Okay, I'll head back to the garage with Matt at one. An hour should be long enough to speak with the remaining staff, unless one of them has something dramatic to tell us. Once we're done, I'll call for a van and ask Hardy to return to the office for a few further questions. Matt can nick him, that'll be a nice little collar for his CV.'

Natalie nodded approvingly.

'Good plan.'

'Who do you want doing the warrant if it's approved?'

'You and Matt. I want you to take Hardy with you when the search is conducted.'

He looked surprised and replied hesitantly.

'Okay…'

'And I'm coming with you. It's just possible I may have met Peter Hardy before, and I'd love to see his face if and when he recognises me.'

Pincent was surprised at this revelation.

'You've met him… where?'

She instantly knew she'd said too much and was

furious with herself at letting it slip. Hardy's possible relationship with her husband was something she didn't want becoming public knowledge.

'It doesn't matter, I'm probably wrong anyway.' She quickly changed tack. 'I'll arrange for a SOCO to meet us at the address. What number Bateman Street is it?'

'56A.'

She noted down the address on a sheet of paper.

'Great, I'll put in the SOCO request to the Met once he's in custody. I'm guessing Soho is West End Central's ground.'

'Yes, it is, but why bother with a SOCO? We might not need one. Wouldn't it be better to wait until we've searched the place ourselves?'

She shook her head firmly.

'No, I want one there from the off. If there's anything there, I want that bastard nailed down.'

Natalie wasn't the type of boss you could challenge and he backed off.

'Fair enough, boss. I'll grab a quick bite, then crack on at the garage with Matt.'

Standing up, he opened the door, offering a small nod to her as he left the room.

Once the door was closed, Natalie sat motionless. She had retaken her seat and was staring hard at her computer, but found herself unable to read anything on the screen. It was just a blur of words with no sense, no meaning.

She was seeing the face of a man mouthing apologies after being caught in the arms of her darling husband... the face of Peter. For three long months she had been desperate for the chance to take revenge on him and now this sweet opportunity had fallen into her lap. In her bones, she felt sure it was the same man and, if so, she would do everything in her power to show that he had

killed Tony Waters, regardless of whether he really was guilty or not.

FOURTEEN

Peter lifted his left arm and tilted his wrist to read the time on his old-fashioned Timex watch, a gift on his 18th birthday from his grandfather, who had owned it for thirty years. It was just after two and he'd been collected in the workshop by Matt Dawes, who escorted him to the sales office, where they apparently had extra questions for him. He'd only just sat down and was about to ask what the problem was, when he saw a police van pulling into the staff car park. He understood what this meant and his heart sank.

Bollocks, they must have found something.

Dawes moved to stand behind Peter and placed his hand on his left shoulder.

'Peter Hardy, I'm arresting you on suspicion of the murder of Tony Waters on Saturday 18th November. You do not have to say anything, but it may harm your defence if you fail to mention, when questioned, something which you later rely on in court. Anything you do say may be given in evidence. Do you understand?'

He wanted to shout and scream, to lash out at the officers and run, but instead he meekly replied, 'Yes.'

The bottom had dropped out of Peter's world. The transformation in his fortunes was hard to take. One minute he'd been elated at finally gaining revenge and ridding himself of Tony Waters; the next he was being arrested for his murder. He felt certain he'd covered his tracks and left no clues, yet here he was under arrest.

The thought of spending twenty or thirty years in

prison for a piece of shit like Waters made his blood boil. He fought to hold back the tears, but still they came, rolling silently down his cheeks.

Dawes grabbed his left arm and hoisted him to his feet. Turning him to face the wall, he placed handcuffs on his wrists behind his back, turned him around once more, checked through his pockets to ensure he had nothing on him that could harm anyone or help him escape, then held his arm and marched him towards the door. Pincent had been in the room throughout, but remained silent. As Peter was escorted past him, he heard Pincent snort dismissively, a distinctly self-satisfied expression on his face. Peter tried pleading with him.

'You've made a big mistake. You've got the wrong man, I'm innocent!'

'You reckon?' smirked Pincent. 'We'll see, won't we?'

The smug faces of the detectives worried him. He was certain they must have found a crucial piece of evidence, something that pointed strongly towards him. The police appeared determined that he was their man, but he wasn't completely cowed, not just yet. He was aware he'd done wrong, but in his mind, *he* was the real victim and had been for many, many years.

He could tell by the way Pincent treated him that he was just as bigoted as Waters; maybe that was the reason he was under arrest and in handcuffs? Whatever the reason, Peter wasn't going down easily. He would fight them all the way.

Peter was escorted across the car park and into the workshop, where his colleagues looked on in astonishment at the sight of him being tightly held by Matt Dawes, hands cuffed securely behind his back. He directed the officers to the area where he'd been working and where his personal property was, including his flat keys.

'Pete, mate, what the fuck's going on?' asked Bill, genuinely confused and alarmed. A weak man, he had gone along with the crowd in teasing Peter, but basically liked the guy and couldn't see him as a brutal killer.

'They think I'm responsible for Tony's murder.'

'That's enough, no talking,' said Dawes. 'Let's go.'

Bill and Vince could scarcely believe what they were witnessing, the hulking great frame of Peter being pulled around by the comparatively diminutive detective. If it wasn't so serious, it would have been comical.

Outside in the car park, Peter was placed into the back of the waiting police van. Sitting inside the cage, he looked out through the open rear door and saw his colleagues watching from outside the workshop. Then the doors were slammed shut, leaving him alone inside the claustrophobically small space. Dawes climbed through the sliding side door into the back of the van, a wall of unbreakable Perspex separating him from Hardy inside the cage. On a signal from Dawes, the driver put the vehicle into gear and drove away.

Two minutes later, Dawes opened the back doors of the van in the rear yard of Sevenoaks Police Station, only 500 yards drive from the garage. He took hold of Peter's left arm and guided him out.

'Mind your head,' he said. 'Don't want you walking into the custody suite with an injury.'

He chuckled at his own joke, as Peter glared at him.

'Think you're hilarious, don't you?'

FIFTEEN

Once inside the custody suite, Peter looked around uneasily as he and Dawes were instructed to sit on a long wooden bench, which ran along the length of one wall. They waited while a very drunk giant of a man was being forcibly searched by two male officers.

As one of them stood behind him to check his rear jeans pockets, the drunk snapped his head backwards, smashing it into the officer's nose and causing it to burst open. The officer cried out in pain, staggering sideways and drawing both hands up to his face where blood was pouring from his nostrils. The custody officer stood up and, in a flash, grabbed the hair of the drunk man, pulling his head hard down onto the counter. A loud crack was followed by a scream of pain, as one of the prisoner's teeth flew across the counter and fell to the floor. The man was yanked upright, blood gushing from his mouth, while another officer ran to replace his injured colleague, who was being helped from the room. As the drunk was arrested for assaulting a police officer, he shouted, 'Fuck you!' Peter watched the unfolding scene with a mixture of horror and disbelief.

The search of the drunk man was eventually completed and the custody officer shouted at the officers restraining him, 'Put him in a fucking cell!' He was dragged away struggling and screaming abuse, until somewhere in the distance, Peter heard the cell door being slammed shut, before the officers reappeared seconds later.

'Tosser,' said one of them. 'He's done a proper fucking job on Steve's nose. I think he's broken it.'

The custody officer was standing up gently rubbing his finger over the surface.

'Jesus Christ! His tooth has chipped the counter.' He smiled broadly. 'I hope it hurt.'

His comments produced a small ripple of laughter. Suddenly turning serious, he addressed the officers involved in the incident.

'Right, party's over, fuck off to the canteen and get your notes done.' He nodded towards Peter. 'I've got one more waiting to be booked in.'

Sitting back in his chair, he started writing up the drunk man's custody record, before pausing and calling to the officers making their way out.

'And let me know how Steve is.'

'Will do, Sarge.'

The custody officer was Sergeant Nick Winter, an efficient and trustworthy officer, well-liked by the Senior Management Team, because whenever a difficult or sensitive job needed doing, he could always be relied upon. A stocky 53-year-old, he was once crowned by a shock of red hair, but now kept his hair cut short, the majority of which had turned grey. He sometimes used spectacles when working on the custody computer, but not always; they were normally called into action after several hours work, when his eyes were getting tired. He peered at the screen now, then looked up at his gaoler, a female officer with a pretty face and a large bun of dark-brown hair tied up neatly on her head.

'Sandy, be a love and make us a coffee.'

'Okay, Sarge.'

Nick Winter looked over to Matt Dawes.

'Won't be a second Matt, I just need to finish writing up that piss-pot.'

'No problem Sarge. Mr Hardy's in no rush, are you?'

Peter glared angrily at him.

'Can't you at least take the cuffs off? They're really hurting and I'm not likely to go anywhere.'

In response to Peter's request, Dawes raised an eyebrow enquiringly at Winter, who nodded his approval and Dawes removed them. Peter rubbed both wrists vigorously, examining the reddening and indentations left by the harsh metal bars.

Sandy handed a steaming cup of coffee to her sergeant in a mug which had *World's best Grandad* written above pictures of Winter cuddling a small girl, which Peter assumed was his granddaughter. He blew some of the steam away and carefully took a tiny sip, sighing with satisfaction.

Looking over the rim of the mug, Winter said, 'All right, bring him up,' and placed the mug carefully on the counter.

Dawes took hold of Peter's right arm and pulled him to his feet, then walked him to the counter. Winter opened both hands with fingers outstretched and gently rubbed his palms together, then he interlocked his fingers and pushed his hands away from his body, producing a cracking sound that made Peter wince.

'Right then, Matt, why have you brought this gentleman in to see me?'

'Sergeant, this is Peter Hardy. He's been arrested on suspicion of murder.'

Raising his eyes to look over the top of his spectacles at Peter, Winter said calmly, 'Time of arrest?'

'2.03pm Sarge.'

He noted the time on the custody record.

'Circumstances of arrest please.'

'Mr Hardy has worked at Duke's Garage on Amhurst Hill for the past three months, where until last

Friday Tony Waters was his supervisor. Mr Hardy is homosexual and transsexual, something which Mr Waters had teased him about since the day he joined. Their relationship was described by everyone who worked at the garage as abrasive, some staff described it as toxic. On two separate occasions, members of staff overheard Mr Hardy threatening to hurt him.

'Mr Waters was last seen leaving a club in Rathbone Place, London, at 2 o'clock on Saturday morning. He didn't join his friends heading back to Kent and walked off towards Soho to continue drinking and to challenge the behaviour of gays in the area. At the same time, Mr Hardy was leaving a club in Old Compton Street, Soho, dressed as a woman. He was in company with another man and heading for his nearby flat in Bateman Street, W1.

'I believe that Mr Hardy encountered Waters in that area, providing him both motive and opportunity to commit the offence. DCI Neider is applying for a warrant to search his flat at the Magistrates Court as we speak. It is believed the search may well show he also had the means. Arrest was necessary to secure and preserve evidence and for the purpose of interview.'

Winter sat back with a concerned look on his face. It was obvious that he was not exactly impressed with the strength of evidence Dawes had presented to him.

'I must say, the necessity for this arrest is questionable to say the least.'

Peter had been listening carefully to the evidence and could see the Sergeant clearly wasn't happy with Dawes and for a moment he felt a glimmer of hope.

Dawes frowned. 'I don't understand, Sarge.'

Nick Winter sat back in his chair, an expression of long-suffering patience on his face.

'Well, let me explain. You see, your job is to

convince me that the arrest was both legal and necessary, but in my view you're barely on the cusp of what's required. There is no direct evidence that Mr Hardy has committed *any* offence, let alone murder. You *have* shown that there is circumstantial evidence pointing towards his possible involvement, but I'm not sure that's enough to justify arresting him.'

Winter rubbed his hands together, carefully considering his decision.

'Just give me a moment. I need to think about this and check a couple of things.'

He stood up, walked into the small rear office and picked up the phone. Dawes and Peter exchanged a glance, both waiting for his verdict.

Two minutes later, he returned to his seat, looking firstly at Dawes, then at Peter. Time seemed to stand still for Peter; he was hopeful, but knew from friends who'd been arrested before that coppers usually stuck together.

'Mr Hardy, I am satisfied there *is* sufficient evidence you have committed an offence. Therefore, I *am* authorising your detention. Do you understand?"

Peter laughed out loud.

'This is ridiculous. You know as well as I do, we've heard nothing that could be considered as evidence to justify my arrest. Just because Tony and I didn't get on, doesn't mean I'd kill him. And both of us being out enjoying ourselves in London on a Friday night hardly proves anything, so were thousands and thousands of other people.'

Winter became annoyed at this challenge to his authority and glared at Peter.

'I've made my decision and in my view DC Dawes' evidence has passed the threshold. That's *my* opinion and it's *my* opinion that counts, not yours. Take off your belt and empty your pockets please, then place all your possessions on the counter.'

Peter shook his head in disbelief, he had no option but to comply with the instruction and Winter directed Dawes to search him. Once he'd been thoroughly searched, Peter's possessions were placed into a plastic property bag, which was sealed with his name and custody record number written on the side.

'You have the right to speak with a solicitor. If you don't have a solicitor, you can speak to the Duty Solicitor. Do you want to speak to a solicitor?'

Peter shook his head and shrugged.

'Do you think I need one?'

'I'm sorry, Mr Hardy, I can't advise you either way, but perhaps you should consider the seriousness of the offence for which you've been arrested.'

'I haven't done anything wrong, Sergeant, but I think I'd better speak to the Duty Solicitor please.'

'Okay,' He looked around for his gaoler, 'Sandy, contact the Duty Solicitor please.'

He turned to Peter. 'I'm authorising that you have your fingerprints and photograph taken. This is done for all persons arrested on suspicion of having committed a recordable offence. Do you understand?'

Peter nodded miserably, desperately trying to keep his spirits up. He needed to stay strong, he wouldn't let them beat him; he *mustn't* let them beat him.

Turning to Dawes, Winter asked, 'Will you be seizing clothing?'

Dawes shook his head, 'No, Sarge, his work clothes are of no evidential value.'

'Okay then, Sandy, please take Mr Hardy for processing.'

She nodded, 'Come with me please Mr Hardy.' She led Peter into a side room and closed the door.

'Matt, crack on with your notes and bring them to

me once you're done.'

'Will do, Sarge.'

Winter then gestured with his index finger for Dawes to come nearer and leaned forward to whisper in the detective's ear, 'And don't you ever bring someone in again with such shit evidence. I had to go out on a limb there, I should really have kicked him straight out.'

Matt nodded, 'Sorry, Sarge. I was just following orders. The DCI really wanted him in, no matter what.'

Winter raised his eyebrows.

'Did she indeed? In that case, I'll be having a word with her later.'

Dawes left the room feeling suitably admonished.

In the side room, Peter stood up to have his fingerprints taken, then sat back down again to have his photograph taken from the front and both sides. It all felt surreal, as if he had somehow stumbled into one of the TV cop shows he was so fond of. The gaoler tried making small talk with him, chatting about the weather, asking if he was married and where he lived. He really wasn't interested in exchanging pleasantries, and responded in monosyllables. Eventually she gave up and, having obtained everything she required, walked Peter down a corridor to cell number two.

The door closed with a loud bang. The gaoler's face briefly appeared through the Perspex wicket, before that too was closed, leaving Peter alone in the spartan cell. Looking around him, he saw only a low bench with a dark blue plastic mattress and pillow, a flimsy light blue blanket, an alcove with a metal toilet with no seat and only single sheets of toilet paper, no loo roll. Not exactly the Ritz.

He slumped down on the bench and thought about the past 48 hours, how things hadn't gone exactly as he'd planned; how if he ended up being charged and convicted, his life may have changed forever. But he found that, whatever happened, he didn't regret killing Tony Waters. Slowly, Peter's mind cleared; he wasn't going down without a fight. Tony Waters had been a bastard who'd deserved everything that had happened to him and he certainly wasn't worth losing his liberty over.

The evidence was thin to say the least, the custody sergeant's reaction showed that only too clearly. They had a very long way to go to prove he'd done anything wrong, let alone murdered Tony Waters. He simply had to stay strong and keep refuting anything put to him. If they managed to produce sufficient evidence to convict him then fair enough but until then, he'd simply deny everything.

SIXTEEN

Peter had been lying on his cell bed for an hour, trying to stop his thoughts descending into a whirlpool of despair, when the wicket was suddenly dropped open and a face peered in. Through the reinforced Perspex he was unable to identify who it was, or even tell if it was male or female. Seconds later, the jangling of keys suggested he was about to have a visitor. The heavy steel door was heaved open and a smartly dressed, middle-aged woman walked in, staring at him without emotion. He vaguely recognised the woman from somewhere and from the intensity of her stare, she seemed to know him. He didn't know her name, but he soon would.

'Hello Mr Hardy, I've been looking forward to seeing you.'

He turned onto one side and lifted himself up into a seated position. The way she spoke, as if there was a personal connection between them, rattled him, leaving him racking his brain, trying desperately to recall who the fuck this woman was. Her hair was tightly pulled back in a ponytail and she was wearing a smart blue suit; she looked nothing like the woman with bobbed hair wearing jeans and tee shirt he'd briefly encountered months before.

'Sorry, you have me at a disadvantage.'

She confidently approached him, her gaze not leaving his face for a second. She was of average build for a woman her age, no more than 5'2", maybe 5'3" tall and he stood 6'4" in his bare feet, yet he was feeling strangely threatened by her.

'Yes, Mr Hardy, I do have you at a disadvantage, a significant disadvantage.'

He passed his tongue over his dry lips. Whoever this woman was, she was trying hard to unnerve him and he simply couldn't let that happen. He had to remain in control, so decided to go on the attack.

'I don't know who the fuck you are, love, but I presume you're a copper.'

She nodded, 'You're right, I am.'

'Well, if they've sent you in to frighten me with a bad-cop routine, you can inform your bosses you're shit at it.'

'That might be rather difficult.'

'Why's that?'

'Because I'm the Detective Chief Inspector in charge of this murder enquiry.' She smiled smugly at Peter's blank stare. 'In other words, Peter, I *am* the boss.'

This had taken him by surprise, but he stayed on the attack.

'Well, bully for you, aren't you the important one?'

She walked closer to him, until her face was only inches from his; although he was seated and she was standing, their heads were roughly equal height.

'Yes Peter, I am the important one. I'm the person who's going to try her level best to prove you killed Tony Waters, and when you go to prison for the rest of your life, I'll laugh my tits off!'

The woman's naked aggression genuinely shocked Peter.

'Sorry, have we met before? If so, I can't remember where and I don't know what your problem is. Have I done something to offend you?'

She slowly shook her head.

'You're fucking unbelievable.'

91

Peter knew he'd seen her somewhere before, of that he was certain, but he just couldn't recall her. Plenty of women brought their cars into the garage; that was probably it. Whatever the truth of their previous encounter was, he wasn't about to allow her bullying to gain the upper hand.

'Sorry, love, you're obviously eminently forgettable.'

He stood up, towering over her.

His snub had enraged Natalie and now *she* struggled to keep her temper. She held up two sheets of paper, unfolding the first one for Peter to read.

'This is a warrant to search your flat at Bateman Street.'

She smiled at the flicker of alarm on Peter's face then unfolded the second sheet of paper.

'And this is a warrant to search your car. Let's see if you're still as cocky once our forensic officers have had a chance to poke around.'

Despite all his best efforts, Peter was becoming increasingly alarmed. He'd done his best to cover his tracks, but was only too aware that murderers rarely, if ever, hide evidence of their offences well enough. The forensic experts always seemed to find evidence from the victim; a single stray hair, a fibre, a fingerprint, something to prove the suspect had been lying all along, something that ultimately convicts them. He wasn't concerned about a search of his Astra - they'd be looking at the wrong car entirely - but was terrified of them searching his flat

He desperately wanted to sit down; his legs felt unusually heavy and they suddenly seemed unhappy at having to continue supporting his weight. Peter tried smiling confidently at Natalie, but knew he was failing miserably.

Natalie noticed his discomfort and fixed him with a satisfied smile.

'You'll be given a meal in an hour or two. After that you'll be coming with me, DS Pincent, and DC Bates to your flat in Soho. Are the keys in your property bag, or will we have to smash your front door off the hinges?'

'They're in my property. Please don't damage my door.'

'Shame, I was looking forward to that.' She backed away to the door. 'I'll be back in a couple of hours, Mr Hardy, make sure you're ready.'

He couldn't let her have the last word.

'I'll look forward to it love. There's nothing of interest at my flat and when I'm released, I'll be coming after you for false imprisonment.'

Natalie moved into the corridor and held the edge of the open cell door in her left hand.

'Okay, Mr Hardy, whatever makes you happy.'

She smiled and nodded at him, before gently pushing the cell door closed, which secured with a soft click; somehow, it felt much worse than when it was slammed.

Peter's meal turned out to be spaghetti bolognaise, followed by pineapple and custard. He pushed his main course around the plate as he contemplated his situation; unsurprisingly, he wasn't very hungry. The custard had congealed with a thick skin on top of the pineapple, so he didn't even bother trying that.

Between DCI Neider closing his cell door and his meal arriving, Peter's emotions had swung between black despair, when he wanted to scream and beat the walls with his fists, and moments of calm, moments during which he reassured himself that the police would struggle to prove anything and that all would be well. He was convinced he didn't deserve being sent to prison for a couple of decades. He just needed to remain resolute and strong.

SEVENTEEN

At 6.40 that evening, Peter's cell door was opened and Natalie walked in with James Pincent; she had a disconcerting smile on her face.

'Hello, Peter, ready for a trip to London?'

'Why are you bothering to search my flat? Shouldn't you be asking me questions or something?'

Pincent laughed, 'You've been watching too many crime dramas. Police work is all about being prepared *before* you start asking questions. We might find things of interest in your flat or your car, things we would need to ask you about.'

Natalie stepped forward.

'There's no great rush, Peter, we'll start the interviews in the morning, once the searches have been completed. Your cottage has already been searched. We didn't find anything, but we weren't expecting to. Your car's been collected from the garage and it's parked in the station yard. After that's been searched, we'll nip up to your flat in Bateman Street.'

Peter couldn't stop the anxiety from showing on his face and Natalie spotted it, tempting her to crack a joke.

'Don't worry about your beauty sleep, Mr Hardy, we'll be back by bed time.'

Pincent extended an arm to direct Peter and they walked together down the short corridor to the custody officer's desk. Sergeant Nick winter was still at his post and nodded at Neider, with whom he'd shared his displeasure about the lack of evidence a few hours earlier.

All that was forgotten now; they were back on the same side and he smiled at her.

'Yes Ma'am, how can I help you?'

'I'd like to book Mr Hardy out for searches please, Sarge, and we'll need the flat keys from his property bag.'

'Okay, no problem.'

He reached under the counter and produced a stamp, which he pressed onto an ink pad before transferring it onto the custody record. He held out a pen for DCI Neider.

'Sign there please.'

Natalie took the pen and signed the declaration produced by the stamp, which transferred responsibility for the security and welfare of Peter from Winter to herself. Finally, once the keys were in Neider's possession, Winter smiled and said, 'He's all yours, have fun.'

Pincent told Peter to put his hands behind his back, before handcuffing him. Out in the station yard, Natalie shook hands with a woman carrying a bright silver case and wearing a white boilersuit who was waiting alongside Peter's Astra.

'Peter, this is Cindy Palmer, she's a scenes of crime officer. After we've had a quick look over your car, she'll dust it for prints and any other forensics which might show that Tony Waters was in there.'

Peter wasn't concerned about the search of his car and gave a resigned shrug.

'Do what you like.'

He thanked heavens he'd used the Escort and not his Astra that weekend. He always left the Escort under a lean-to in the farmyard, so they would have been unlikely to link it to him when they searched his house. They could search his Astra as much as they wanted, but they were checking the wrong vehicle.

Matt Dawes appeared from a separate door that led out to the yard from the station's canteen and joined them, pulling on a pair of rubber gloves.

'Sorry I'm late, Ma'am. Had to queue for ages to get served.'

Dawes walked around the vehicle opening all four doors, the bonnet lid and the boot. He checked under the seats, under the carpets, inside the door panels, the glove compartment, the boot, and the engine compartment. Once he was satisfied that nothing incriminating had been found, Natalie said to the SOCO, 'All yours Cindy.'

Cindy Palmer had been a SOCO for 25 years. A painfully thin woman, with sunken cheeks and a permanent hollow expression, she rarely smiled. However, she was bloody good at her job, probably the best in Kent and had assisted DCI Neider several times in the past. Natalie worked on the assumption that if Cindy couldn't find the evidence, it probably wasn't there.

The minutes crept by and the yard was getting very dark. Luckily it wasn't too cold for a November evening but Peter was already shivering through nerves about having his flat searched. After almost an hour, Cindy turned to Natalie and said, 'All done here.'

'Anything of interest?'

'I've lifted a few decent prints and a couple of fibres. I'll get them off to the lab for comparison.'

Peter smiled.

'Nobody else has been near that vehicle for months. Anything you've found will be mine.'

Natalie looked searchingly at him, noting the uneasy shuffling of his feet.

'Oh dear, Sergeant Pincent, I do believe Mr Hardy's feeling the pressure. He's shaking. Are you feeling unwell, Mr Hardy?'

Peter didn't respond. He knew Natalie was pulling his chain, but he had no intention of giving her the pleasure of knowing she'd got him rattled.

Peter didn't respond. His back Natalie was pulling his chair, but he had no intention of giving her the pleasure of knowing she'd got him rattled.

EIGHTEEN

An hour later, the unmarked police car pulled up behind a white scenes of crime van parked outside 56 Bateman Street. The journey into London had been uneventful, with Peter sitting in the rear near-side seat, handcuffed to Matt Dawes. James Pincent drove and Natalie was in the front passenger seat. He was thankful that they'd hardly spoken a word to him throughout the journey, not even bothering to taunt him, which was something he'd fully expected. Their talk seemed to revolve around various villains they'd nicked over the years and how most uniformed officers, or "woodentops", were *fucking useless*.

Jumping quickly from the car Natalie opened Peter's door and held out her arm.

'Slide your arse across Matt, we'll unload him from this side.'

Pincent made his way to the pavement, where he spoke to the young SOCO, who gave his name as Archie. He'd been supplied by the Metropolitan Police at Natalie's request. Dawes closed the rear door and Pincent pressed his key fob to lock the car. He waved the keys to the flat.

'Ready to go, Ma'am?'

She nodded, 'Yes, let's get on with it.'

Peter looked around at the familiar street with sadness; would he ever be able to return here and enjoy the freedom he had before Waters came and invaded his world?

Two minutes later they were inside the flat. Dawes

uncuffed himself from Peter then removed the other handcuff, freeing him completely. Pincent locked the door and slid the flat keys into his trouser pocket, ensuring their prisoner couldn't escape. Natalie told Peter to stand by the settee and keep quiet. He was becoming increasingly edgy, his earlier confidence about covering up the crime steadily evaporating.

'Fucking hell,' said Pincent, 'this is like living in a shoe box!'

'It suits me,' replied Peter.

The DS looked slowly around the room, sizing it up. 'What does it measure, about four yards by eight?'

'Something like that, but it's got everything I need.'

Natalie interrupted their conversation.

'That's enough chat. Matt, you search the kitchen cupboards, toilet and shower. James, you check the bed, settee and anything else. Make sure you're gloved-up and don't be too long, the SOCO doesn't want too much disturbed, do you?'

Archie grinned and shook his head.

'Touch as little as possible please, guys, and if you don't need to disturb something, leave it.'

Dawes and Pincent set to work, peering into cupboards, in the wardrobe, under the bed, underneath the settee cushions, inside the toilet, everywhere, while Peter watched, with a burning unease in the pit of his stomach, terrified something would be found to reveal Tony Waters' presence in his flat. Two and a half days ago, he had brutally beaten Tony in that very room, before drugging him and driving him away to his death. He might very soon be suffering the consequences of his actions.

Pincent seemed to be paying particular attention to the newly created dining area, carefully inspecting the photographs on the laminate wall; then he flapped up the rug and ran his fingers over the newly laid flooring. He hated this faggot who'd almost certainly killed one of his mates, so didn't want to miss anything important. Peter watched his every move with bated breath, anticipating questions about when that area of the flat had been completed.

'All done here, Ma'am,' said Dawes. 'Nothing to report.'

'Thanks Matt.'

Flapping the rug back down while resting on one knee, Pincent glared accusingly at Peter, who matched the hostility in his look, while at the same time fighting to keep his breathing regular and stable. Pincent rose slowly to his feet, moving his gaze to Natalie as he did so.

'Nothing found here either, Ma'am.'

'Thanks James.' She turned to Archie, 'Right young man, it's all yours. We'll be waiting in the car.'

Archie nodded.

'Thank you. Shouldn't be too long, there's not much in here.'

Not being present while the forensic search was carried out didn't seem right to Peter and he felt compelled to say something.

'So, I'm not permitted to witness the forensic examination of my own property… when I'm suspected of murder?'

'That's right,' said Natalie.

He glared angrily at her.

'Okay, you're the person with all the power right now, but once he's found nothing, I'll be passing this on to my solicitor.'

Natalie heaved a sigh of frustration and rolled her eyes.

'Look, if you really want to stay in here for the next hour, watching this gentleman dusting for prints and other equally boring tasks, then you can.'

Thinking about what she'd just said, she turned to Archie.

'No offence.'

He chuckled, 'None taken. Most coppers seem to think this work is mind-numbingly boring, but I love it.' He looked sympathetically at Peter.

'I don't mind having your company. Take a seat on the settee. I might be a while though.'

'Thank you.'

Sitting down, Peter was hoping against hope he'd done a good enough job of cleaning the flat.

Dawes groaned, 'That'll mean me staying in here too, then?'

'Spot on,' said Pincent snorting with laughter. 'Don't want Mr Hardy going AWOL, do we?'

'Tell you what,' said Neider, 'James can go and get fish and chips for everyone and we'll claim it back on expenses. After all, we do have a prisoner in custody for murder. I'll wait outside in the car.'

'Would you like something Peter?' she said, in a voice of mock concern.

'No,' he replied, coldly. 'I want nothing from you!'

'Are you sure? Could be your last evening meal as a free man, depending on what Archie finds, of course.'

Something in the way Neider was looking at him, as if he was something she had just wiped from her shoe, made him shiver. He was sure that this woman loathed him and that her feelings went deeper than the usual homophobic distaste.

'Yes… I'm sure. Nothing for me… thanks.'

Neider was thoroughly enjoying the effect she was having on the man in front of her; she loved having him at her mercy, unable to work out the connection between them, why she had such obvious hatred for him. She laughed and turned her back on Peter.

'Come on, let's leave them to it and get the food. I'm starving.'

'Okay, boss,' said Pincent, slightly perplexed by her evident amusement. He opened the door and stepped aside to let her pass through first. Before leaving, he turned back to Dawes and raised his eyebrows as if to say "What the fuck's going on?" then followed her out into the night.

NINETEEN

Pincent was taking his time fetching the fish and chips and, meanwhile, Neider waited in the car, thinking about Peter Hardy and his impact on her life. She replayed the wonderful times she'd shared with Thomas before that fateful day in the car park. Their wedding day had been the happiest of her life.

Having previously been married to her police career, the longest relationship she'd enjoyed with any man prior to meeting Thomas was eight months. Previous to that she'd been happy enough living a solo life, always content with her own company. Then came the day that Thomas accidentally bumped into her at a rugby match in Sevenoaks and, in an instant, her life changed for the better – or so she thought.

Images of her husband making love with Hardy flashed persistently in her head, as they'd done every night for months. How could Thomas have done this to her? The thought of him having sex with Hardy, then coming home and touching her was disgusting. She wanted revenge, wanted it so badly.

Forcing her anger back down inside, she battled hard to calm down. Fate had smiled on her; she had Peter Hardy, the bastard who'd seduced her husband, the man who'd ruined her life and destroyed her happiness, precisely where she wanted him. The evidence against him at present was weak to say the least, but she was convinced he was responsible for the murder of Tony Waters. She just needed the tiniest scrap of forensic evidence proving that Waters had been inside either the car or the flat; that, combined with CCTV and circumstantial evidence, should be sufficient to convict him.

If insufficient evidence was found, then she'd personally conduct his interview and she'd carry out the best fucking interview she'd ever done. Hopefully, once she'd put him under pressure, he would either slip up… or let his guard down.

There was just one tiny fly in the ointment. Although she would dearly love to have been able to confront Peter with her identity, to see the shock on his face when he realised who exactly he had to deal with, this would risk exposing the truth she had worked so hard to hide for many months. If it all came out, not only would she be immediately removed from the case, severely damaging her previously unblemished record as a straightforward and honest detective, but the shame and humiliation of her husband's affair and her subsequent cover-up would turn her into a laughing stock among her colleagues. She'd be a figure of fun wherever she went in what was still a largely homophobic, and male-chauvinistic profession. That was something she just couldn't allow to happen. She would just have to stay in control of her emotions and play the long game; she was good at that.

By the time Pincent returned with the fish and chips, she was ready to play her part. They re-entered the flat to find Archie had finished his checks of the settee and bed, meaning they now had somewhere to sit. Natalie and James chose the settee, leaving Matt to perch on the edge of the bed, while Peter stretched out on it.

At one point, while all three detectives were concentrating on their food, rather than what the SOCO was doing, Peter noticed Archie paying close attention to a small stain near the bottom of the curtain; something which he hadn't noticed when he'd cleaned the flat. He knew that if the stain was caused by Tony's blood, or other bodily fluids, then his freedom was forfeit and a long stretch of imprisonment awaited him. He held his breath, trying not to betray any signs of anxiety.

Archie shone a UV light onto the stain, which was barely visible with the naked eye, but illuminated brightly for a split second under the UV's penetrating beam. Peter's heart sank; he knew enough to realise that the stain was probably blood and it certainly wasn't his. At that moment, Neider noticed the SOCO's interest in something on the curtain and quickly swallowed down a piece of battered cod.

'Have you found something?'

The SOCO met Natalie's gaze with a serious look on his face, momentarily transferred his attention to Peter then he looked back at the DCI.

'No Ma'am, just a food stain, nothing of interest.'

Natalie glared at Peter, who inwardly breathed a huge sigh of relief; he truly thought his time had come. 'Shame.'

Once Natalie's attention had completely returned to her meal, Archie glanced back at Peter and gave him the merest, almost imperceptible nod. Peter wasn't sure if his eyes had deceived him.

In that moment, Peter knew he owed Archie a huge debt, but he had no idea, if it was indeed a blood stain, why he would cover for him. That might be something he would never know the answer to.

Twenty minutes later, Archie started packing his equipment into his suitcase. 'All done, Ma'am. Apart from a few prints and hair samples, there's nothing of interest I'm afraid.'

'Could you possibly…?'

'Hurry the checks through? Yes, I'll get started on them in the morning.'

TWENTY

A light drizzle was falling as their car pulled into the rear yard of Sevenoaks Police Station, the gloomy weather perfectly matching Natalie's mood. The searches had thus far proved entirely fruitless, a fact that Peter knew was entirely down to the whim of a SOCO he'd never even met before.

Peter was handed into the care of Custody Officer Cynthia Moore, who had taken over from Nick Winter at ten, the start of the night duty shift. The time was now approaching midnight and Peter was feeling the effects of the previous twenty-four hours; he was mentally and physically shattered.

Natalie walked him into the custody suite and once he was safely inside, she turned to James and Matt.

'You guys head off home, I'll take care of booking him back in.'

Neither of them needed asking twice and within a moment they were gone. Once Peter's flat keys had been returned to the Custody Officer and placed back into his property bag, Natalie signed the relevant paperwork. She told the gaoler to relax, insisting she would personally escort him back to his cell.

At the cell door she turned to face Peter square on.

'I think you're a disgusting piece of shit and I'm going to prove you killed Tony Waters if it's the last thing I do.'

Although he already knew that Neider, for reasons best known to herself, seemed to have some serious personal issues with him, he was nevertheless taken aback by her open aggression, but he towered over her, matching her hatred.

'Good luck with that darling, but you've got one major problem.'

She raised an enquiring eyebrow.

'You've got no evidence, so you won't be able to prove it.'

He paused, letting his words sink in then decided to torment her by going one stage further.

'It might also interest you to know that once I've been fully released, I'll be looking for compensation. Not only are you holding me for no good reason, but you're also clearly motivated by personal dislike and prejudice. I'm being persecuted just for being gay.'

Her gut feeling was that this man was guilty. She wanted him to be guilty, she was desperate for him to be guilty. But just for a moment she wondered whether her loathing of him really was affecting her judgement. Could he be innocent of Waters' murder? As if reading her thoughts and sensing her doubts, Peter smiled.

'You can't prove a fucking thing can you Detective Chief Inspector Neider? As for Tony Waters, he had it coming, darling. He *really* was a disgusting bastard.'

Not bothering to respond, Neider forced herself to hold his stare for several seconds before slowly pushing the cell door shut until the lock clicked into place. In that moment, she knew that tomorrow morning's interview would be merely going through the motions, something to satisfy the custody officer and her bosses that she was taking the matter seriously.

If none of the forensics came back with a positive trace on Tony Waters, she knew that Hardy could simply lie his way through it, or say "No comment" to each question and she'd have to release him almost immediately afterwards. She knew he'd won this battle, but somehow, in some way, she fully intended to win the war.

TWENTY-ONE

Peter was left alone in his cell with his thoughts and his memories. He'd had many lovers in recent years and didn't regret any of them. There had been the gorgeous guy at the health club, Dan, who had got him into pulling weights, in between energetic bouts of sex in the guy's home gym; that's where he'd got the idea to create one of his own. Jamie had been a laugh; he was an actor and sex with him had always been imaginative and fun; that is, until Jamie's regular boyfriend got wind of the affair and their role-playing sessions came to an abrupt end. Then there was Thomas. He remembered the first time Thomas had brought him home.

Thomas's car had pulled up on the gravel surface of the in-and-out driveway of 'Tall Trees,' an imposing six-bedroomed house with 1½ acres of land on a heavily wooded private road where the rich and powerful chose to live, not far from Sevenoaks. Privacy was provided by large trees on three sides while the winding driveway and thick leylandii hedge prevented prying eyes from anyone using the road. Anyone driving up to the house had first to negotiate the large wooden electronic gates which had opened at Thomas's command.

Petra had stared open-mouthed at the massive mock-Tudor property in front of her; the patio was huge and there was a triple garage to one side of the main house, which had another whole floor above it.

Thomas noticed Petra's interest in the area above the garage.

'It's a self-contained flat, for when we have large numbers staying over and they can't all fit in the house.'

Petra shook her head.

'I shouldn't think that's very often. How many bedrooms are there?'

'Six, seven if you include the flat.'

'Unbelievable. Talk about how the other half live.'

Thomas smiled broadly and leaned across to kiss her.

'Well, for the next two or three hours you're going to enjoy the benefits this kind of life can provide.'

Petra smiled and returned his kiss.

'Come on,' said Thomas, 'let's get indoors.'

Thomas Neider had been bisexual for almost thirty years. Since the age of sixteen, he'd had several long-term 'going steady' relationships with women. That had always been the persona he wanted the world to see and it had served him well. Over the past ten years it had complemented his image as a well-respected, powerful and uncompromising businessman. He had started investing in mobile phone technology in his mid-twenties and, by his mid-thirties, owned one of the leading mobile phone circuit-board manufacturers and distributors, rapidly making him a multi-millionaire - and a very eligible bachelor.

But despite his outward appearance to the world as a full-on heterosexual alpha-male, Thomas nearly always had a male sexual partner on the go. He loved the deception he was perpetrating on the world, the sordidness of the encounters, the animal lust he felt whenever he was with a man. He knew he was being a total bastard to the women who had loved and trusted him, but he simply didn't care. Being with a man was different, exciting; it was like a drug and he had no intention of giving up any time soon.

Meeting Natalie and falling in love with her had taken him completely by surprise. He first met her while watching rugby at the nearby Sevenoaks Rugby Club. Both enjoyed the sport and would occasionally enjoy watching a game down at the team's ground. They bumped into each other in the clubhouse on a cold, wet winter day in 1987. It was half-time and at first they chatted about the game, Thomas being mightily impressed with her knowledge of the sport, before they walked back out from the clubhouse to watch the second half together.

He learned that she was a Detective Inspector in the Kent Constabulary and that she'd dealt with some very serious and well-known cases. However, he was a little surprised she'd never had a long-term relationship. She wasn't the archetypal stunningly attractive female that he'd spent his life pursuing, but there was something about her, something different, something he'd been seeking for a long time. Fundamentally, she was a female version of him, strong, ruthless, and driven, and he was captivated. At the end of the game, he asked if she would like to go for a drink and the rest, as they say, is history. However, it hadn't been long before Thomas was on the hunt once again, he longed for extra-marital diversions.

By the time of the visit to Thomas's home, he and Peter had been seeing each other for almost a month. They'd met in a pub in Sevenoaks, when they were both buying drinks at the bar. Peter had instantly picked up on the more than friendly vibes Thomas was emitting and before long, they had begun seeing each other regularly. Thomas was soon introduced to Peter's alter-ego, Petra, and was fascinated by her.

Thomas was 46, Petra 21; he was a wealthy businessman, she was unemployed, having just lost her job as a mechanic. Sometimes Thomas would ask her to come as Peter, sometimes as Petra, depending on how he felt at the time. Their previous meetings had been in car parks, lay-bys and twice in small hotels in the Medway Towns, like most of Petra's liaisons. However, this time was different, this time he was taking her into his home, safe in the knowledge that his wife was giving evidence at the Old Bailey all day.

Thomas initially walked her through the palatial ground floor of the house and out of the back door, where she gasped on seeing the heated swimming pool with adjoining pool house. The rear patio was even larger than the one at the front. Pulling her inside the pool house, Thomas kissed her savagely on the mouth. Even though Petra liked dressing as a woman, she preferred being the penetrator during sex, although she would occasionally allow a partner to be dominant and always enjoyed Thomas's aggression.

Thirty minutes later, armed with a bottle of red wine, Thomas led Petra to the sumptuous master bedroom. Thomas had prepared the area by removing the duvet and placing what looked like a large groundsheet over the whole bed. Glancing at it, Petra raised her eyes enquiringly.

'I don't want the problem of having to explain stains away,' Thomas said.

She giggled. Then, as her gaze shifted to the bedside cabinet, she noticed a polaroid camera.

'Is that for us?'

He smiled. 'I like to keep a record of men I've had back here, for private viewing. Don't worry, my wife will never find them. You can have some of the photos if you'd like.'

An hour and a half later, they lay in each other's arms. They'd taken dozens of pictures: intimate close-ups of them in various sexual positions, pictures that left nothing to the imagination. Then, after only a couple of minutes and a shared cigarette, Thomas, as he always did, suddenly changed.

'Right, you'd better get going. I've got work I need to be getting on with and I'll need to tidy this place up before the missus gets home.'

Petra smiled to herself. This was the normal reaction for married men and Thomas was no different. She detached herself from his arms and slid from the bed, not in the slightest bit upset by his change of mood. She'd accepted that this was how it would be when she first started seeing him. She was having fun, great sex, and had no commitment; it was almost perfect.

'Okay, I'll get dressed and be gone before the little lady gets home.'

She blew him a kiss and he smiled broadly at her. He had found the perfect balance in his life in Natalie and Petra and intended to maintain that balance and make sure his two worlds never collided.

TWENTY-TWO

Peter's interview began at 8.20 and just as he'd anticipated, Natalie didn't mention their conversation at the cell door the previous evening. She was accompanied by DS Pincent, who, during the interview, was clearly infuriated by Peter's decision to answer 'No comment' to every question.

Peter would have preferred to answer their questions and provide Natalie with his fake version of events. He suspected that deep down, Natalie knew the truth about Tony Water's death and hearing him spouting lies would have driven her crazy. However, his solicitor strongly advised him against that degree of openness and he reluctantly bowed to her wisdom.

Natalie ended the interview at 9.25, and Peter was taken back to the custody counter, where Custody Sergeant Cornel Stephens was enjoying his tea and toast. Unlike Winter, Stephens was badly overweight and looked scruffy, even in his police uniform.

Peter was briefly returned to his cell while Natalie hastened back to her office to check her email for results from the two SOCOs. Both had sent her messages informing her that every sample or fingerprint taken matched Peter Hardy. Nothing had been found to indicate Tony Waters, had ever been in his car or flat.

Sitting back in her chair she raged inside; it all seemed so wrong, so unfair. The man who'd destroyed her marriage was a murderer, she was sure of that, but she had no way of proving it. Two minutes later, she'd managed to pull herself together and returned to the custody suite, looking her usual, composed self.

Stephens was brushing toast crumbs from the counter and smiled at Natalie as she approached.

'Yes, Ma'am, how can I help?'

'I'd like to bail Mr Hardy for four weeks please.'

Looking at the calendar, Stephens said, 'Wednesday 15th December?'

'Yes, that's fine.'

Stephens lifted Peter's custody record from its hook and laid it on the counter.

'Reasons for bail?'

'Mr Hardy is a murder suspect who has answered 'no comment' to every question during interview. However, he has previously given an account of his movements to DS Pincent and DC Dawes, the veracity of which now needs to be checked. Extensive CCTV enquiries are necessary to confirm not only his movements, but also the movements of the victim. These enquiries will cover a substantial area of the West End of London. Additionally, we need to check all CCTV bordering roads surrounding the area where the victim's body was found.'

'Do you want to apply any bail conditions?'

She sighed and said reluctantly, 'No, unconditional bail.'

Stephens turned to the gaoler.

'Get me cell two's property please, Gerry, and arrange for his vehicle to be taken round to the front.'

Five minutes later, Peter was being ushered out of a side door next to the front counter of the police station. Natalie managed a frosty smile for him.

'It's not over yet, Hardy. You'll be back here before you know it.'

Peter was grinning from ear to ear, elated at being

released; he was walking on cloud nine.

'I admire your optimism, but you'll soon discover that I'm too good for you... way too good.'

It was Natalie's turn to smile.

'Are you so confident because you know that Westminster Council's CCTV was down in that area?'

Her smile unnerved Peter, but he replied with a sneer, 'Took your time finding that out.'

'It makes no difference. My officers are checking the outside CCTV's of all the bars and clubs. I'm sure we'll pick you up on one of those.'

That was a hard blow. She was right, they might well pick him up and if they did, it could also show the meeting with Waters. His concern was showing on his face, but he had to remain calm.

'Do your worst love, I'm not bothered.'

He turned and with his head held high, walked quickly from the building and approached the officer standing alongside his car. The officer handed him the keys and he jumped inside; seconds later the engine roared into life and he drove away.

Natalie stood by the door watching him drive off. The corners of her mouth beginning to turn up with the ghost of a smile. This was a game of chess and she'd just taken one of his important pieces. She had seen the flicker of fear in his eyes when she'd mentioned the bars' and clubs' CCTV; she'd found his weak spot and would now pour all her teams' efforts into checking those images.

TWENTY-THREE

Deciding against going home for a change of clothes, Peter drove straight to Duke's garage, pulling into the staff car park at 10.35. He turned off the engine and stared through the rain-streaked windscreen for several seconds before finally getting his act together and hauling himself out of his car.

A loud banging made him look towards the office window, where he could see the angry face of his boss, Des Thayer, looking back at him. Thayer gestured with a crooked finger that he wanted to speak to Peter and he was looking none too pleased.

Once again, Peter's heart slumped. This would be an uncomfortable meeting; he was hoping for the best but feared the worst. Des Thayer was every bit as homophobic as Tony Waters, every bit as transphobic, every bit as bigoted. He locked his car and moved slowly towards the offices with no idea what he could say to placate him.

Throughout his time at the garage, Thayer had easily matched the level of Tony Waters' abuse, but because he was the boss and Peter didn't want to lose his job, he'd never responded in the same way. When Tony taunted, Peter would sometimes shout back at him, even once or twice threatening him with reprisals, but with Des Thayer he tended to accept whatever was thrown at him and skulk away from the situation. He didn't like accepting the abuse, it really stuck in his throat, but he needed this job and couldn't afford risking the sack.

The eyes of the five all-female office staff followed him with interest as he walked through their open-plan office space, past four huge posters of 'nearly new' second hand cars, until he reached Thayer's office, which occupied a corner of the sales floor. Peter was on first name terms with all the women, but none of them spoke to him as he moved through.

He knocked on the office door and received a harsh shout, 'Come in!'

Des Thayer was standing behind his desk, which in itself was strange as he hardly ever moved from his chair, often lounging with his feet on the desk. Peter closed the door and took in his boss's grim face and the clenched fists at his sides.

Shit, this doesn't look good.

Thayer was a huge man, about an inch shorter than Peter and just as well built. He'd been a mechanic most of his life and been cautious with his money. At the age of 45 he'd rented the land where the garage now stood and opened a small car lot. He'd slowly built up the business for twelve years into the thriving concern it was today, not only selling used cars, but also offering repairs and MOT checks. Despite his success, however, he was a man who seemed permanently at war with the world, prone to often random rages, which had led to the ominous first signs of an ulcer.

Des didn't offer Peter the chance to sit down, instead growling at him.

'Well, what happened?'

Peter shrugged.

'They've searched my house, my car and my flat.'

'And?'

"Nothing… because there's nothing to find, Des.'

'They must've thought there was enough to arrest you.'

'Yes, but they're relying solely on circumstantial evidence. I've done nothing wrong. There are two reasons they've arrested me: firstly, because Tony used to harass me and call me names at work and, secondly, because we both happened to be in London on Friday night. Otherwise, they've got nothing. They haven't thought it through, they've just put two and two together and made five.'

Des banged his clenched fist against his desk, causing it to visibly reverberate.

'Harass… fucking harass…? It was banter you soft tosser. I've always given you as much shit as he did! Fucking hell, Pete, you're a fudge packer working in a garage workshop full of hairy-arsed blokes, what the fuck did you expect?'

Peter gave a small, almost imperceptible shake of his head.

'A little respect would have been nice.'

Des snorted.

'Don't be such a fucking girl. Look, if you're queer, then you're queer. As long as you perform well in the workshop then I'm okay with that. But it doesn't mean we have to like you, the lads in the workshop have every right to take the piss.'

'Not every minute of every day. It's upsetting, it's boring and it makes me angry.'

'Oh really? Angry enough to kill someone? Angry enough to kill *Tony*?'

'Don't be ridiculous, of course not. If the police had found evidence to show I'd done it, don't you think they'd have charged me? The reason they haven't is because I didn't do it!' Peter's voice was becoming raised and he took a deep breath to calm himself.

Des slumped down into his chair.

'This is not good publicity for the business. We've

had a purchase order and two repairs cancelled already and that's probably just for starters.'

'I'm really sorry, Des, but it's not my fault, the police have got it wrong.'

'So, you're released without charge, are you?'

'Not yet, I'm on bail.'

'Bail! Why?'

'The fingerprints and forensic results have come back negative, but more CCTV needs to be checked. Once that's done, I'll be released without charge.'

Des tipped his head back and closed his eyes.

'This is a fucking nightmare. It's my own fault for not spotting it when I interviewed you. Gays always cause problems working somewhere like this. Tony picked it up the minute you walked into the workshop.'

'What?'

'That you're a fucking bog-trotter!'

It sounded like Des was thinking about sacking him and Peter's heart sank.

Not again, I don't want to have to start all over again.

Tony Waters had made his day-to-day existence in the workshop hard to bear, but that problem had now been dealt with. Although Des was just as bad, Peter only saw him a couple of times a week; most days he didn't see him at all, so his occasional vile abuse was much easier to tolerate.

Des could see the concern on Peter's face.

'Don't worry, I'm not sacking you. Your job's safe.'

'Thanks Des. I won't cause you any more problems, I promise.'

Des glared at Peter with barely concealed contempt.

'The only reason you're not picking up your cards is because the press and the union would be on my case if I sacked you.'

He stood up again and moved to the side of his

desk. Peter felt apprehensive and took a step back as Des jabbed a finger in his face.

'I don't like poofs and I don't like you, but I'm not stupid. Getting rid of you would stir up a hornets' nest and, at the moment, I could do without any more aggro. You're a bloody good mechanic and we're one light until I can replace Tony, so I'll overlook that fact for a while, but I'd advise you to start looking elsewhere for employment. Do I make myself clear?'

Peter nodded his head resignedly. Yet again, he would be forced to move on because of bigotry, small mindedness, and homophobia.

Thayer's voice oozed hatred.

'Get back to work, and stay out of my fucking way.'

Peter turned and opened the door, just as Des handed out more bad news.

'And I'm docking you a day's wages for missing the past 24 hours.'

Peter walked out with his shoulders slumped and made his way to the workshop.

Sliding open the heavy side door, Peter entered nervously. He wasn't really looking forward to the barrage of questions he knew would be coming his way. Bill, Andy, and Vince were sitting in the small rest area that occupied one corner of the workshop, where there was a kettle, tea and coffee, odds and sods of cutlery, an old Quality Street tin containing biscuits, and five white plastic chairs in a semi-circle. Peter looked at the clock on the wall; it was 10.50, so the lads were on their tea break. Bill and Vince stood up to greet him but Andy sat holding his cup, eyes focused on the steam rising. Bill was first to speak.

'Good to see you back mate. What's going on?'

Touching the kettle to see if it was still hot and removing his plain blue mug from its hook, Peter dropped in a teabag and poured himself a brew. Only once he'd added the milk and taken his first sip did he bother replying.

'Usual Old Bill. They've tried their very best to fit me up with something I had nothing to do with.'

'So why the fuck did they arrest you?' asked Vince.

Peter wrapped both hands around his mug and gave a heavy sigh.

'Because... rather like Tony and Des... the DCI and the Sergeant are nasty fuckers who hate people like me.'

Andy chuckled and nodded.

'Got something to say. Andy?' asked Peter.

Andy turned slowly to look at Peter, his loathing written across his face.

'Yes, I've got plenty to say, but nothing to your kind.'

His anger beginning to boil over, Peter sat forward.

'What do you mean *my kind*?'

Vince tried to calm the situation.

'Forget it, Pete, he didn't mean it. He's just really upset about Tony. That's right, isn't it, Andy?'

'If you say so.'

Andy removed his gaze from Peter and returned it to the liquid in his cup, his body language screaming 'just leave me alone.'

'Come on Pete,' urged Bill, 'don't leave us hanging, tell us what happened.'

Over the next few minutes Peter told the whole story, from his arrest up to his release. The only things he kept under wraps were SOCO Archie keeping quiet about the stain on the curtain and the conversation with Natalie Neider.

By the time he'd finished, tea break was over and they rose as one from their chairs.

'Fucking hell, sounds like they really had it in for

you,' said Vince.

Bill rested a hand on Peter's shoulder.

'For the record mate, I know I've taken the piss along with the others, but for me it stops now. I was bang out of order.'

Peter looked up at him, genuinely surprised and moved; he knew how hard that must have been to say that in front of their colleagues.

'Thanks, Bill, that means a lot.'

'That's okay. I've never meant any of it nastily, it was just banter.'

Vince was busily rinsing his cup in the sink.

'That goes for me, too. I suppose I was just following Tony's lead. I did it to keep in his good books… like a fucking idiot.'

Peter stood and patted Vince on the back.

'It's okay. I'm grateful for the apology. Let's move on, shall we?'

Andy sullenly rinsed his cup after Vince, and returned to his work area without saying a word. He was in complete agreement with the police's viewpoint: that Peter was responsible for Tony's death, and if he could help them prove it, he would.

TWENTY-FOUR

Natalie called her officers together for an 11 o'clock catch-up on Wednesday morning.

'Right, before we go around the teams, I can inform you that fingerprints and hairs lifted from the suspect's car and flat all belong to him. Additionally, clothes fibres collected by both SOCOs match clothing found in his wardrobe, so that's a dead-end too.'

She dropped the papers she was carrying onto a table and looked around at her troops.

'Right, let's see where we are. Give me some good news! Team 1, what have you found?'

DI Peter Plant rose to his feet.

'We firstly considered whether the victim may have secretly been involved in homosexual encounters. Our findings have shown that Waters appears to have been 100% heterosexual, in fact, his closest friends say he was seeing at least three different women. There's no chance he may have been a closet gay. On the contrary, everything we've discovered about him shows that he had a serious problem with homosexuals. Almost every person we've spoken to, both friends and family, included that in their description of him.'

Feeling very uncomfortable and hoping he hadn't been spotted in the Concord Rooms, James Pincent nevertheless felt obliged to speak up in support of his friend.

'That's fair enough, there's no law saying you've got to like them.'

Plant glared at him in disapproval; he'd got openly gay officers on his team and didn't appreciate the comment.

'No, there's not James, but that doesn't mean you can abuse someone because of it.'

Pincent persisted.

'Doesn't sound like he did. Just a bit of banter according to their colleagues at the garage.'

Shaking his head in exasperation, Plant continued.

'We've spoken to two friends he was with on Friday night. They insist there was nothing strange about his behaviour, and nothing unusual about him going off, drinking in Soho once they'd finished. He'd done the same thing at least three times before.'

James was grateful that everyone had kept schtum about his attendance at the Concord Rooms and the KBS meeting.

Natalie tapped the table loudly to draw Plant's attention.

'Yes, Ma'am?'

'Any luck tracing the third friend? The one with the baseball cap?'

Pincent held his breath and could feel his palms become sweaty.

'No. We've been given the name Michael Smith, but apparently they know nothing about his private life, no phone number, address, nothing.'

'Hmmm, not sure I believe that. Keep digging on that one, it doesn't sound quite right to me. Do we know yet whether Waters had any enemies, or if someone wished him harm?'

'No, apparently not. Everyone spoke about what a great bloke he was, life and soul of any night out, apparently didn't have an enemy in the world. Usual story!'

Natalie grimaced.

'Apart from Peter Hardy?'

Plant reluctantly agreed with her.

'Yes, Ma'am.'

'Okay, thanks for that.' She looked around for her female colleague. 'Team 2, what have you got for me?'

DI Jameson rose slowly to her feet.

'We've checked CCTV from the Concord Rooms, both inside and outside. From what we could see, Waters seems to be enjoying a thoroughly good night out with his mates. However, a large chunk of the evening inside the club, from nine through to just before midnight, wasn't on CCTV.'

Natalie frowned.

'Why's that?'

'About fifty people moved upstairs into a private function room, Ma'am, it's not covered by CCTV.'

'What function did they move upstairs for?'

'Apparently they were holding a meeting of the anti-gay group, KBS.'

James again fidgeted uncomfortably.

'What does KBS stand for?'

'Keep Britain Straight.'

Looking thoughtful, Natalie said, 'Okay. Are we certain nobody from that meeting followed Waters into Soho?'

'Absolutely certain, Ma'am. Once they'd split up outside The Concord Rooms, we used Westminster Council's CCTV to follow him down Rathbone Place, across Oxford Street, down Soho Street and into Soho Square. Nobody else from the club headed in that direction, he was alone.'

'Okay, where did he go?'

'He walked around the left side of Soho Square, past the junction with Sutton Row and was last seen entering

127

the top end of Greek Street at 2.02.'

'How do you know that? I thought cameras in Soho were down.'

'They were, but a camera on the edge of the down area caught him walking into the square, lost him as he turned left to walk around the square, then picked him up again at a distance passing the junction with Sutton Row.'

'Is that where he goes out of range?' asked Natalie.

'Yes, just as he entered the top end of Greek Street.'

'Does he reappear anywhere?'

'No. We've checked every place he could possibly have left the area from two up until six. He never reappeared.'

One of the detective constables spoke up.

'Unless he was in a car or van.'

Jameson nodded. 'We're on that already. We're currently working through images to see if Hardy's Astra leaves the area.'

'What about images of Hardy?' asked Matt Dawes.

'Going by what Hardy said when he was spoken to at the garage, we knew where to look for him. It took a while for us to spot him because he was heavily made up and dressed in a bright blue trouser suit. The trousers were outrageously flared, but you could just about see a pair of black flat shoes underneath. He was getting very pally with a man as he left the My Pink Life nightclub. They left together around two.'

'Then what?' asked Natalie.

'They walked arm-in-arm from the club, turned left out of the club onto Old Compton Street, then left into Greek Street, into the area where CCTV was out. A couple of minutes later the other man is seen walking back out of Greek Street, which sort of ties in with what Hardy said.'

Natalie looked thoughtful.

'And what's happening regarding our collection of CCTV from private premises?'

'We should have everything in by tomorrow afternoon. We're already checking through what we've obtained so far, nothing yet though.'

'Brilliant. Thank you, Carolyn.'

Carolyn nodded and sat down.

Pacing across the front of the room, Natalie looked pleased.

'So, at almost exactly the same time, we have Tony Waters entering the north end of Greek Street and Peter Hardy entering the south end, two hundred yards apart and heading straight towards each other.'

She stopped pacing and faced the assembled officers.

'I'm certain he's our man. We've just got to find that meeting point!'

She turned her attention to DI Tim Waterman.

'Any luck with Team 3?'

Tim Waterman shook his head disappointedly.

'Sorry, Ma'am, nothing yet. We've only managed to trace five vehicles that entered the area and then left in the timeframe. All the drivers have solid alibis, two of them were taxis.'

'So that's a dead-end?'

'Looks like it. We'll know for sure within the next couple of days.'

'Right then, it looks like all our eggs are in one basket, we simply *have* to find that meeting between Hardy and Waters. Once we've got concrete evidence that the meeting took place, we can show he definitely lied to us and that will help us nail the bastard.'

TWENTY-FIVE

The events regarding the investigation into Tony Waters' murder were weighing heavily on James Pincent's mind. Firstly, he was worried about being spotted on CCTV in The Concord Rooms in company with Waters and the others; he knew he may have placed his career in peril, fully realising the deep shit he would be in if he was identified attending the KBS meeting. What's more, he was totally convinced that Peter Hardy was the murderer and was desperate to help prove it.

Popping into his boss's office, a ten-minute meeting with DCI Neider quickly reinforced that belief. She was grim faced when he arrived.

'Come in and close the door. I don't want us being overheard.'

Natalie was stressed; her face looked tired and lined, showing the strain of command. Senior management wanted a result and they wanted it quickly, but she was struggling. James walked in, closed the door and sat down opposite her, determined to make something happen.

'Any luck with getting a surveillance team?'

She shook her head. 'No.'

His face dropped; this was terrible news.

'How did you pitch it?'

'I told the Super that Hardy was a creature of habit. I asked for permission to run a short follow this weekend, in case he'd return to a place where he'd hidden evidence. I explained that murderers often hide things in a panic then return within a few days to collect them and discard of them properly.'

James nodded, she'd clearly made a good pitch.

'We'll never know now,' she said with a lengthy sigh. 'He won't authorise it and that's the end of the matter. Apparently, a surveillance team is too costly and there's not enough evidence to justify it.'

Pincent shook his head in disgust.

'For fuck's sake, there's plenty of evidence, what more does he want?'

'A lot more apparently.'

He angrily itemised the evidence so far, turning over a finger with each piece to stress its importance.

'We've got three months of bad blood between Hardy and Waters and two of the staff at the garage overheard Hardy threatening him. When Waters was last seen alive, they were 200 yards apart walking straight towards each other and would have met close by Hardy's flat. The next time Waters is seen he's brown bread in a fucking stream. What's the matter with him, does he want Hardy to get away with it?'

Natalie sadly shrugged her shoulders.

'I think he doesn't want to rock the boat. Too busy chasing the next rank to be a proper copper.'

Pincent was silent for a moment; he was carefully weighing up whether to put an idea to her. He was angry: one of his mates was dead and something *had* to be done to prosecute his killer. Sensing that Natalie wanted to get Hardy every bit as much as him, he decided to go for it.

'I was on a surveillance team for four years. If you could spare me this weekend, I'll follow him on my own. He just might slip up and lead me to something we don't know about, something he doesn't want us to find.'

She stared at him in disbelief.

'Are you crazy? That would be a disciplinary offence.

131

You'd be ignoring the refusal of a surveillance request by the Super. You'd be carrying out an unlawful and unauthorised activity, quite apart from the fact it would be horrendously difficult carrying out a covert follow on your own, it would normally need at least ten officers and at least three vehicles.'

He smiled conspiratorially.

'So, you'll let me do it?'

She returned his smile and nodded.

'You're fucking right I will. I'll tell Matt you're otherwise engaged this weekend.'

'Might be tricky. He'll want to know what I'm doing.'

'Leave that to me. I'll tell him you're carrying out a private job for me and to keep his nose out.'

He laughed. 'Thanks for this, Ma'am. I'm sure Hardy's hiding something and we need to know what it is.'

Her expression quickly became serious, and she fixed him with a stern expression.

'Be *very* careful. We don't need that wanker spotting you tailing him, that would fuck everything up.'

'Don't worry, I'll keep a long eye. It helps with cold weather being forecast for the weekend. I'll use different coats and hats so he won't spot me. It'll be fine.'

'Sounds good.' She shook her head. 'I can't believe how much he's affecting me. I've always played by the book, always stayed within the rules… now I'm breaking them, all for the sake of nailing this fucker'

'It'll be worth it if I can discover something.'

'Maybe Carolyn's team will come up trumps and spot their meeting. If that happens before the weekend, your follow won't be needed.'

James noticed her clenching her jaw, she was clearly annoyed.

'You okay Ma'am?'

'Yes… I'm fine. We have to catch him out James, we really have. I've not been sleeping too well. This case has got to me, but I'm fine.'

He gave her a reassuring smile.

'We'll nail him. It might take a while, but we'll nail him.'

'Thanks James, I hope you're right. We'll speak again before the weekend.'

Pincent moved to get up, but she waved him back into his seat.

'There's one last thing.'

'Ma'am?'

'If it all goes tits up, I know nothing about this. You're on your own. Sorry, James, that's how it's got to be.'

He smiled.

'I thought that might be the case.'

With that, she returned her attention to her computer screen which he took as the cue for him to leave. He stood and walked to the door, turned and gave her a reassuring nod, before leaving and gently closing the door.

TWENTY-SIX

On Friday morning, Carolyn Jameson stood in front of the officers gathered for the latest briefing.

'Every available piece of CCTV from private premises has now been seized. Unfortunately, there were only seven premises with working CCTV systems and nine others had dummy cameras fitted. Five of the seven working systems picked up images of our subjects and between them they showed some interesting developments. They have all been viewed and assessed.'

She turned to one of her DC's and nodded, he clicked the mouse on his computer and the station's new power-point screen burst into life.

'The first film is from the Pillars of Hercules public house. Tony Waters is here.' She pointed to Waters walking down Greek Street on the east pavement and crossing a side junction. The image changed. 'And at the same time, on the opposite footpath, Hardy can briefly be seen walking past the front door of Café Bella, about forty yards into Greek Street from Old Compton Street.'

The assembled officers watched with interest, several of them sniggering as they saw a flamboyantly dressed Peter Hardy proudly displaying as a woman; he was accompanied by an unknown male as they passed the front of the café arm-in-arm, only in view for a couple of seconds, but it was undoubtedly him.

'Next clip please, Steve.' The DC clicked his mouse again and Carolyn pointed at the screen. 'Here's Waters thirty yards further down Greek Street, passing the door of Bar Canto. Watch the young couple kissing, and he's… there,' she pointed at him, 'walking past the couple, still heading towards Hardy. At this point, Waters is almost directly opposite the junction with Bateman Street. Next clip please.'

'The next image shows a rear view of Hardy and his friend walking with linked arms outside The Covex Group, a graphic design company.' They all watched as the men walked from the bottom to the top of the screen and out of view within seven seconds. 'Next clip please.'

The image on the screen flicked over.

'This shows Waters from the door system of Eat Not Meat, a vegetarian restaurant. He appears to be happily walking towards Old Compton Street when he spots something on the opposite footpath. He slows his pace then stops completely, before changing direction and crossing the road. Watch his expression change.'

Although not perfectly clear, it was obvious that Waters' face which had worn a look of disgust gradually broke into a grin of amusement. Several officers murmured to those around them, and Natalie, who was standing quietly to one side with a triumphant smile on her face said, 'It gets better.'

Carolyn smiled at her boss before continuing.

'They would now have been directly opposite each other, and I'm convinced seeing Hardy was the reason Waters crossed the street.' She paused and checked through her notes. 'Only 25-30% of the street is covered by these images, so it's not really surprising that their meeting, which we're fairly certain took place, was out of view.'

She glanced at Natalie and raised her eyebrows, offering her the chance to step in and say something. Natalie shook her head and lifted her chin indicating for Carolyn to continue.

'About two minutes after Waters crosses the road, this happens.' The image changed again. 'As you can see, it's Hardy's boyfriend looking very flustered and upset hurrying back towards Old Compton Street past The Covex Group. Almost certainly because Waters had said something to Hardy.

'Nothing happens for almost five minutes, then this…' The next clip started. 'This shows Waters crossing back over the road to Eat Not Meat and walking back towards the junction with Bateman Street, now watch carefully.'

Complete silence descended on the room as the image was stopped just before Waters disappeared off the right-hand side of the screen.

'Now, look carefully at the very top of the screen…' she indicated the very tall figure in the flowing blue trouser suit. 'That's Peter Hardy.'

Excited murmurs erupted around the room.

Carolyn spread her arms with her hands facing downwards in a 'calm down' gesture until quiet was restored.

'If you look a little more closely, Hardy appears to look directly across the road at Waters before he disappears from the screen.'

She looked at her DC operating the power-point and span her right index finger round and round. He rewound the image and played it again, clearly showing Peter's quick glance at Waters, reinforcing her point.

'Final clip please.'

The image on the screen changed.

'This clip shows Waters still walking up Greek Street past Bar Canto and then he does this…' the officers watched with intense concentration as Tony Waters looked across the road and nodded at someone out of shot, before stepping off the pavement and heading towards Bateman Street.

'After that, they disappeared. They weren't picked up on either pavement heading further north on Greek Street and they didn't turn back on themselves and head south, so they both must have turned into Bateman Street, where Hardy's flat is situated only fifteen yards on the left. Unfortunately, there are no CCTV systems on that section of Bateman Street, which is between Greek Street and Frith Street. There is an alleyway called Bateman Buildings a few yards past Hardy's flat that leads from Bateman Street to Soho Square, but if either of them had gone down there, we would have picked them up on the council's CCTV system as they left Soho Square.'

Her shoulders slumped slightly.

'At the moment, we can't prove where they went, but Hardy's flat must be a strong probability.'

She nodded at Natalie, handing over control of the room to her boss. Natalie was smiling as she strode to the front of the room and took Carolyn's place.

'The circumstantial evidence we've amassed against Hardy is almost overwhelming, but sadly we're still missing that vital piece of *direct* evidence that would prove conclusively he met and killed Tony Waters.'

A young Detective Constable raised his hand, Natalie nodded at him.

'Yes, Clive?'

'Once we've put this video evidence forward, surely the CPS will run with it. It looks pretty damning to me.'

His comment bought sniggers from more experienced detectives.

She replied ruefully, 'You've got a lot more faith in them than me, Clive, it's nowhere near enough yet.'

Natalie became quiet and thoughtful before continuing.

'I want every piece of CCTV viewed again over the weekend. We must ensure we haven't missed anything. I'll make my decision on Monday about where we go from here. Any other questions?'

A female DS raised a hand.

'Yes, Karen?'

'Why aren't we following Hardy this weekend? We don't know exactly what he gets up to when he's up there. We might discover something that he's trying to hide.'

Natalie deliberately avoided looking at James.

'I've requested a surveillance team for this weekend, but the boss won't pay for it. I'll re-submit the request with this video evidence straight after this meeting, but I wouldn't get your hopes up.'

The room fell silent.

'Right, if there are no more questions, let's get back to work.'

She looked at Pincent.

'James, my office, now.'

Just along the corridor from the briefing room, Natalie held the door to her office open. James walked inside and she quietly closed the door. She lowered her voice, ensuring nobody overheard.

'Keep working until three then make your excuses and leave. Go home and pack yourself a case with whatever clothes you need, I'll cover for you.'

'Okay, Ma'am… and thanks.'

'Hardy finishes work at half-five, so you'll need to be well positioned to follow, whichever direction he drives off in.'

'Will do. He'll either be heading home or straight up to his flat in London. Either way, I'll have it covered.'

'He might not. He might travel up by train, have you considered that?'

He shrugged, 'I'll worry about that if it happens. We'll find out soon, won't we?'

She nodded. 'Good luck, James, and thanks. That bum bandit has got away with things for far too long.'

'*Things*? You mean the murder?'

'S... sorry... figure of speech. I really do need a good night's sleep!'

She had let her personal feelings slip yet again.

'Anyway, get going, let's hope you find something.'

'I don't know why he pisses you off so much and I don't want to know, that's your business. But believe me, I hate that bastard every bit as much as you do. I'll carry out a professional tail on him and if there's anything worth finding out about Peter Hardy, rest assured, I'll find it.'

TWENTY-SEVEN

Two national newspapers had picked up the story and were running lurid headlines about the 6'4" transgender mechanic accused of murdering his tormentor at a garage in Sevenoaks. *The Mail* ran with the angle that the police were struggling to gather sufficient evidence to charge and demanded more funding for the police. Meanwhile, *The Guardian* interviewed gay and transsexual support groups about their experiences of being persecuted. They voiced their support for Peter, and one small group with placards had travelled to the garage on Thursday, gathering outside to shout their backing for Peter, something which enraged Des Thayer.

Peter, on the other hand, greatly appreciated their support; it had been a tough week and his nerves were in shreds. For a short while he'd wondered whether he should have simply done what he'd always done, and run away from the problem. Tony Waters would still be alive, he wouldn't be fretting about being re-arrested every waking minute and he could probably have found employment at another garage. Starting his life over from scratch somewhere else might have been a good option on the face of it.

But that wasn't him anymore; he was no longer the weak, cowering pushover he once was. He wasn't prepared to tolerate the abuse he'd suffered throughout his life. He wanted to be accepted as a woman whenever he felt like being a woman, and a man when he felt like being a man, and if his work colleagues couldn't hack that and started persecuting him again, he'd be the toughest, meanest bastard they'd ever encountered.

The atmosphere in the workshop was strained. Bill and Vince had been pleasant enough but Andy kept his distance, refusing to speak to Peter and rarely exchanging words with the others. He seemed to be furious with Bill and Vince for even communicating with Peter, let alone showing him any kindness and understanding.

Always arriving at the workshop wearing his work overalls, Peter had little opportunity to openly express his lifestyle choices at work. However, on Friday he turned up at the workshop wearing eye makeup, causing intrigued glances from Bill, Vince, and the two ladies from the office who popped in during the day. When Andy arrived and saw him, he couldn't conceal his disgust; he was bursting to say something but nervous about Peter's reaction.

At lunchtime, Deborah from the sales team turned up at the workshop with the message Peter had been anticipating and dreading.

'Pete, when you've finished lunch Des wants to see you in his office. A word of warning, he's not happy.'

Thirty minutes later, Peter rapped hard on the door of his boss's office; he was quaking with nerves, but had no intention of being a doormat. Those days were over.

'Come in.'

Peter walked in and without being invited to sit down, pulled a chair from the edge of the room. Placing it alongside Des Thayer's desk, he sat down opposite him.

'You wanted to see me?'

Des stared in disbelief and barely concealed fury at the makeup on Peter's face and his confident manner. He'd never seen this level of cockiness from him before and for a moment it knocked him off guard. Anger was building inside and he vented his fury.

'What the fuck is that shit on your face?'

Peter narrowed his eyes.

'What did you say?'

'I said, what the fuck is that shit on your face?'

'It's makeup.'

'I can see that... but you're a bloke.'

'I am, but I like wearing makeup. Anyway, I might be a man now, but hopefully that's just a temporary state of affairs.'

Rocking his chair back onto two legs, Des chuckled dismissively.

'A fucking great lump like you, turning into a bird? Don't make me laugh.'

Peter held his gaze.

'Why not?'

'Because you'll be a laughing stock everywhere you go. You'll always look like a man in women's clothes, you'll never look like a real woman.'

'Why shouldn't I? Why can't people accept me for the person I am?'

'That's exactly the point, it's not the person you are. You're a bloke, a bloody great strapping bloke. More importantly, you're a bloke who I'm paying fucking good wages to work.'

Peter angrily leaned forward across the desk.

'I know and I'm a fucking good mechanic turning out fucking good work, aren't I?'

Des puffed out a long sigh.

'I'm not complaining about the standard of your work, but I'm not prepared to allow male workers in my garage to dress up like tarts, it doesn't look good.'

'Why not? It doesn't affect my work, does it?'

'Maybe not, but it affects those who work with you. They feel uncomfortable with it. They complain to me

142

about you and that means I might not be getting the best out of them. I want a happy workforce.'

Now it was Peter's turn to let out a heavy sigh; he knew that someone must have taken it further than garage gossip and he knew exactly who that someone was, but he needed to hear it from Des's lips.

'Come on then, how many people have put in complaints?'

Des shifted uneasily on his chair.

'There's only been one official complaint, but the others are always talking about it and it's affecting the work rate.'

'I'll ask again, who's put in the complaint?'

'I can't tell you that, but it's a member of the workshop.'

Nodding to himself, Peter said, 'Oh right, so it's Andy.'

Des reacted angrily.

'Okay, yes, it's Andy and I'm in total fucking agreement with him. It's bad enough that I made the mistake of employing you in the first place, but that poor fucker has to work with you and look at you every day.' His face reddened, 'And don't you dare say a word to him, he was only doing what he thought was right.'

Staring at his boss with incredulity, Peter said, 'Why don't you sack me then?'

Des's aggressive finger pointing stopped and his voice softened.

'Because I'm not stupid. The gay lobby and the papers would tear me up for arsehole paper, so for the moment I'm stuck with you.'

Peter grinned, 'Good, shall I get back to work then?'

'Yes, just get that shit off your face first.'

Not willing to back down, Peter stood his ground.

'No, I won't, I like it. It makes me feel comfortable,

in fact, it makes me feel great.'

Des practically exploded with anger.

'What's wrong with this fucking world? A shit-stabber telling his boss that he's going to behave however he wants!' He pointed at the door. 'Just fuck off out of my office.'

Peter glared at Des defiantly; he wanted to reach over the desk and throttle him right there and then. Instead, he smiled, calmly lifted himself from the chair and walked quietly from the office. He controlled his desire to slam the door shut, quietly pulling it closed instead. The time would come for dealing with Des Thayer.

Back inside the workshop, his three colleagues stopped working on their vehicles and regarded him with interest. Peter deliberately walked over to his workbench and opened his holdall, removed a brush and combed his hair, then applied a new layer of lipstick, before picking up a torque wrench and reaching down inside the car's engine compartment.

'Still here then?'

Peter didn't look up but recognised the voice as Andy's. He rested the wrench on the engine and unfolded himself from underneath the bonnet.

'Sorry, did somebody speak?'

Bill was looking directly at Andy and shaking his head.

Vince said, 'Leave it, Andy.'

But Andy didn't leave it; he pinned his shoulders back and raised himself to his full five feet six inches.

'Thought you'd have realised by now that you're not wanted here.'

Raising his eyebrows, Peter acted surprised.

'No, I haven't. Who doesn't want me here?'

'I don't, Des doesn't, Vince and Bill can't stand shirt

lifters like you but they're both too fucking pussy to admit it. Even the girls in the office think you're a joke.'

Andy's words were brutal and for a moment Peter was too shocked to speak. He badly wanted to hurt Andy but, in the circumstances, understood the stupidity of such a move. He forced a smile, sat on the wing of the car and folded his arms.

'The boss has told me to stop wearing makeup but I refused, told him to shove it. He's like you Andy, pathetic and weak. He hasn't got the balls to sack me, so unfortunately, you're stuck with me until *I* choose to leave.'

A look of astonishment spread across Andy's face.

'He wouldn't sack you?'

'Nope. Go and ask him yourself if you like.'

'But... I thought you'd be gone.'

'Like I said, the man's got no bottle.'

Shaking his head, Andy lay down on a trolley and wheeled himself back underneath a Mercedes van, without speaking.

For a moment there was silence in the workshop apart from the noise of Andy angrily wrestling with a rusty exhaust. Then, first Vince and then Bill put down the tools they were working with and walked over to Peter.

Bill put a hand on Peter's shoulder.

'Don't listen to him, Pete. What he said about Vince and me just now, it's not true.'

Peter smiled, 'I know that, you've both treated me well this week.'

'I'm truly sorry if we've upset you in the past,' said Vince, 'but keeping in Tony's good books was important if we wanted overtime. I know that sounds pathetic, but...'

Peter was genuinely touched. It took a big person to

admit they'd behaved badly in the past and he was happy to forgive them both. He held out a hand to Vince and shook hands with him, then did the same to Bill.

'Right,' said Bill, 'we don't get paid for standing round chatting, so let's get back to work.'

TWENTY-EIGHT

At 5.30, Peter walked from the workshop with Bill and Vince. Andy had downed tools five minutes before knocking-off time and his car had already left the staff car park.

'What are you two up to this weekend?' asked Vince.

'My wife wants me to help put the fucking garden to bed for the winter,' moaned Bill.

'No footy this weekend then?' asked Peter.

'Christ, I wish. What about you, Pete? Celebrating not being charged for murder?'

Peter laughed. 'Sort of. I'm going up to my flat in Soho to celebrate. I'm going to be Petra for the weekend.'

Bill and Vince had never heard Peter refer to himself as Petra before.

Vince's face bore a bemused look, 'You mean…'

'Yep, I'll be fully made up and dressed as a woman all weekend… and believe me, I'll look gorgeous!' He tossed his hair to one side provocatively.

Peter's workmates exchanged an uneasy glance before Bill laughed and said, 'Oh well, each to their own, have a great time mate.'

'Yeah,' said Vince, 'you enjoy yourself.'

Peter suddenly felt real warmth at these simple good wishes from his workmates; he'd had so little positive reaction from the straight community.

'Thanks lads, I appreciate that. See you Monday.'

As Peter drove out onto Amhurst Hill, he didn't

spot the blue Ford Granada parked in the lay-by thirty yards down the hill. It was on the opposite side of the road, with Detective Sergeant James Pincent at the wheel. Moments later, he didn't notice as the same Granada pulled out into the traffic two vehicles behind him.

Peter headed straight home to the cottage, took a shower, packed a suitcase for the weekend, mainly consisting of female clothing and food, then loaded up his Vauxhall Astra and set off. He drove down the isolated bumpy track, continuing past the collection of farm buildings that nestled 150 yards from his little cottage, then through the farmyard and down a rough concrete track for a further 100 yards to the narrow country lane. If he turned right, the lane went nowhere, a dead-end, so, as he always did, Peter turned left.

Considering the stupendous events in his life over the past week and the fact that he remained on bail for murder, he was feeling remarkably relaxed and happy. He'd spent many sleepless nights worrying about his future, nights where sleep wouldn't come and he had lain in bed assessing his predicament. He'd killed Tony Waters, but still had Andy Clark and Des Thayer being unpleasant to him at work. Both were disgustingly homophobic and transphobic, and both were seemingly hell-bent on making his life miserable.

One problem down, two to go.

Neider and Pincent also appeared to be of the same opinion. Between them, they seemed determined to convict him, but thus far they were missing one vital thing – evidence. His problems were slowly receding but he wasn't out of the woods just yet. If he made a single mistake, just one, his future life would be spent rotting in a prison cell.

Slowing down to allow a tractor to pass in the narrow lane, he spotted a blue Ford Granada parked in a lay-by on his side of the road fifty yards ahead. He'd never seen a car in that lay-by before and assumed it was someone lost and checking their map. Once the tractor had passed, he sped up again and, looking through the rear windscreen of the Granada, saw the driver was slouching down in his seat. As he passed, Peter glanced briefly to his left to see if he recognised the driver, but was unable to do so as the man now appeared to be leaning across the front passenger seat, his face obscured. He shrugged, not understanding the relevance of what he'd just seen, and happily continued his journey to London.

Having parked in his private space just off Soho Square an hour and a half later, Peter hurried through the cold drizzle to his flat. After the week he'd had, he intended to forget his troubles and thoroughly enjoy himself; he would drink plenty, dance the night away and hopefully pick up a fit bloke.

***

James Pincent hadn't tailed anyone for a few years and soon realised he was distinctly rusty. Picking up Hardy's car as it pulled out of the garage had been simple enough, but he'd soon lost him twice in the heavy Friday rush hour traffic. It was only because he'd turned left out of the garage and not right towards the motorway, that he knew Peter was driving to his home in Underriver, meaning he could relax a little, as he was already well acquainted with the location of Hardy's cottage.

He'd done some research and selected the lay-by to wait in while Hardy got changed. Cars parked up in lay-bys were a common sight in the country lanes of Kent, so he'd decided waiting there would be the perfect cover. He assumed that Hardy would be heading for his flat in

London for the weekend but knew he couldn't take that fact for granted.

He had spotted Hardy's car approaching in his rear-view mirror just as a huge red tractor passed by, and slouched down in his seat so he wouldn't be recognised. However, his face would still be visible if Hardy happened to glance across, so to make sure, he had leaned down across the front passenger seat, wrongly assuming his actions wouldn't be seen by Peter as he passed.

Following Peter's Astra at a discreet distance, Pincent saw him join the M25. Satisfied that Hardy was heading for his flat, he then waited until Peter was on the inside lane doing about sixty, before accelerating to eighty down the outside lane. He wanted to ensure he arrived in Soho first and had time to park his car before Peter arrived.

An hour and a half later, Pincent had parked his vehicle in a nearby NCP car park and was seated in a comfortable little café, with a great view of Hardy's flat, tucking into a slice of pizza and a mocha; he was feeling quietly happy with his work so far. Light rain had been falling since he arrived, but the streets were still busy with people heading out for the night.

A woman politely enquired whether the other seat on the table for two was free and James smiled warmly, indicating it was hers if she wanted it. That one act of chivalry almost made him miss his target. As the woman gratefully took her seat and James returned to his observation, he caught a glimpse of Peter carrying a small suitcase as he disappeared from view down the black iron staircase to his flat. Peter had entered Bateman Street from the Greek Street end and James had very nearly missed him.

TWENTY-NINE

Petra left her flat at 9.30, dressed to kill, and headed for her favourite café, La Belle Homme in Wardour Street. She was relaxed and carefree, having no idea that her every move was being monitored by James Pincent. At the café, she drank a beer and chatted with fellow Soho free spirits before moving on. The next two hours were spent dancing with a couple of friends at Madam JoJo's, after which she moved, as she always did shortly after midnight, to My Pink Life. It was *the* place for people like Petra to gather and it was a magnet for men who were attracted by them.

Dressed in a dazzling yellow knee-length dress, with a thick lilac stripe across the front from left shoulder to right hip, lilac stockings and bright yellow shoes, Petra was making a real statement: she was gay, she was trans, she was a woman, and she was proud. She'd had fun chatting and dancing with a few of the many friends she'd made over the weeks, but by 1.15 was feeling disappointed she hadn't managed to pull a man since arriving at the club.

She was normally approached within minutes of taking up her regular seat at the corner of the bar, but this night, for whatever reason, her luck was out. Her seat looked along the length of the long bar, allowing her a view of the majority of the club; it also allowed men in the bar a good view of her.

A small seating area behind her usual seat could accommodate around 15 people, but the seats there were nearly always taken up by couples wanting a little privacy. A man stood up from one of the tables there and approached her.

'Buy you a drink?'

As she heard the words, Petra felt a hand gently tracing the length of her spine from neck to buttocks. She shivered with anticipation. Without turning around to see who was offering, she replied, 'Rum and black, please.'

'Don't you want to see who's asking?'

Something in the tone of the voice seemed familiar, it was a young voice but sounded confident and assured. Then it hit her; Petra remembered with a shock where she'd heard the voice before and span round in her seat to face him.

'Hello, Archie. What brings you into a place like this?'

'Like I said, I want to buy you a drink.'

Petra grinned and tapped the stool next to hers. Archie climbed onto it and sat facing her. Looking at him closely for the first time, Petra was quietly impressed. She had been too preoccupied to notice in his flat, but Archie was handsome: slim, about 5'10" with jet-black curly hair. He was smartly dressed in cream Chinos, white shirt and a trendy grey Suede jacket.

'So, is this a chance meeting, or were you looking for me?'

Archie held a hand up by way of delaying his reply for a moment, while he ordered the two rum and blacks and handed one of them to Petra.

'Let's say I was hoping I might find you here.'

Petra fixed him with an enquiring stare, remembering the look they'd exchanged when Archie found the stain on the curtain; she wanted, needed, to know more.

'Well, you've found me, so what now?'

'I think you're looking very attractive tonight.'

His supremely confident manner took Petra by surprise.

'I'm very pleased to hear that… so are you.'

A nasty thought was forming in Petra's mind and a shiver of fear ran up her spine. She looked around nervously. Spotting her concern, Archie laughed.

'You don't have to worry, I'm all alone.'

Petra wasn't sure whether to believe him.

'Isn't all this rather risky in your job?'

'Why should it be?'

'Well, you work around here for a largely homophobic organisation, I'm a trans guy currently on bail for murder, yet here you are, chatting me up in a gay club. You figure it out.'

Smiling and taking a sip of his drink, Archie leaned close to Petra. 'You'd be a charged murder suspect if it wasn't for me. You'd be in custody awaiting trial, probably facing a life sentence, so I think it's only fair you trust me and give me a chance, don't you?'

The colour drained from Petra's face. So she was right, Archie *had* identified the stain on the curtain as blood, but for some reason he'd said nothing to the detectives. Almost imperceptibly, she nodded her understanding, struggling to take in what this meant, unable to speak. Archie could see her unease and confusion.

'I was given details of your case before the search at your flat was carried out. Sounded to me like Tony Waters was a complete bastard who had it coming to him. I'm not surprised you took revenge.'

He took a sip from his drink, not taking his eyes from hers for a second.

While she was deeply grateful to Archie for his

153

actions, Petra was astonished at the casual manner in which Archie spoke; after all, she had killed another human being... and he worked for the police! She shook her head, bemused.

'I still don't get it. Why are you helping me?'

Archie reached a hand over and stroked the back of Petra's right hand, which was resting on the bar.

'I would think that was obvious. Look, I've felt confused about my sexuality ever since I was a kid. I suppose I knew for certain I was gay soon after starting secondary school. I came out to my family and closest friends when I was fifteen and since then life has been difficult, to put it mildly.' He looked down at his glass, clearly trying to control his feelings.

Gently pulling him towards her, Petra wrapped a strong arm around his shoulders and hugged him tightly.

'Hey, hey, come on, it's okay.'

After a few seconds, Archie drew a deep breath pulled away from Petra's encircling arm and sat upright again, taking a deep swallow of rum and black.

'The request for a SOCO came through to my boss. We aren't normally given too many details, just the basic job description and the address, nothing more. But because it was a request from a separate force, the full case details were faxed through. The boss would normally be the only one to read those details, but she was busy, so she quickly authorised our help, assigned me the case and dropped the whole thing on my desk.'

He took another long gulp of his drink and gently placed the glass back on the bar.

'Once I'd learned about the abuse you'd suffered and why you were suspected of killing him, I made my mind up there and then to help if I could.'

Petra held his left hand with her right hand.

'Would you believe me if I swore to you that they've

154

got it all wrong, that I didn't kill him?'

'Don't say that. Don't lie to me. No… you killed him, I'm certain of that.'

Petra stared at him. 'And you're comfortable holding hands in a gay bar with a transgender killer in a yellow dress?'

'Yes, very comfortable,' Archie laughed. 'In fact, I feel right at home.'

Petra again began to feel a prickle of unease. Was this a trap? Had he been sent into the club wearing a microphone to lure her into saying something incriminating? Was he even telling the truth about his own life? A life that sounded surprisingly similar to hers, it all seemed so unlikely. She looked steadily into his dark brown eyes and all her instincts told her to believe him.

Having someone like Archie on her side was unexpected to say the least. Although she had no idea how, she knew that befriending him could prove extremely helpful in the days and weeks ahead. Tossing all her eggs into one basket, she took the plunge.

'Would you like to come back for a coffee?'

Archie leaned forward to plant a kiss on her cheek.

'I was hoping for something a little more… exciting than coffee, but that would be good for starters.'

Petra raised her eyebrows.

'Archie, you're sure about this, are you?'

'Why shouldn't I be?'

'Well, the position I'm now in makes me quite a dangerous person to be with, doesn't it?'

Archie smiled and shrugged.

'So?'

'Aren't you at all worried?'

He flashed her a wicked smile.

'I might be being stupid, but I like living dangerously. I'm sure I'll manage.'

THIRTY

They stayed for another drink, then rolled out of the club together at 2.20. Archie was on a high; he got a massive kick from deceiving his bosses and those homophobic bastards from Sevenoaks. He laughed aloud as he imagined their faces if they could see him now! He knew that if he had done his job properly at the flat, Petra would have been charged with murder. Instead, Archie had been able to help somebody who'd taken the same crap he had ever since he was a teenager. He had helped Petra to fight back and that made him feel great.

Turning left out of the club onto Old Compton Street, Archie was still laughing, the rum and blacks beginning to kick in as the cold air hit him, but his smile quickly faded as he spotted someone sitting at a table in a café across the road. He'd only met this person once before in his life, but was certain he knew who it was, and his blood ran cold.

He said, 'Follow me!' and, setting off through the crowds, rapidly increased his pace. Following behind, Petra couldn't understand what he was playing at and struggled to keep up. Without slowing down, Archie turned his head to warn her.

'We're in trouble. Just keep walking!'

'What's wrong?'

'I've just seen that Detective Sergeant, the one who came to your flat last week.'

Knowing that the chances of his presence in the area being a coincidence were negligible, Petra quickly realised she'd been followed. Her thoughts returned to earlier in the evening.

The blue Ford Granada, the man ducking down, trying not to be seen... Pincent!

'Are you absolutely sure it was him?'

'One hundred percent.'

'Fuck. That's not good for either of us.'

They dashed into Greek Street, Petra's speed seriously hampered by her high heels, but her flat was now only 100 yards away, just around the corner. Archie had picked up a few tips on surveillance from his colleagues and looked towards a delicatessen window on the street's corner where he saw Pincent in the reflection, leaving the café in a hurry, shrugging himself into his overcoat.

Archie's voice broke.

'He's coming.'

Petra hurried to catch up, moving close behind him. 'When we turn into my road, run to Frith Street and head off home,' she gasped. 'Don't worry, you'll be around the corner before he reaches the junction, so he won't see where you went. I'll meet you in La Belle Homme at noon tomorrow.'

Archie nodded; he knew his career was in jeopardy now he'd been seen in the company of a suspected murderer. Especially one whose premises he had recently searched. Turning into Bateman Street, Archie ran for the junction with Frith Street, just fifty yards away.

Petra was even more worried than Archie. Being caught socialising with the young SOCO could be seen by DCI Neider as grounds to have the flat searched by a different officer, one who would look far more closely than Archie had, one who might well find evidence of her home gym. On top of that, she quietly cursed herself for not removing the stained curtain and disposing of it.

But Petra had a plan: she was going on the offensive. Once Archie had set off, she turned back into Greek Street and retraced her steps, heading straight towards Pincent, who was almost upon her as he struggled through the crowds milling around on the pavement. The moment he saw Petra, Pincent stopped dead and turned around, hoping she hadn't seen him but Petra accelerated, quickly closing the distance between them.

'Hello Sergeant, fancy meeting you here. I didn't know you were this way inclined. I thought you hated us gays, you've certainly kept your *true* preferences quiet.'

Pincent was infuriated at being caught out so early in the weekend and bristled with anger at Petra's teasing. This was not how the surveillance was meant to go.

'I'm here to make enquiries about any CCTV we might have missed.'

She knew he was lying and, thoroughly enjoying his obvious discomfort, continued winding him up.

'Oh, I thought you might be out for a good time. You know what it's like, it's always the ones who protest the loudest who are the queerest.'

Pincent snorted angrily.

'You needn't worry about that, you creep.' He looked her up and down with disdain. 'What the fuck do you think you look like?'

Petra knew she had him rattled and ignored the insult.

'I think I look fabulous, darling. You must think so too, or you wouldn't be following me.' She ran her hands over her fake breasts, down the sides of her body and across her hips. 'Admit it James, you'd like a piece of this, wouldn't you?'

Pincent wasn't getting drawn into any more of this obscene conversation and changed the subject.

'Who was that you were with earlier?'

Petra had planned out her strategy. She couldn't risk lying about her companion; if Pincent had identified Archie, denial would only look more suspicious. Understanding the need to protect Archie and prevent him getting into trouble, she had her answer ready.

'So, you *were* following me. I thought so. It was Archie, the forensics guy you used to search my flat, as if you don't know. I saw him in the club and approached him. He acted as if he was shocked to see me and when I asked him a direct question, he told me he was gay. We had an uncomfortable chat for about thirty seconds and then he left.'

'So why did you come out together?'

'We didn't. He was ready to move on to a different club, and I followed him out, I thought I'd have a laugh with him.'

'A laugh?'

'Yes, I asked him to come back to my place for some fun,' she laughed. 'He was crapping himself! You should have seen the look on his face. He couldn't get away from me fast enough. He wouldn't be part of this ludicrous surveillance operation by any chance, would he?'

Pincent shook his head. Her story seemed to make sense going by what he'd seen, but if Archie was keeping tabs on Petra, he was doing it independently.

'I wondered why he was walking so quickly.'

Petra laughed. 'He couldn't walk quickly enough. Eventually, he ran off to get away from me, so I gave up and decided to go back to the club. That's when I spotted you.'

She leaned close to Pincent's face and whispered.

'Now we're alone together, I could do with a really good seeinto from a dishy man... but you'll have to do. I don't mind giving or receiving, your choice.'

Pincent visibly shuddered at the thought.

'Go fuck yourself, Peter,' he said, coldly.

'It's Petra.'

Pincent's hatred blazed in his eyes. Through gritted teeth he repeated, 'Go fuck yourself, *Peter*. I've got to go.' Then he smiled, 'Oh, and by the way, we've found the moment you and Tony Waters bumped onto each other that night. We've got it on CCTV.'

Their gazes locked in a silent stand-off until Pincent could stand it no more.

'People like you really do disgust me.'

He raised his voice, spitting venom, and jabbed a finger in Petra's face.

'There's no doubt in our minds that you killed Tony Waters and we're confident we'll soon have enough to prove it. You'll be banged up for life soon, *Peter*, and when that happens, I'll be standing there laughing.'

He pushed past her and walked off through the crowds, quickly disappearing from sight.

Anger coursed through Petra, but her mind was clear.

I'll show you who's disgusting, you little prick. You just wait.

THIRTY-ONE

Petra made her way back to her flat, feeling deflated; she didn't feel like going to another club, the night was ruined. The Detective Sergeant had rattled her more than she cared to admit, and the news about her meeting with Waters being found on CCTV was devastating. She threw herself onto her bed and lay there sobbing, a familiar rage building inside her. She considered putting in a complaint about Pincent's abuse, but decided against it; she was, after all, on bail for murder. She couldn't rock the boat, not yet, and any conversation would only be her word against his.

Not only had he upset her, his intrusion also meant another wasted opportunity. She'd been so excited at the thought of spending time with Archie and now it might never happen. She felt an overwhelming urge to hurt Pincent, the same rage she'd felt when she'd killed Tony Waters, but this was different; she'd only met Pincent a few times - and he was a serving police officer.

Eventually Petra started to calm down, stopped crying and sat up on the bed, going over in her head what to do about the two officers who seemed so desperate to see her in prison. Clearly, both Neider and Pincent had serious issues with gay people, bordering on fanaticism, but Neider's attitude seemed more personal, more visceral, than her colleague's. She wondered whether Pincent's comment about the CCTV meeting between herself and Waters was bullshit. After all, if it was true, why hadn't she been arrested?

She stood up, made her way to the kitchen and put the kettle on, hoping that a strong cup of coffee might steady her nerves. Suddenly, something snapped, her mind was made up, she wouldn't take the bullying anymore. She had fought back against Tony Waters, now it was time to fight back against the likes of Neider, Pincent, Des Thayer and Andy Clark. The police were desperate to take her down, but she wasn't going to make it easy for them. As she sat on the settee with her coffee, she thought carefully about her next move. Then it came to her. It was obvious when she thought about it: she needed to turn the tables on those pursuing her; become the predator, not the prey.

Knowing that Pincent would be watching from somewhere nearby, she carefully removed all her make-up, threw off her yellow dress and lilac tights, replacing them with dark grey tracksuit bottoms and a black hooded top; a pair of trainers replaced the high heels she had worn earlier. He needed to be Peter once again for his plan to succeed. Pulling his hood up, he turned off the light, opened the front door and crept quietly up a few steps, just far enough to give him a view towards Frith Street, through the gaps of the closely spaced black railings.

Just as he'd suspected, there was Pincent leaning on a wall at the junction, smoking a cigarette, like a character from a Raymond Chandler movie.

You're really not very good at this, are you, James?

Peter remained perfectly still, confident he couldn't possibly be seen from that distance, because he was so well hidden by the railings. Pincent was expecting him to come bounding back up the stairs in a bright yellow dress; that wasn't about to happen.

Peter's hatred for him was burning inside him like acid, an intense loathing that he'd felt so many times

162

before in his life, a loathing he'd felt for so many people who'd made his life hell just for being himself. He smiled, pleased with the plan he'd hatched. He was about to turn the tables.

Pincent had not moved too far away from Hardy's flat. He was keeping a long eye from fifty yards away at the junction with Frith Street, standing outside the café he'd used earlier in the evening. After walking away from Petra, he'd watched her return to the flat, assuming that she would soon be out and about again. Nothing had happened though, so after thirty minutes of inactivity, at 3am, he called it a night.

Making his way through the early morning crowds, trying not to touch or be touched by any of the creatures around him, he headed to the car park to collect his suitcase, then retraced his steps past the cafe to Hotel Boyle, a small hotel at the top end of Frith Street. He'd chosen the hotel himself and booked a room for two nights at his own expense. It was an almost perfect location; 100 yards from Hardy's flat, but hidden from view around the corner.

It never occurred to Pincent that he might be followed by Peter, who was moving unseen through the crowds in a dark hoodie, watching his every move. Following him back up Frith Street, Peter watched with interest as he entered the front lobby of Hotel Boyle, a hotel with a unique reputation in Soho. It was the favourite haunt of MP's, judges, senior police officers, powerful businessmen, senior council officials, and even a couple of bishops.

It was a popular place with the "great and the good" of London society for very good reasons: it was well known for turning a blind eye to customers bringing "friends" into their rooms for a few hours. In addition to its discretion, the hotel had no CCTV system, something

163

which their regular customers greatly appreciated and was the main reason many of them frequented the hotel in the first place. An unobtrusive building, it was situated between two large private town houses and could easily be missed by passers-by. Unless you looked directly at the tiny *Hotel Boyle* sign etched into glass above the door, there was no indication of the hotel being there.

Petra had been taken there one night a couple of months ago, after being picked up in a club by a very handsome senior police officer from the Surrey Constabulary. He remembered being asked by the officer to punch a number into a keypad outside the hotel's front door, because the officer was too drunk himself, and he also remembered the number – 5 6 7 8. Once in the bedroom, the man had wanted very kinky, rough sex, something which Petra was more than happy to provide.

Peter ran across the road and peered through a tiny window, just in time to see Pincent press a button on the counter and hear a bell ring. Within twenty seconds, a man appeared from a back room. After seeing some identification, he turned to a wooden board behind the counter containing twenty small squares, five across and four deep, reached into the second box from the top on the right-hand side and withdrew a key. Assuming they were in order, Peter worked out that the key was for room number ten. The man passed Pincent the key, which he took with his right hand, tossed it into the air then caught it with a theatrical flourish, before walking to the bottom of the staircase and disappearing from view.

There were still a few people passing along Frith Street, no more than twenty yards from Soho Square, but nobody seemed to be paying attention to him, so Peter strolled casually away from the window and back to his flat.

One hour and fifteen minutes later he climbed the

stairs from his flat once more and stepped into the now deserted but still dark street; it was time to initiate part two of his plan.

THIRTY-TWO

Instead of going round to the front door of the hotel where he would be conspicuous, Peter turned right off Bateman Street and headed into Bateman Buildings, a quiet alleyway leading through to Soho Square. Towards the far end of the alleyway, between industrial-sized rubbish bins, he found what he was looking for: the rear door of Hotel Boyle. He had passed the door many times before and knew it had a keypad entry system, identical to the one on the front door.

Hoping against hope that the hotel would be as lax about security as most other hotels in the West End, Peter used his gloved hands to slowly and carefully punch in the numbers he remembered from two months ago - 5 6 7 8, nothing happened for a second, then the door made a satisfying 'click' and Peter pushed it open.

He found himself in a narrow corridor, at the end of which he could see a half-glass door leading into the lobby. He swiftly made his way down the corridor, his feet falling quietly on the thick patterned carpet. On reaching the door, he had a cautious look through the glass to ensure the coast was clear. The lobby was silent and empty, so he quietly opened the door, walked quickly through the lobby and hurried up the stairs to the first floor where he was faced with a choice: turn right, or left? He turned right and to his relief saw that the first door was number 8, then 9, then 10. He stared at the number.

It's almost five in the morning. What do I say if I've got the wrong room?

He'd come too far, he couldn't back out now. Breathing in deeply through his nose and exhaling through his mouth, he rapped hard with his knuckles on the door. Surprisingly, Pincent was still awake and answered in a clearly very annoyed voice.

'Who is it?'

Peter's mum was from Norwich and over the years he'd perfected the accent, disguising his own 'home counties' voice perfectly.

'It's the police, can you open the door please sir?'

There was a brief pause then, 'Hang on a second.'

Moments later, Pincent swung the door open, wearing grey boxer shorts and a light-blue t-shirt. He stared in astonishment at seeing Peter standing there and opened his mouth to speak but before any words came out Peter landed a powerful kick to his groin, knocking him backwards. He let out a deep groan of pain and writhed on the floor in agony as he watched Peter quietly close the door, panic and pain coursing through him in equal measure.

Keeping his voice down, so as not to waken people asleep in neighbouring rooms, Peter straddled Pincent's prone body, his right hand feeling in his hoodie pocket for the item he'd picked up just before leaving his flat.

'Right, you filthy piece of shit. I'm going to talk and you're going to listen, understand?'

Pincent was having trouble breathing, so hard had been the impact of Peter's kick on his balls, but he managed to grunt and nodded his head.

'I'm not going to hurt you anymore, but I've got to make sure you don't shout for help, so I'm going to have to gag you.'

Trying to roll away, Pincent's eyes were wide with terror; he shook his head and managed to muster a low and breathless, 'Help!'

Shaking his head, Peter said, 'Naughty boy,' and stamped hard on the side of his ribcage with his heel. Pincent let out an involuntary gasp of breath and moaned with pain.

Peter quickly grabbed a pair of black socks from the open suitcase resting on a chair and stuffed them roughly into Pincent's mouth. Then he picked out a plain white shirt, folded it into a single band, pulled it tight across his victim's mouth and tied it firmly at the back of his head.

Tears were forming in Pincent's eyes, giving Peter intense satisfaction. To make sure he couldn't suddenly gather enough strength to fight back, Peter punched the bicep of his upper arm, once again causing Pincent numbing pain, while rendering the arm almost useless for a few minutes. With the gag, he was now incapable of crying out, only making pitiful groaning sounds.

After allowing a couple of minutes for his victim to bring the pain under control, Peter crouched down by his side.

'Right, I'm going to explain how people like you destroy lives like mine... and you're going to listen. Understand?'

Despite the pain he was suffering, Pincent nodded.

'If you move from that position, I'll stand on your throat and kill you. Understand?'

Pincent's breathing was ragged and painful, as tears streamed down his face. He had no idea where all this was leading but had no choice but to comply. He nodded again.

For the next ten minutes, Peter spoke in a quiet voice, describing, just as he had for Waters, how miserable his life had been through no fault of his own, placing the blame entirely at the feet of people like Pincent. He explained how hard it had been to continually move on and start again; how he'd now reached a position where he wasn't prepared to simply sit back, take the abuse and move on any more.

At no stage did Peter sit on the bed or the chair, he crouched or stood at all times, not wanting to leave any unnecessary forensic evidence which might link him to the scene. Pincent wasn't able to reply to what Peter was saying, his job was just to lie there and listen.

When he'd finished, Peter knelt down on one knee close to Pincent's head, leaned close and whispered directly into his ear.

'Now you know what it feels like to be abused and threatened, don't you James?'

Pincent nodded. The pain was still excruciating, but at least his ordeal might be coming to an end; his tormentor sounded like he'd finally finished making his point.

'Good.'

Peter reached into an inside pocket, pulled out a small serrated knife, yanked up Pincent's right arm, allowing access to his torso and calmly stabbed him in the stomach. He watched as Pincent's eyes widened with fear and his body writhed in agony, then stabbed him again and again, his ripped and torn t-shirt staining and soaking with deep red blood. Finally, as Pincent stared pleadingly at him, begging him to show mercy, he plunged the knife into his right eye, the blade penetrating through to his brain.

A feeling of euphoria washed over him as he watched his enemy's body go limp and lifeless but it was soon replaced by a wave of panic as the reality of what he'd just done hit him. He pulled the knife from Pincent's eye, trying to block out the revolting sound as it freed itself from the eye socket, then quickly checked around the room until he was happy he'd left nothing for the police forensic teams to get their teeth into.

Peter put the blood-soaked knife into his hoodie pocket, took one last look at his tormentor and with great satisfaction, smiled grimly. With his clean and unbloodied left glove, he picked up the 'Do Not Disturb' sign. He opened the door, stepped as silently as he could into the corridor then closed the door, before hanging the sign on the handle.

One week ago, he had been leading a reasonably normal life as a garage mechanic called Peter Hardy; now he was a double murderer... what's more, the murderer of a police officer! The stress and tension were exhausting but he knew he had to remain focused. With any luck, the remains of Detective Sergeant James Pincent wouldn't be discovered for several hours at the very least, leaving Peter plenty of time to carry out part three of his plan: covering his tracks.

170

THIRTY-THREE

Safely back inside his flat, Peter stripped off every piece of clothing; trainers, socks, underpants, tracksuit bottoms, t-shirt, sweatshirt, hoodie, and gloves. He shoved them all into a bin-liner then stayed awake watching videos until morning light fell on the outside staircase and forced its way in through the small window.

Two hours after daybreak, his watch told him it was 9.15. For around four hours he had been half expecting a knock at the door, a knock which would have indicated his life was over. If the police arrived now, they would capture him with all the evidence they needed to convict him in a black plastic bin-liner, and he would have no choice but to confess. Staying inside his flat had been a risk, but Peter was well aware that once the body was found, they would be able to estimate the time of death to within about an hour, so it was a chance he had to take. Disposing of the evidence so soon after the murder, and before Soho's morning bustle commenced, would have looked hugely suspicious during the subsequent investigation. He knew for certain they would spot him on CCTV. How would he explain moving around in the streets just after the murder had been committed, carrying a large bin bag?

No, he was satisfied he'd made the right decision; the chances of Pincent's body being discovered before late morning were practically non-existent. But now he'd waited long enough and it was finally time to dispose of the evidence. At this time in the morning, it wouldn't look remotely unusual if he left the flat and disposed of his rubbish in a bin-bag.

Ten minutes later, Peter walked back into his flat. He had found one of the many refuse lorries that operate in the West End on Saturday and Sunday mornings, clearing up the debris from the previous night. He'd waited until the refuse workers' attention was distracted and when they were all busy picking up black bin sacks, he casually threw his own bag into the back, watching with mounting relief as it was crushed and swallowed by the mechanism.

Satisfied he'd now done all he could to cover his tracks, Peter headed swiftly back to his flat. He felt terrified and nauseous, but willed himself to stay calm and follow his plan. Killing a copper meant the investigating officers were searching for not just anyone, but the person who'd murdered their colleague, their friend; no doubt they would be pulling out all the stops to find his killer.

He shook involuntarily from time to time on the short walk back and unusually for him, avoided eye contact with people he passed in the street. Whether he was Peter or Petra, he was usually relaxed and outgoing on his weekends in London, but now he was suddenly acting withdrawn, something which could make people who knew him ask difficult questions. If they did, it could cause him a problem, so he had to snap himself out of it, right now, and play a part.

Peter kept plenty of spare clothing in his flat, including a navy-blue hoodie very similar to the one he'd just disposed of, and two further pairs of tracksuit bottoms, one a slightly lighter grey than the pair he'd worn the previous night and one dark blue pair. He also had two pairs of trainers, one of which was almost identical to the pair he'd worn earlier. All in all, he was confident that when they came to arrest him, which they undoubtedly would, he'd covered all bases.

Suddenly aware he was ravenous, he set about making a belated breakfast, demolishing a bowl of Weetabix and two rounds of toast and jam in double quick time, washing it all down with two cups of coffee. He had to stay alert.

Every minute, he expected the knock at his door, but when it hadn't come by 11.45, he smartened himself up, pulling on a pair of expensive Wranglers, his brown leather shoes, a tailored flower pattern shirt and a black quilted puffer jacket. He was beginning to feel paranoid and checked through the railings to see whether he was being watched by someone else, but the coast appeared to be clear. Bounding up the stairs two at a time, he went out to keep his noon appointment with Archie, in La Belle Homme.

THIRTY-FOUR

Peter had experienced an unexpected thrill when killing James Pincent, just like when he was brutally beating Tony Waters. It was wrong, he knew that, but he couldn't control it. He would have loved to take Archie back to his flat, but that would have been playing straight into the hands of the police when they eventually came looking for him. If they were caught together, it would be game over. Spotting Archie sitting at a table at the back left hand corner of the café, Peter threaded his way carefully through the crowded tables and sat down opposite him.

A nervous smile appeared on Archie's face the moment he saw Peter entering the café, and as he sat down, he couldn't help commenting on his appearance.

'Good Morning, Petra, you look a little different to the last time I saw you.'

'Don't take the piss, darling, I'm still better looking than you.' He squeezed Archie's arm affectionately, then leaned in and said in a whisper, 'Probably better if you call me Peter.'

Archie nodded, 'Understood.' His face looked like he hadn't slept well and he looked nervously around from time to time.

'We're fucked, aren't we?'

'Why?'

'That detective seeing us together last night.'

'Don't worry, I've covered it.'

'How?'

'After you ran off, I turned round and confronted

him.'

'Did you? Shit! What did he say?'

'He wanted to know what we were doing together.'

'What did you tell him?'

'I told him we'd bumped into each other by chance and that I was trying to get you to come back to my flat, but you didn't want anything to do with me. I explained that was the reason you were hurrying away.'

'Did he believe you?'

'Yep. Hook, line and sinker, he's a typical thick copper. I even said I had wondered if you were part of his pathetic little operation. Don't worry, gorgeous, you're in the clear.'

Archie heaved a sigh of relief; he'd been fretting about losing his job ever since running off into Frith Street and felt, for the first time since being with Petra the previous night, that he could relax.

'I don't know how to thank you.'

'You don't have to, we're quits. How about you buy me a coffee?'

'I will, but I need to know exactly what was said between you and him.'

Peter smiled reassuringly.

'Get me that coffee and I'll tell you everything.'

Catching the eye of a waitress, Archie ordered Peter his coffee, which arrived a couple of minutes later.

'Well?'

Sipping the foam off the top of his steaming drink, Peter gazed at Archie.

'Well what?'

'What happened with that officer?'

Peter licked his lips clear of foam and sat back.

'I confronted him about following me but he denied it. He said he was checking for CCTV systems they'd missed regarding Tony Waters' murder.'

'Do you believe him?'

Peter shook his head.

'He's talking shit. He was definitely following me and looked extremely pissed off that I'd sussed him.'

'How long did you talk to him?'

'A couple of minutes, maybe more. I started making jokey suggestions that he might be gay, at which point he nearly had a fit!' Peter laughed then his voice became more serious. 'I hope I did enough to throw him off the scent. Anyway, he walked off and I didn't see him again.'

Archie reached over and held his hand.

'Look, he's groping in the dark for clues and he doesn't know about us, so let's keep it that way.'

Peter raised an eyebrow.

'Us? I didn't know there was an *us*.'

Archie smiled seductively.

'There might be if you're a good boy.'

Peter smiled back but, aware that the less Archie knew about what had occurred during the early hours, the better for both of them, he realised he would have to lie through his teeth.

'I wasn't in the best mood after talking to that scum, so I went back to the flat. I looked out through the railings half an hour later and he was still standing on the corner, watching, so I went to bed.'

'Was he still there this morning?'

'I don't know, I don't think so. I looked outside but couldn't see him anywhere, so he may have gone back to Kent because his cover was blown.'

Nodding, Archie took a gulp of coffee.

Peter continued, reassuringly, 'I hurried down here to meet you, so even if he was following, he would have lost me once I turned into Wardour Street. There's no way he'd have seen me enter the café and we're well hidden at the back here.'

Archie visibly relaxed and his eyes locked onto Peter's.

'It was a shame about last night. I was quite merry and would definitely have been up for some fun. What about you?'

Peter was feeling more attracted to Archie by the minute, but he'd killed a police officer only a few hours earlier: a police officer who he was convinced absolutely deserved to be killed, but a police officer nonetheless. He knew the shit was about to not only hit the fan, but that he was standing up close to it. Fighting his natural urges, he tried to let Archie down gently.

'Yes, I would, and please don't take this the wrong way, but now is not the right time.'

'Oh.' Archie's voice betrayed his disappointment.

'I'm sure we'll get together soon, but him following me last night has shaken me up. They're desperate to convict me for Tony Waters' murder and…'

Smiling and nodding understandingly, Archie interrupted.

'Don't you dare say you're innocent.'

'Sorry, forgot who I was talking to there for a second. What I meant was, I don't want to get *you* into any trouble.'

Archie laughed. They chatted for a further half an hour, making plans to get together the following weekend and exchanging mobile phone numbers.

Saying goodbye, Peter leaned forward and placed a kiss on Archie's cheek.

'You're the best, darling. I'd be doing time for that evil bastard if it wasn't for you.'

'Shame you couldn't have done the same thing to that wanker last night. Our lives would be much easier with him out of the picture.'

Looking at him thoughtfully, Peter wondered

whether Archie was being serious and for a brief moment considered telling all, but caution got the better of him. He gave Archie one final bit of advice.

'Don't forget, if they ask questions, I was bothering you and you were simply trying to get away from me.'

Archie nodded.

Peter looked longingly into his eyes as he lifted himself from his chair, ran a finger slowly down Archie's cheek, lingering for a moment on his lips, then turned and walked out.

THIRTY-FIVE

Natalie stared at the Mickey Mouse clock which hung in pride of place on the wall opposite her desk. It had been a Christmas gift from her niece, Isabel, and was now giving her serious cause for concern: Mickey's big hand was pointing straight up and Minnie's smaller hand was pointing at one.

Pincent had called her at 3.15 in the morning, something she'd instructed him to do, whatever time he finished. Once he'd given her an account of how the night had gone and that Hardy had confronted him in Greek Street, she considered things for a moment before making a decision.

'Right, I'm calling it off now. I want you back here. I'll see you in my office at eleven and we'll have to think of something else,' she had said.

Pincent realised there was no point in arguing; he was disappointed, but had to acknowledge that she was making the right call.

'Okay boss, see you at eleven. Sorry for letting you down.'

Neider had hung up the call without replying... and now he was two hours late. Knowing what a stickler he was for punctuality; an alarm bell was ringing in her head. Something wasn't right.

After contacting directory enquiries for the phone number of the hotel where James was staying, she dialled Hotel Boyle's number and a pleasant sounding woman answered.

'Hotel Boyle, Anna speaking, how can I help you?'

'Good afternoon, it's Sevenoaks police here. I'm Detective Chief Inspector Neider and I'm trying to trace one of my officers. I believe he was staying with you last night.'

'I see. Under what name please?'

'James Pincent.'

Anna checked through her booking-in ledger and within seconds had found him.

'Yes, Mr Pincent is in room 10. He's booked in for two nights, last night and tonight.'

'Are you saying he hasn't checked out yet?'

'No, not yet, is that a problem?'

Natalie drummed her fingers on the table. Something had happened, she could smell it.

'Has anyone checked his room this morning?'

'Hang on.'

Anna checked through the cleaning records.

'His room wasn't cleaned this morning because he'd left the *Do not Disturb* sign on his door handle.'

An icy finger ran the length of her spine.

'Could someone please go and check his room - now!'

One thought was running through her head, *Hardy, it's fucking Hardy, it's got to him.* If anything had happened, the bosses would want to know what he was doing up there and she needed to have a good answer.

'I'm on my own here,' said Anna, plaintively. 'I really shouldn't leave the front desk. My boss will…'

Natalie cut her short.

'It's of vital importance that I contact him as soon as possible.'

With a sigh of exasperation, Anna said, 'Okay, I'll get back to you in a minute.'

Two minutes later, a hysterical Anna was back on

the phone shouting and screaming. Through the sobs, Natalie had trouble deciphering her words.

'He's dead… blood everywhere… it's horrible!'

'Stay calm, Anna, I'll call the local station. Officers will be with you very soon.' She thought for a moment. 'You're absolutely certain he's dead?'

'Yes… one of his eyes is open… the other one is just a mess. There's blood everywhere… he's dead!'

For the briefest of moments, Natalie was stunned into silence, then her police training took over.

'Okay. Keep the door to his room closed. Don't go back in and make sure nobody else does, it's vitally important. I'm putting the phone down now, Anna. Don't worry, help will be with you very soon.'

After contacting West End Central Police Station, Natalie sat back in her chair and stared up at the clock. James was a bloody good officer and now, because she'd stupidly given him permission to tail Hardy, he was dead. In that moment, she knew she had to cover her tracks and protect herself. She phoned her boss, Detective Superintendent Kelly.

'Sir, I've got some bad news.'

'Go on.'

'DS Pincent has been found dead.'

'Fuck! Where? What happened?'

'In a hotel room in London.'

'Shit! What was he doing up there?'

'I don't know, Sir. I suspect he may have been following Peter Hardy.'

His voice became steely.

'What? How dare you countermand my orders.'

'No… you don't understand, Sir. He came to me asking how my request for a surveillance team went. I explained it had been refused. He protested, but I told him that was the end of the matter and didn't think any

181

more of it. Then he phoned my home in the early hours to tell me he'd been watching Hardy in Soho.'

'What did you say?'

'I shouted at him for waking me and for disobeying orders and told him I wanted him back at the office this morning. When he didn't show up, I phoned the hotel. His body's only just been discovered, I contacted the Met and local officers are on their way.'

'I don't believe it! What the fuck was he thinking of?'

'I don't know, Sir. This case has really got to him.'

'Get your arse up there and liaise with their CID. We're going to need a substantial amount of cooperation on this. I'd better let the Chief know.'

'Okay. Sir.'

'Oh, and Natalie.'

'Yes, Sir?'

'Until you've ascertained exactly what's happened, let's keep this tightly under wraps. Not a word to anyone on the Waters investigation team.'

'Understood, Sir.'

'And I'll be expecting constant updates… at least every couple of hours.'

'No problem.'

Putting the phone down, Natalie sat forward with her head in her hands, steaming with anger. Although they weren't friends outside of work, James was a good police officer and now, partly because of her, he was dead. She pulled out an A-Z to check the exact location of Hotel Boyle and was stunned when she saw its proximity to Bateman Street. It left no doubt in her mind.

Hardy, Peter fucking Hardy. You did this, but you won't get away with it, you bastard. I will get you!

THIRTY-SIX

It was approaching three in the afternoon when an unremarkable but fit-looking young man greeted Natalie outside Hotel Boyle, wearing black trainers, scruffy blue jeans and a tight t-shirt with a picture of the rock band *Led Zeppelin* on the front, with their 1980 European Tour dates emblazoned across the back. His hair was mousey brown with a neat side parting and he had tiny freckles dotted over his nose.

He offered his hand to Natalie and she shook it firmly.

'DI Bernie Tanner, pleased to meet you.'

'DCI Natalie Neider. I got here as quickly as I could.'

'Sorry about the casual clothes, Ma'am. I'd already got changed and was about to head home when the call came in.'

'No problem, you look fine.' Neider was so preoccupied with the job in hand, she hadn't even noticed the man's clothes.

Bernie smiled politely then became serious.

'I understand the victim is one of your officers?'

'Yes, James Pincent, a DS on my team.'

'You're certain it's him?'

'As certain as I can be without seeing the body.'

'Would you like to see the scene? It's rather gruesome and might be upsetting if he's one of your own, so please don't feel obliged.'

She replied, crisply, 'I'll be fine, just take me to the

room.'

Bernie nodded and led her into the foyer, then up the stairs, giving their names to a young detective writing up the crime scene log on the landing directly outside the room. Two forensic officers in full protective garb were busy inside the bedroom; they stopped on seeing the DI and Natalie in the doorway, seemingly waiting for his permission to continue.

'It's okay guys. This is DCI Neider from Kent Police, please carry on.'

Despite all her years of experience, on entering the room Natalie was shocked; she had seen many murder victims in her career, but never one she knew personally. The terrible sight of James's mutilated body made her stomach turn over and she felt the room spin.

He was lying on his left side in a foetal position, his t-shirt punctured and torn in several places, the material completely soaked in blood. His left eye was staring lifelessly across the floor, his right eye was missing, the eye socket where it once sat, a disgusting mixture of flesh, congealed blood, and ripped open eyeball. Blood had run from his eye socket and down over his nose and face, tracing its path to the floor. The heavily patterned carpet couldn't hide the deep red blood stain stretching from his knees to his head.

Bernie viewed Natalie with concern, 'Are you sure you're okay?'

She gulped, nodded, and pulled her shoulders back. 'I'm fine, just hard when it's one of your own.'

'Come on, we'll have a quick look around, but please don't touch anything.'

She looked at him coldly and snapped, 'I know how to behave at a crime scene.'

'Sorry, of course you do… habit.'

Neider relented and managed a thin smile. 'And a

very good habit.' She held her arm out, 'Shall we?'

Careful where they placed their feet, Bernie and Natalie spent ten minutes checking only what was easily visible, leaving the majority of the search to the SOCOs.

Back in the corridor, Bernie said, 'I'll have a really good look through James's personal items for any potential clues with my DS once these boys have finished. You're welcome to be involved if you'd like?'

'No thanks, I've already got a good idea who did this.'

Raising his eyebrows, he sounded surprised and excited in equal measure.

'Really, who?'

'Sorry, Bernie, I could do with a coffee and something to eat. Is there somewhere local? I'll explain everything there.'

Five minutes later they were in a window seat of Carlo's Pantry, a café that would have been at home in 1950's Italy, nestling quietly in a corner of Soho Square.

'Here you go, Ma'am.'

Bernie handed her the coffee and shortbread biscuit she'd requested.

'Thank you.'

'You're welcome. So who is this suspect?'

'His name's Peter Hardy and he has a basement flat in Bateman Street.'

Bernie's eyes widened. 'The guy under suspicion for the murder on your patch?'

'We haven't got enough to charge him yet but as far as I'm concerned, he did it. James was desperate to find the missing piece that would prove it was him, that's why he was up here, to tail him.'

Bernie frowned. 'What, on his own?'

'Afraid so. My boss refused a surveillance team, so James asked to follow Hardy alone.' She took another

185

sip. 'I refused, of course, but it seems he took matters into his own hands.'

'Didn't he say anything?'

'Nope. I knew nothing about it until I received a call from him in the early hours. He'd been following Hardy, saw him leaving a nightclub, witnessed him pestering an off-duty SOCO of yours, then got confronted by him in the street.'

Bernie listened intently then leaned in towards Natalie.

'I need to know full details of everything he told you, timings, locations, everything. If we work quickly on this, we just might get a result. He pulled out an A4 notebook from his bag.'

Over the next thirty minutes, Natalie went over everything about the Waters murder and the ongoing investigation: the arrest of Hardy and search of his flat; the CCTV evidence they'd obtained; everything that James had seen during his unauthorised surveillance and finally contacting the hotel and learning he'd been murdered.

Sitting back in his chair, Bernie shook the sensation back into his right hand, which was aching after writing for such a long time. He quickly read through his notes without speaking, then gave a low whistle.

'If we can find CCTV of them together anywhere near here, we've got enough to bring him in.'

Natalie smiled inwardly; Peter Hardy had totally fucked up her life and she intended to repay him by fucking up his. He'd killed James, of that she was certain. He had been lucky with his murder of Tony Waters, but this time he'd pushed his luck too far.

She'd been quietly impressed with Bernie Tanner; he was calm, efficient, methodical. Looking more closely at him, she estimated his age to be no more than thirty, young for a Detective Inspector in the Met, but she had confidence in his ability and, if she were completely honest with herself, had rather enjoyed his company.

THIRTY-SEVEN

Bernie Tanner moved quickly, posting officers into the surrounding streets to seize CCTV from private premises, while sending a separate officer to Westminster CCTV Control Room for the council recordings.

The day had passed quickly and by 7.15, in company with Bernie and two of his DS's, Natalie was at Vine Street Police Station watching CCTV of Hardy and Pincent in animated conversation in Greek Street. The images were taken less than 100 yards from Hardy's flat and only 200 yards from Hotel Boyle. Their body language looked combative and something Hardy said had clearly upset Pincent before he stormed off.

Turning to DS Graham Carter who oversaw reviewing CCTV, Bernie said, 'What happened after that?'

'The victim stands on the corner of Frith Street and Bateman Street until about three, he doesn't move. After that, we've tracked him all the way down to the Shaftesbury Avenue car park, then straight back up Frith Street, pulling a suitcase back to his hotel. There's no CCTV in the hotel, so our last image of him is going through the front door.'

'And Hardy?'

'There's nothing covering his flat and the bright yellow dress isn't seen again.'

'Fuck, so we've got nothing to put him at the hotel?'

The two DS's exchanged a glance, 'We might have, Sir.'

Bernie raised his eyebrows and looked over to Natalie, who impatiently said, 'Well? What is it?'

Carter removed the video cassette and replaced it with another.

'Unfortunately, Westminster Council CCTV was facing away from the hotel at the vital moment, but this was seized from a residential property next door.'

He pressed the play button.

'The main part of the image is of people passing the front of the house but pay close attention to the top right of the screen.'

Bernie and Natalie sat forward on their chairs, eager to see what was coming. The first ten seconds showed nothing at all, then Pincent walked with his suitcase from the bottom centre of the screen to the top right-hand corner, where you could just see the hotel entrance. He opened the door and walked in. Seconds later, a large man wearing a dark hooded top and dark tracksuit bottoms jogged across the road to the door, his hood up, obscuring his face. The man seemed to peer through the door into the hotel, before walking down Frith Street straight towards the camera. Unfortunately, his hood was pulled well forward, hiding his identity until he disappeared from view.

Natalie was intrigued. 'Is that it?'

'No, there's a little more, Ma'am.'

He changed the cassette and pressed play.

'This image is from a vegetarian cafe in Frith Street and shows the junction with Bateman Street. The man in the hooded top briefly appears on the screen,' he pointed to the suspect on the right of the screen, 'but immediately turns into Bateman Street, heading straight towards Hardy's flat.' He leaned forward and turned the machine off.

'Does hoodie man reappear on Greek Street?' asked

Natalie.

'No ma'am, he doesn't.'

Bernie turned to his DS's.

'Thanks for your help, lads. Could you give us a moment?'

The DS's left the room and Natalie was quick to assess what they'd seen.

'Fucking hell, it's him, I'm sure of it. He's tall, well-built and he's got the same lolloping gait. Looks like he was following James and checking the lay of the land before topping him.'

'I think you might be right. Don't get too excited though, if forensics have found nothing at the scene, we've got nowhere near enough for the CPS yet.'

THIRTY-EIGHT

After leaving Archie at the café, Peter walked back to his flat feeling more alive than he'd felt for years. He knew the police would come looking for him and arrest him, but was surprised at how little he cared; he wasn't going to be bullied and abused just because of who he was. Those days were over. He was fighting back and it felt fucking brilliant. If he'd covered his tracks as well as he thought he had, all should be well; there was certainly no way he'd be confessing anything.

After wandering around Soho to clear his head, he returned to his flat at two and lay on his bed, staring up at a cobweb in the corner of the room. Normally, he was very house-proud and would have swept it away with his broom in an instant, but this time he smiled to himself as the long-legged spider stayed completely motionless in the web's centre, a killer prepared to do whatever was necessary to survive in a difficult world. His previous revulsion at seeing a spider in his flat had been replaced by empathy, a grudging respect and an understanding of why it behaved so ruthlessly. It did what it did to survive - and so would he.

Slowly, he drifted off into a deep sleep. Over 24 hours without any sleep, combined with the exhausting physical and mental efforts of the night had finally caught up with him.

Hearing distant voices, Peter slowly came to. Through the kitchenette window he noticed a shadow passing, then another, followed by the sound of heavy footsteps on the metal stairs to his door. He rubbed his tired eyes and glanced up at the clock, it was 7.55 and dark outside, apart from the distinctive orange glow of the streetlights on the windowpanes.

There was a loud banging on the door, accompanied by, 'Police! Police! Open the door, please!'

Sitting upright on the bed, he started grinning.

Come on then you fuckers, let's see what you've got!

Another loud bang on the door followed, with an officer shouting, 'Five seconds and we'll break the door down!'

'Okay, okay, I'm coming!'

Sliding off the bed, Peter walked four steps to the door, unlocked and opened it, then stood smiling at the four burly police officers crowded into the small area outside. A uniformed officer almost as tall as Peter roughly turned him around, pushed him up against a wall and, with the assistance of another officer, pulled Peter's arms behind his back and handcuffed him. He was turned around to face them and saw that the four uniformed officers had been joined by one in plain clothes.

It was this officer who said, 'Peter Hardy, I am arresting you on suspicion of the murder of Detective Sergeant James Pincent,' and proceeded to caution Peter, who was surprised to find he was almost enjoying himself.

'You said that very well, darling. Have you been practising?'

The officer remained expressionless.

'Get this fucking faggot in the van.'

'Aren't you going to tell me your name, sweetheart?'

'I'm Detective Sergeant Christopher Carter and you're going to prison for the rest of your life.'

Peter pouted and replied mockingly, 'I doubt that

very much. You need to have committed a crime to be sent to prison and I haven't done anything.'

Carter jerked his head towards the door and the first uniformed officer to grab hold of Peter walked him up the stairs and into the police van. Ten minutes later, the van backed into Vine Street, a tiny dead-end road housing the police station. Peter was feeling remarkably confident, considering he'd just been arrested for the murder of a police officer, a police officer who, at the time of his death, was in the process of investigating him for another murder!

An hour later, Peter had been booked in by the custody sergeant, a surly, sarcastic officer who seemed to be as homophobic as Pincent had been. His fingerprints and photograph were taken, he was searched, then strip searched and had all his property, including his outer clothing, removed and placed into property bags. He was given a white paper boiler-suit and a pair of black plimsoles to wear instead.

He noticed all the officers were being markedly more aggressive to him than the ones he'd encountered in Sevenoaks Police Station. This was to be expected; after all, this time they thought he'd killed one of their own.

Just before being placed into a cell, two officers returned from searching his flat. They told the custody officer they'd found clothing that matched what the suspect was seen wearing on CCTV. They'd also found a set of four different sized carving knives in a drawer, with a fifth knife, the second smallest, missing. These items were also placed into bags and added to his custody record.

Peter was offered the assistance of a solicitor but declined, confident in his own ability to fend off any line of questioning they might throw at him. He was then roughly pushed into cell 3 by a particularly unpleasant and aggressive gaoler, and the door slammed shut behind him. He hated being enclosed and the stark grey of the cell walls added to the mild sensation of claustrophobia. Unlike his cell at Sevenoaks, the bare wooden bench had no mattress and no pillow and the strip light overhead buzzed annoyingly… they obviously meant to make him suffer.

So, this is how cop killers get treated.

Sitting down on the hard bench, he clenched his fists and repeated over and over in his head:

They can do what they fucking like, they can be as mean as they like, I'm walking out of here and carrying on with my life.

Less than ten minutes later he heard footsteps outside in the cell passage. A face appeared at the wicket then a key turned in the lock. The door was swung open by an incongruously baby-faced man in torn jeans and a *Led Zeppelin* t-shirt, carrying a bundle of papers and several video cassettes.

'Hello Peter. I'm Detective Inspector Tanner and I'm the OIC for the murder of James Pincent.'

'You're very young to be in charge.'

Tanner ignored Peter's remark.

'Please, come with me.' He held out an arm, indicating for Peter to go first.

'It's rather late. I was about to turn in.'

'This is a murder enquiry, Mr Hardy, and you're going to be interviewed right now whether you like it or not.'

As they entered the interview room, he saw a woman seated at the table with her back to him. As she turned her head, he was dismayed to see Natalie Neider smiling at him.

'Hello, Peter, lovely to see you again.'

Her voice was dripping with sarcasm. Determined not to show weakness, he faced her down.

'You're determined to stitch me up with the murder of someone, aren't you, love? I'm sorry, but you'll fail again. I haven't done anything.'

Her hatred of him oozed from every pore of her body. Unable to control her anger, she snapped, 'Let's see if you're as cocky once you've seen our evidence!'

Bernie stepped forward to break up the confrontation.

'Okay, let's just calm down, shall we?'

Natalie was furious.

'Calm down! He's just killed one of my officers!'

Peter relished the fact that he had her rattled.

'You can't say that, you stupid cow, I haven't killed anyone!'

Natalie's eyes glared with fury but she remained silent. Peter saw this as a perfect opportunity to wind her up.

'I've been told that it was poor old Detective Sergeant Pincent. Nobody wanted to see that.'

She jumped to her feet, 'You fucking…'

Bernie quickly placed a hand on her shoulder and gently pushed her back into her seat.

Grinning widely and pleased he'd won this small battle, Peter took his seat on the opposite side of the table.

Settling into his chair, Bernie looked at him coldly for a few moments before saying, 'I've been informed by the Custody Sergeant you don't want a solicitor, Mr Hardy, is that correct?'

'Yes.'

'Are you ready to begin the interview now?'

'Yes.'

THIRTY-NINE

This was it; the moment that really mattered. The next hour or two could dictate the rest of his life. He needed to stay calm and stay as close to the truth as possible, as often as possible. Whatever else happened, he mustn't let Neider get to him.

The tape started with the familiar long buzzing sound, followed by the participants introducing themselves for the benefit of the tape, before Bernie asked the first question.

'Could you tell me your movements from finishing work on Friday afternoon, through to being arrested this evening?'

Peter sat back, pursed his lips, then leaned forward with his forearms on the table and his fingers interlinked. He spoke thoughtfully and carefully. He described how he left work and travelled to London; getting changed into his yellow dress and his movements during the evening, ending up at My Pink Life; meeting Archie in the club and how he'd teased him and that Archie had tried to get away from him; the encounter with Pincent, repeating the conversation exactly as it happened, and finally how, feeling pissed off after the meeting with Pincent, he'd headed back to his flat and gone to bed.

Natalie glanced at Bernie, who nodded to say the floor was hers.

'So, you admit you were pissed off after meeting DS Pincent.'

'Yes.'

'Was that solely because of the conversation you'd just had, or was there something more?'

Peter breathed out slowly to calm himself then held her gaze for several seconds before answering.

'Partly because of the conversation, but meeting him again reminded me of how vile he was when he interviewed me at the garage.'

She stared back at him.

'Would you say you hated DS Pincent?'

Seeing no reason to deny the obvious, Peter answered truthfully.

'Yes, I hated him. He was a bigoted pig and I'm glad he's dead… but I didn't kill him.'

Their eyes locked, neither of them blinking or backing down, until Natalie slowly turned to Bernie.

'Thank you, he's all yours.'

Selecting one of the video cassettes, Bernie slid it into the recorder, turned on the monitor and pressed play. The screen burst into life with images showing the front door of My Pink Life. After a few seconds, Archie could be seen emerging from the club, closely followed by Peter.

'Wow, I look great in that dress, don't I?'

Bernie allowed the tape to roll on then paused the image at a particular moment.

'Can you identify this person?'

He pointed at Archie Cowper.

'Yes, that's the SOCO that DCI Neider used to search my flat last week. His name is Archie, I believe.'

'And where are you?'

'Seriously? You need me to point myself out, in that fabulous dress?'

'Yes, please.'

He leaned forward and pointed at himself in the bright yellow dress, then leaned back and eyed Natalie.

'Voila! Don't I look exquisite?'

She continued to stare at him, no expression on her face.

Bernie continued, 'Anything unusual about Archie in this picture?'

The tone of the question was pointed and it wasn't a question Peter had anticipated. Leaning towards the screen, he looked carefully at Archie. Was there something he'd missed?

'No, I don't think so. Why?'

'Let me rewind and show you those few seconds again.'

Peter watched the re-run and his heart sank as he realised what Bernie was referring to. He acted dumb, giving nothing away.

'No, I've got no idea what you're going on about.'

Bernie tapped the image of Archie.

'He comes through the door looking carefree, laughing and smiling. Then, as he steps into the street, he appears to recognise someone across the road and his expression changes - dramatically.'

Peter swallowed; he could feel his face going red. Bernie noticed his discomfort and tapped the screen hard.

'He looks worried, almost frightened and after saying something to you, he moves quickly through the crowds to get away from whatever it was he saw. Why did he do that, Mr Hardy? What do you think he saw?'

Peter shrugged.

'Come on, Peter, you can do better than that.'

'How should I know what he saw?'

He was feeling the pressure building and Bernie could see it; Bernie rubbed his chin thoughtfully.

'He saw Sergeant Pincent, didn't he? And he knew he'd be in deep shit, being seen leaving a club with you.'

Peter somehow managed to keep his outward composure, while his insides were knotted tight.

'I only found out that Sergeant Pincent had seen us after speaking to him. I'd no idea at that point that Archie had seen him.'

Bernie kept slowly increasing the pressure, as he inserted two further tapes, showing Peter and Archie moving quickly up Greek Street.

'As you were struggling to keep up with Archie, he looked over his shoulder several times and you exchanged words. What was said?'

This was a much easier question and Peter batted it away.

'He kept telling me to fuck off and leave him alone. I was asking him to come to mine. It was just a joke; I was only winding him up.'

Bernie and Natalie exchanged glances, Bernie lifting a single sheet of paper from the bundle.

'I find that difficult to believe, but we'll move on.'

The next tape showed Archie running into Frith Street and the one after that showed Peter moving back down Greek Street before confronting Pincent. Bernie stopped the tape and replayed the same section again, then asked his question.

'You seemed to be making a beeline for Sergeant Pincent, Mr Hardy.'

It was a statement, not a question; he took a slow sip of water from a glass while watching for a reaction. When he didn't get one, he asked, 'How is that possible if you weren't previously aware of his presence?'

Peter could feel the noose tightening. None of this was direct evidence of him killing Pincent, but the circumstantial evidence was mounting and they'd only just started. He tried to control the involuntary twitching of his left leg.

How much more do they know?

'I saw him through the crowds as soon as I was back in Greek Street because he was almost directly in front of me. I'm tall, so I spot people in crowds quite easily. I'm a friendly bloke, Detective Inspector, so I thought I'd say hello, just for a laugh, but it didn't go as well as I'd expected.'

'You say you were "pissed off" after meeting Sergeant Pincent and that you headed home to bed. Is that right?'

'Yes.'

He felt relieved; he was back on safe ground.

'Why pissed off?'

'Because I've never done anything to annoy him, but he was a real bitch; he's hated me from the moment he first set eyes on me.'

'And that really upsets you?'

'Of course, it does. Wouldn't it upset you if someone hated you and did their damnedest to make life difficult, for no other reason than you're gay?'

Bernie considered asking whether it had upset him enough to want revenge, enough to kill, but instead he changed tack.

'You say you headed back to your flat?'

'Yes.'

'And you didn't go out again?'

'I didn't say that.'

Natalie sat bolt upright and broke in, 'Yes, you did, you said you returned to the flat and went to bed.'

By her tone and the way Bernie's questions were leading, Peter realised they'd probably got CCTV of him in his hoodie, and he had to think quickly.

'That's right.'

His eyes burned into her.

'Now, you're a brilliant detective, DCI Neider, so tell

me… where in my statement do I say I didn't go out again?'

He was taking the piss and she was beginning to lose her cool.

'Alright smart arse, I'll ask the question this way: did you go out again?'

'I did, actually.'

'Why?'

Natalie was in her groove now and although Bernie was frowning uncomfortably, unsure in which direction this might be going, he allowed her to continue.

'I was wired and couldn't sleep, so I went for a walk.'

'At what time?'

'No idea, maybe 3 o'clock, I didn't check.'

'Where did you go?'

'I wandered down Frith Street towards Shaftesbury Avenue, then back up to Soho Square.'

Natalie looked at Bernie, then back to Peter.

'That's interesting.'

Peter could see in her face that she knew something and it made him distinctly uncomfortable.

'Why?'

'Because that's the route Sergeant Pincent took, going to his car to collect his suitcase, before heading back up Frith Street to his hotel.'

Shaking his head and shrugging, Peter struggled for something believable to say.

'I didn't see him until I caught a glimpse of him going into Hotel Boyle.'

Natalie's eyes widened; this was the breakthrough she'd been hoping for - she'd got him.

'So, you admit following him to the hotel?'

'No! I didn't follow him; I just saw him going in. In fact, I wasn't even sure it *was* him, so I went and looked through the window by the entrance door.'

Bernie and Natalie exchanged a glance and Peter spotted it. He'd taken a chance by admitting going out again, but looking at their reactions, it might have backfired on him.

'Why? Is that important?'

Natalie viewed him with an element of exasperation at such a stupid question.

'Is it important that you were watching someone in a hotel foyer? A man who *you* stated had upset you earlier that evening? A man who was murdered in his hotel room a couple of hours later...? Why do *you* think that's important?'

Peter had walked into a trap and he knew it.

'I... look, you've got to believe me, I didn't kill him. I went straight home. You can check the CCTV, it will show me going home.' He knew his voice was becoming shriller and stopped abruptly.

Before Natalie could ask another question, Bernie intervened.

'I think this is a good moment to take a short break.'

He suspended the interview and switched the tape off, leaving Natalie staring at him open mouthed.

FORTY

Once Peter had been returned to his cell, Natalie followed Bernie out of the custody suite and into the main CID office. On the way through, he informed DS Carter of what Hardy had said in the interview so far. Natalie watched, listened, but said nothing, then she followed him into his small side office at one end of the room, closed the door and they stood facing each other. She didn't look happy.

'What the fuck, Bernie? I had him on the ropes there. I would've had him nailed with a few more questions.'

Bernie heaved out an exasperated sigh.

'Sit down, Natalie. We need to talk.'

She dragged a chair irritably up to his desk and dropped into it with a loud sigh.

After a few moments, Bernie said, 'What's the story between you two?'

She frowned, 'What do you mean?'

'There are issues here that I'm not aware of, issues that I need to know about because it's affecting your judgement.'

She bristled and looked pointedly out of the window.

'I don't know what you mean. There's nothing wrong with my judgement. That interview was going well until you stopped it.'

Bernie waved at an officer through the glass in the main office and beckoned him to come in. A skinny young officer opened the door and entered the room.

'Make us a couple of coffees please, Dave, one sugar for me... Ma'am?'

'None for me, thanks.'

'No problem, Guv.'

Once the young policeman had left the room, Bernie leaned forward, fixing Natalie with a hard stare.

'He was goading you in there. He was even taking the piss at one point after you butted in... and instead of ignoring him, you took the bait."

Surprised at the forthrightness of his remarks, Natalie became defensive.

'Anybody would have reacted the same way.'

'No, they wouldn't. I wouldn't, but then I don't have a personal issue with him. Which takes me back to my earlier question...'

Natalie shrugged without replying.

'You gave him details of where James went to get his suitcase, ruining our chances of gathering further evidence and challenging him later.' He shook his head. 'You were asking him closed questions, not open ones, and it was clear from your tone that you were becoming agitated. I know from your reputation that you're a brilliant detective, but it's almost as though you'd never conducted an interview before.'

Natalie looked down at her hands, frustration with herself beginning to overtake her anger at Hardy. Bernie was right and she knew it.

At that moment, Dave returned with a tray containing two cups of coffee, a sugar bowl, a small jug of milk and a plate of chocolate digestives.

'Thanks, Dave, leave it on the desk please.'

As Dave walked out, Bernie stood up and closed the blinds, hiding their meeting from the main office. In an attempt to bring her emotions back under control and give herself time to think, Natalie poured the milk, handed him his cup and offered him a biscuit, which he refused.

Bernie took a deep gulp of coffee and continued, but in a gentler tone.

'You were about to put it to him that he'd killed James because of their previous clashes, am I right?'

She nodded, 'Yes, I was.'

'And what would he have said?'

'He'd have denied it and I couldn't have proved a thing.'

'Exactly!'

He picked up his cup and warmed his hands around it. 'Come on, I give you my word it will go no further, what's going on between you two?'

The coffee had helped Natalie think hard about her next step. Although she trusted Bernie and didn't think for a moment that he would spread gossip, she realised that to reveal the true nature of her connection with Hardy could be massively damaging. Bernie was a straight cop and would have no choice but to report her involvement, and she would lose control of the case, perhaps even facing disciplinary action for not disclosing the situation. She had to tread very carefully.

Over the next few minutes, Natalie told Bernie the truth, but certainly not the whole truth. She explained how finding her husband in a clinch with another man in a car park had ruined their marriage and probably coloured her judgement in any matters involving homosexuality; how Peter Hardy reminded her painfully of Thomas's infidelity. She then told him of the provocative comments made by Peter as she had returned him to his cell in Sevenoaks Police Station.

When she'd finished, she sat back in her chair, watching for his reaction. It had been hard for her to admit any weakness, even to herself, but the partial confession had to be convincing. Bernie didn't say anything. Instead, he got up, walked around his chair and perched on the desk alongside her.

'Well then, we need to work hard to make sure of a conviction, don't we?'

Natalie felt a wave of relief at Bernie's acceptance of her story and looked at him gratefully.

'It's true, this case has just got to me. I can't think straight any more. I *am* a bloody good detective and people have always looked up to me, but he's able to jerk my strings, I admit it.'

'Look,' said Bernie, 'it's obvious he killed James, but he's a clever fucker, so we've got to be just as clever.' He thought for a few seconds. 'We're going to nail him, Natalie, but it might take a little while. I want you to be patient and whatever he says or does, don't let him rile you.'

Bernie walked back around the desk to his own chair, a thoughtful expression on his face.

'I wish you'd told me all this earlier. I'd never have allowed you in on the interview, I'd have used Graham Carter instead.'

She nodded. 'I know, I should have said something, I'm sorry.'

'But if we remove you from the interview process now, he'll know he's got to you, so we'll keep you in there. But this time leave the whole interview to me.'

Holding his gaze, she nodded. At that moment a loud rapping at the office door interrupted them.

'Come in.'

It was Graham Carter and he looked like the cat who'd got a very large bowl of cream.

'We've found him, Guv. We've got the fucker following Jim Pincent.'

Natalie and Bernie exchanged excited looks and followed Carter to a prepared monitor to re-view tapes they'd already seen, showing James Pincent's route to the car park and back to the hotel. Fifteen minutes later, Bernie had collected the tapes, noted down the relevant recording times and beamed at Natalie.

'Well, that's given us some more ammunition, hasn't it? I'm ready and raring if you are?'

She stood up and returned his smile.

'I'm going to enjoy this. Let's go.'

FORTY-ONE

'Interview resumed at 23:20. Interviewing officers are DI Bernard Tanner and…' he looked at Natalie.

'DCI Natalie Neider.'

'We are continuing the interview of…' He raised his eyebrows at Peter, who remained silent. 'Could you please introduce yourself for the tape?'

Smiling at Natalie he said, 'Peter, AKA Petra Hardy, gay, trans, and proud.'

'Is there anything you wish to correct, alter, or add to the answers you gave earlier?' Bernie fixed Peter with an icy stare.

'No, everything I said was the truth.'

Bernie placed a tape into the video recorder and pushed the play button.

'Please watch this tape, Mr Hardy. My questions will follow.'

The images were from the Westminster Council CCTV system and very high quality. The first tape looked straight down Frith Street; the second tape looked from Shaftesbury Avenue back up Frith Street towards Old Compton Street.

Watching the images, Peter's heart sank. James Pincent was easily identifiable walking quickly down the street in both images. Unfortunately for Peter, he too was easily identifiable, following the same route as Pincent at a distance of about thirty yards. On reaching Shaftesbury Avenue, he could be seen standing on a street corner, while Pincent entered the NCP car park forty yards away.

Then, once he'd left the car park, Peter could be seen turning his back to conceal his identity from him, before following at the same thirty-yard distance all the way back to the hotel.

Bernie didn't speak all the time the tapes were running, allowing the pressure on his prisoner to slowly build. Finally, he leaned forward, staring at Peter, removed the final tape, replaced the first tape again to play the first minute or so, then paused the image.

He pointed at James Pincent.

'Can you identify this person for me?'

A tight knot was forming in Peter's stomach. This was a classic interrogation tactic, just like he'd seen on so many cop shows on TV, allowing the suspect to slowly bury themselves by their own admissions, before the serious questions have even started. Suddenly, he felt totally exposed; he knew what questions were coming next and there was nothing he could do but tell the truth.

'It's Sergeant Pincent.'

'Thank you.'

Bernie wound the tape on a further fifteen seconds.

'And can you identify this person please?'

Peter glanced at Natalie, whose face was a mask. He looked back at Bernie.

'Er… I'm not really sure.'

Bernie leaned forward, interlinking his fingers on the table top.

'Really? Take another look, there's no rush.'

Having already seen that the images from the next camera clearly showed his face, he moved on to damage limitation.

'Okay, it's me.'

A trace of a smile appeared on Natalie's face and she quietly released a sigh, but remained silent. Bernie checked back through his notes, feigning puzzlement and confusion.

'Sorry, I thought you hadn't seen Sergeant Pincent until he entered the hotel.'

Peter was in trouble, of that there was no doubt. The cocky arrogance from earlier was rapidly evaporating. His mouth had gone dry, he shuffled uncomfortably on his seat and took a drink of water from the glass in front of him, but said nothing.

Bernie used the pressure of silence to encourage him to answer, sitting back in his chair and absent-mindedly looking at his notes until, after about a minute, he snapped.

'Okay, I lied.'

Bernie finally looked up from his notes, a satisfied expression on his face.

'There, that wasn't too difficult, was it?'

Detecting a distinct tone of triumph in the DI's voice, Peter's initial optimism dipped even further. He'd been spotted following a murder victim in the build-up to the offence and now he'd been shown to have lied about it. This was not looking good. Realising he was being too defensive, he decided he might as well open up.

'I know what it looks like, but I didn't kill him. I just wanted to turn the tables on him. I looked through the railings from my flat and could see he was watching from the street corner. I hadn't done anything wrong and it really pissed me off that I was being treated like a common criminal. I didn't kill Tony Waters and I didn't deserve the treatment I was getting.'

Tears of self-pity were forming in his eyes.

Looking on impassively, Bernie said, 'Go on.'

Wiping his nose on his sleeve as Bernie looked down at his notes, Peter turned his head imperceptibly towards Natalie and gave a sly smile before continuing.

You bastard, she thought, *you're just fucking acting.* But remembering Bernie's instructions, she remained silent.

Peter continued speaking with a noticeable fracture in his voice.

'I wanted to be the one in charge for a change, to be the hunter, not the hunted. So I thought I'd follow him. And I'm glad I did, it made me feel great. It made me feel like *I* was in charge for once, seeing what he was up to and where he went, without his knowledge. But that's all I did. I didn't kill him, I went home to bed and stayed there until the morning. You can check the CCTV in the area, you won't see me leave my flat.'

Bernie appeared to be listening but not really paying too much attention, he seemed more interested in reading through his notes.

'Uh huh.' He waited a few seconds then asked, almost as an afterthought, 'Do you know Bateman Buildings?'

Shit, was there a CCTV camera I've missed?

'Of course. It runs from almost opposite my flat through to Soho Square. Why?'

'Because there are no cameras covering the route from your flat to Soho Square… at least not if you walk through Bateman Buildings.'

Peter's leg began to twitch nervously again. In that moment, he felt sure that Bernie Tanner knew he'd killed Pincent, and how he'd managed to carry it out. It was like being trapped on a railway line with no way of escaping the oncoming train. He was finding it difficult to remain in control of his emotions, fighting hard to remain calm. Fixing Bernie with a determined stare, he shrugged.

'So?'

Returning Peter's stare, Bernie sighed.

'So, you could easily have left your flat armed with a knife, walked into Bateman Buildings, entered via the hotel's rear door then made your way to Sergeant

Pincent's room.'

'How would I know there weren't any cameras in Bateman's Buildings?' he lied. 'In any case, the cameras in the hotel would have filmed me.'

Bernie made a face showing he didn't believe him and raised his eyebrows.

'You're bullshitting, Mr Hardy. You know very well the hotel doesn't have CCTV.'

Peter shrugged and held his hands out wide.

'How on earth should I know it didn't have CCTV? I couldn't have been expected to know that.'

Peter knew he was coming across as increasingly desperate, but didn't seem able to control his words.

Glancing at Natalie before speaking, Bernie leaned across the table.

'I think you did.'

His gaze was so intense that it felt to Peter like his eyes were downloading the truth from his very soul. Fidgeting on his chair, Peter closed his eyes, desperately hoping the moment would pass, but knew deep down inside that hope would prove to be pointless. After ten seconds, he opened his eyes again, and transferred his gaze across to Natalie, to see her lips part to form the silent words, 'Fuck you.'

It was as if he had received an electric shock. The intensity of this woman's hatred was beyond anything he had ever experienced and frankly terrified him. He badly wanted to respond with aggression, but realised that keeping calm and answering their questions was probably his best bet.

'Well, I didn't. Why should I know anything about CCTV in local hotels?'

Instead of replying, Bernie suddenly changed tack, asking further questions about when Peter first started going to Soho, about his flat and about why he went to certain venues.

These questions were much easier for Peter to answer; the tight knots in his stomach became looser and he slowly began to relax. For once, he could speak truthfully and without fear of incriminating himself. The questions continued in this vein for over twenty minutes and Bernie's manner had become affable, almost friendly. Peter began to feel confident he'd beaten them.

Then, after an innocuous question about My Pink Life, which Peter easily answered, Bernie suddenly asked, 'Where did you buy the cutlery for your flat?'

Taken aback by the sudden change of tone and line of questioning, Peter mumbled, 'I… I can't remember.'

Bernie regarded him inscrutably for a few seconds.

'The reason I'm asking, Mr Hardy, is that we've recovered a set of cooking knives from the kitchen drawer in your flat, four of them. Do you know which ones I'm talking about?'

Peter's mood of relief, almost elation vanished in an instant. Tanner had been sucking him into an ambush and he'd fallen for it. He slowly nodded his head.

'Yes.'

'It's just that the three largest knives are there, and the smallest knife is there, but the second smallest is missing. Any idea where it might have gone?'

Stay calm Pete, for fuck's sake stay calm.

'It hasn't gone anywhere. I got them from a boot fair in Kent and there was one missing when I bought them.'

'I see,' he looked through his notes. 'It's just that the forensic department will be able to tell me by tomorrow exactly what type of knife killed Sergeant Pincent. They'll know the width of blade, whether it had a serrated edge, even how long the blade was.'

Peter's stomach was knotting and churning, but he had to remain calm. He shrugged again, 'So?'

'I'm willing to bet that the type of knife used to kill Detective Sergeant Pincent will be exactly the same as the one that's missing from the set in your kitchen. Added to the rest of the evidence, what do you think a reasonable member of the public sitting on a jury would make of that?'

'If it's the same sized knife, it's just a coincidence. Anyway, a jury can think what they like, it's just circumstantial.'

As soon as the words had left his mouth, Peter regretted them and wished he'd kept his mouth shut. He'd made the same mistake when being interviewed by Pincent and was furious with himself for not learning his lesson.

Bernie sat back in his chair and folded his arms.

'Oh, I see. You're an expert on circumstantial evidence now, are you?'

'No... it's just that... I'm sorry, that's not what I meant.'

Bernie leaned forward to rest his forearms on the table.

'I'm going to explain how it's stacking up as I see it, Mr Hardy. You're already under investigation for another murder and the previous victim was in Soho at the same time as you, shortly before he died. You and Sergeant Pincent clearly did not like each other and you'd argued with him in the street in the hours before his death. You followed him to his car, then back up to his hotel, shortly before he was killed. Your flat is nearby. The route to the hotel's rear entrance from your flat is not covered by CCTV, so you could have made it to his room and back without being seen. Finally, a knife that I'm betting will be the type that killed him is missing from a set in your kitchen. Doesn't look good for you, does it?'

Listening to the litany of circumstantial evidence,

Peter had to agree it sounded damning. His face must have shown the officers they had him on the ropes, but he chose to remain silent.

'You see, Peter, that's rather a lot of evidence stacked up against you. It's circumstantial, I'll give you that, but people have been convicted of murder on overwhelming circumstantial evidence many times before.'

Peter had had enough, the anger building inside exploded out of him.

'I've got nothing more to say to you bastards. I want to go back to my cell.'

Surprisingly, considering he hadn't yet asked any questions about being inside the hotel, or the murder itself, Bernie paused for a moment before saying, 'Okay then,' and promptly terminated the interview.

Natalie remained silent throughout and was pleased she had, although she too was surprised at his abrupt termination of the interview. She'd been impressed at Bernie's interrogation skills so decided to trust his instincts.

'Follow me please, Mr Hardy.'

Bernie opened the door and left the room, holding the door for Peter and Natalie to follow. Peter walked down the corridor between the two detectives, the familiar rage churning like acid in his stomach. Suddenly he could control himself no longer and, turning for a second towards Natalie, made a single, sharp stabbing motion towards her eye, before turning back and continuing to follow Bernie.

Unable to believe what she had just seen, she called out, 'Bernie, stop!'

He span around, alarmed at her tone.

'What's up?'

'He just did this!' She copied his action and Bernie's

eyes widened in shock and surprise.

They both knew Peter couldn't possibly have known that Pincent had been stabbed in the eye… unless he was the murderer. Walking up close to Peter, a furious Bernie glared up at him.

'You bastard.'

Peter looked down at Bernie, a sneer on his face. He knew he might just have blown it, but right now he didn't really give a damn.

'Fuck you, Detective Inspector, fuck the pair of you. That venomous piece of shit had it coming. If either of you repeat this to the CPS, they'll just assume you're trying to fit me up. It's her word against mine. You've got nothing on me… so let me go.'

Seething with rage, Bernie grabbed Peter's arm, frogmarched him back to the custody officer, signed the stamp on the custody record showing him returned from interview then walked him to his cell and pushed him inside. Slamming the door shut and closing the wicket, he leaned heavily on the door, breathing hard. He was angry with himself for letting Hardy get to him in the same way he'd infuriated Natalie.

'I told you he was an evil bastard, didn't I?' Natalie was standing behind him. 'Come on, I'll buy you a tea.'

FORTY-TWO

Peter was woken at 7.30 the following morning with a cooked breakfast on a white cardboard plate and a cup of tea. He ate and drank slowly and thoughtfully, wondering what delights the day would bring for him. He'd spent a restless night, cursing himself for being so stupid during his interview, falling into every trap Bernie Tanner had set. His loss of control in the corridor also weighed on his mind. It was becoming harder to keep his feelings from breaking through the surface and, despite his bravado the evening before, he feared what the outcome might be. On the other hand, he had really enjoyed letting them know he'd killed their colleague.

Fuck 'em, they knew I did it, so what does it matter?

Trying to sleep had been almost impossible. A combination of the noise from prisoners in adjoining cells, officers chatting loudly in the custody suite, the painfully thin mattress that had been grudgingly provided, and fears about his future, all conspired to make it a thoroughly miserable night.

At 8.30 he was taken once more to the interview room, where this time he was met by two detectives he'd never seen before. He answered "no comment" to each question, and after almost an hour was returned to his cell, where he remained until an officer came with his lunch at 12.30. By this point, the stress he was under had resulted in a blinding headache, for which he was given some paracetamol by the divisional surgeon.

As soon as he'd finished his lunch, he was taken out

for interview again, this time by Bernie and Natalie. Bernie had changed his tee shirt, but appeared to be wearing the same jeans and looked for all the world as though he'd slept at the police station. Natalie had travelled up to London prepared for an overnight stay and had taken a change of clothes; she looked her usual immaculate self.

They produced the four knives from his kitchen and laid them out on the interview room table. Bernie Tanner told him that the puncture wounds showed the knife used to kill Sergeant Pincent had a serrated edge on one side; not only that, it would have been exactly the same size as the one missing from the set in his kitchen. This wasn't exactly unexpected, but it was yet more compelling evidence to pile up against him.

This time Bernie asked questions about the hotel and the murder scene. Once again, Peter answered, "no comment" to their questions. As he was returned to his cell, Bernie thanked him.

"I was hoping you wouldn't answer our questions today, because that was your last opportunity to explain your fantasy version of events. I'm confident we've got enough to convict you, Mr Hardy, and the papers are being submitted to the Crown Prosecution Service as we speak."

Peter could feel panic bubbling up inside him, but forced himself to adopt an air of confidence.

"Better hurry up and get on with it then darling. The sooner the decision comes back, the sooner I'm out of here."

Natalie spoke to Peter for the first time that morning.

"You're pure evil, aren't you? I can't wait until you're sent down."

"Get over yourself love, you've not got enough evidence and you know you haven't. Even if I get

218

charged, I'll never be convicted by a jury. When it comes to the crunch, you're not very clever, are you?"

Quietly closing the cell door, Bernie steered Natalie away.

"Come on, he's not worth it."

FORTY-THREE

Shortly after 4.30, Natalie and Bernie were staring at each other in disbelief at the case decision, which had been faxed through from a lawyer called William Shortland at the CPS. Natalie was almost apoplectic.

'I don't fucking believe it!'

'I know,' said Bernie. 'I've just spoken to the lawyer and asked for an explanation.'

'What did he say?'

'He said there was almost enough, but "the days of relying entirely on circumstantial evidence" had gone. They needed a little more direct evidence to pass the charging threshold and sadly, we don't have it.'

'So, what... we've got to release him?'

He nodded, 'Sorry, no choice.'

'But he's practically admitted killing Tony Waters and one of my officers. He's murdered my friend!'

'I agree, but you know as well as I do that what he has said and done don't amount to an actual confession.'

He offered her a sympathetic smile, which he knew wouldn't be much help.

'But we'll get him eventually. We'll bail him for a month... that should be enough to find the missing piece that will bury him.'

'We'd better do, he's murdered two decent men.'

*

Thirty minutes later, Peter walked free from the front

entrance of Vine Street Police Station. He'd been bailed to return on 20th December pending further enquiries. Bernie and Natalie had sent a young detective down to the Custody Suite with the job of releasing him, something which gave Peter great satisfaction; it meant they couldn't face him as he walked out of the station a free man.

His weekend had been ruined yet again, but at least he'd successfully disposed of another tormentor, another bigoted, intolerant prick and that made him exceedingly happy. The only thing he could think of to rescue something pleasurable from the weekend was to give Archie a call.

FORTY-FOUR

The workshop door slid open, causing the mechanics to glance up from their work. It was Des Thayer and he looked even more aggressive than usual.

'Bill, Andy, Vince, my office now!' His voice and body language conveyed the clear message that all was not well. It was five minutes before lunch on Monday morning, a very ordinary Monday morning as far as anyone in the workshop was concerned, so what could possibly have made him so angry?

All four mechanics downed tools, exchanging confused glances and shrugs as they made their way to the door.

Pointing at Peter, Des shouted, 'Not you! Did I call your fucking name?'

Shaking his head, Peter said quietly, 'No.'

'Well don't be a twat! Get back to work. I'll speak to you later... alone.'

Des and the other mechanics walked out, leaving Peter alone in the workshop with a nasty feeling in his bones.

He'd had a great time with Archie at a flat belonging to one of the SOCO's friends the previous evening. They couldn't risk being found together at either of their own places and the friend was more than happy to help out. They obviously didn't reveal the real reason for needing to hide from the police, saying it was purely because Archie didn't want the grief at work if his colleagues found out he was gay.

Following a thoroughly enjoyable and exhausting couple of hours, they agreed to meet up again the following weekend. Archie had been briefly interviewed by two DC's at his home address, and stuck to the story he'd agreed with Peter, which seemed to satisfy them. Before Peter left, Archie wanted to know chapter and verse about his arrest and interrogation, but once again, Peter was careful not to disclose everything.

He arrived back in Underriver just after midnight on Sunday and went straight to bed. He felt no remorse for murdering James Pincent, on the contrary, he was feeling proud of himself; he'd stood up for his gay and trans friends, for everyone victimized for the way they lived and felt. Lying on his bed, his head resting on the pillow as he stared up into the inky blackness of the night, he thought that too much had happened over the weekend for sleep to come, but the next thing he knew, it was morning.

Arriving at the garage, it seemed as though nothing had changed. He was pleased to be back dealing with cars and was looking forward to getting stuck into his work, which would help take his mind off the police investigation. Bill and Vince were still pleasant enough to him, being their usual chatty selves, but Andy continued to ignore him, looking daggers in his direction whenever he got the chance and blanking him whenever he spoke, a state of affairs Peter was more than happy with. Radio 2 had been blaring out as normal, with people joining in on the odd song, just like they always did. Nothing unusual had occurred since the morning tea-break, so what could possibly have rattled Des's cage?

At lunchtime, Peter sat by himself, his lunchbox on his knees, eating his sandwiches and crisps. The events of Friday night played over and over in his head, despite his desperate attempts to think of something else.

Another twenty minutes passed before his three colleagues returned to the workshop. As they walked in, he instantly realised there was something going on… something bad. Bill and Vince's manner had changed. Somehow, they were looking at him differently, not being themselves; nobody was smiling.

'All right, lads? What was all that about?'

All three looked away, nobody replied, even Bill and Vince didn't appear to want contact. Peter banged his fist down hard on the plastic table and opened his arms wide.

'For fuck's sake, will somebody please tell me what's going on?'

Before anyone could reply, the workshop door slid open and Caroline from the office came in.

'Pete, Des wants to see you in his office… now.'

Looking at Bill for some kind of idea as to what was happening, Peter raised his eyebrows and shrugged enquiringly. But Bill just pursed his lips and shook his head. Peter's shoulders slumped and he followed Caroline out through the door; this did not look good.

As he knocked firmly on Des Thayer's door, his heart was hammering. For some reason, he was more stressed about this meeting than when he was being interviewed about the murder at the weekend.

'Come in.'

He pinned his shoulders back, lifted his head high and pushed the door open. He detested Des Thayer with a passion, and wasn't about to allow him to throw his weight around again.

I've disposed of Waters and a copper, so he'd better watch his fucking step.

Des was on the phone and motioned impatiently for Peter to take a seat. He growled down the phone.

'Okay, okay, I'll get it sorted right away. Sorry, I'm a bit busy just now, I'll have to call you back.'

Banging the receiver down hard, Des shouted, 'Useless cunt!' He scraped his chair back and stood up.

'Wait here, I'll deal with you in a minute.'

He rushed from the room shouting, 'Caroline!'

Peter watched him through the glass as he left the building and headed out into the yard.

He's obviously pissed off another punter.

On the cluttered desktop, Peter noticed the edge of a photograph sticking out from between two sheets of paper and, leaning forward for a better view, he saw the face of Andy Clark at the edge of the picture. Intrigued, he checked over his shoulder to make sure Des wasn't returning and pulled the photo free.

He couldn't believe what he was seeing. In the photo, six men posed under a banner saying *Keep Britain Straight* and underneath the slogan was the group's logo – a clenched red fist emblazoned with the white letters KBS. All the men in the photo had their right arms raised with fists clenched, posing for the camera; all of them were smiling broadly. The men, from left to right, were Tony Waters, Des Thayer, unknown, James Pincent, unknown, and Andy Clark. Peter assumed that the two men he didn't know were Tony's Friday night drinking pals Duncan and Stan.

So… they're part of that anti-gay group! Of course, it makes sense now. No wonder they all hate me so much.

FORTY-FIVE

The unmistakable sound of Des's booming voice could be heard, re-entering the building, so Peter hastily pushed the photograph back between the sheets of paper and sat back in his chair, his face a picture of innocence, but now armed with the knowledge of exactly what he was up against.

Slamming the door closed as he walked back into the room, Des mumbled to himself, 'Fucking people.'

Peter was uninterested in Des's problems and cut to the chase.

'You wanted to see me?'

'Yes.' He threw himself down into his worn office chair and he spoke through gritted teeth. 'I'm getting rid of you. You're causing too much trouble and it's not good publicity for the firm.'

Even though he'd guessed what was coming, the old feelings of rage and incomprehension came roaring back. He was being rejected yet again; he would have to move to a new job, meet new work colleagues and make new relationships. These were things he'd done time after time in his life, through primary school, secondary school, in his private life, and in the workplace. He simply couldn't stand the thought of having to do it all over again.

'That's not fair. I've been arrested for something I didn't do. I didn't kill Tony!'

'Yes, you fucking did! And now you've killed one of the police officers investigating it!'

Des's words stunned Peter into silence.

How the fuck did he know I'd been arrested again?

He stared at his boss with undisguised dismay.

'There, that's fucking shut you up, hasn't it? That female DCI's been on the phone to me this morning asking questions. She told me all about your arrest at the weekend. The police are absolutely certain you killed that copper.'

Peter's eyes filled with tears, Neider couldn't get him for the murders, so she was destroying his private life, starting by getting him the sack.

'But I didn't kill him.'

'Well, she's fucking convinced you did. The press were all over this garage last week so fuck knows how bad it'll be once they hear about this weekend's arrest on top. They'll have a fucking field day. I've decided to take whatever shit I get from the union, the press, and the queer lobby. I want you out of here right now. Pack your bags and go.'

Peter looked at Des, pleading for some compassion and understanding.

'I know you hate me, but do you really believe I'm capable of murder?'

'I'm fucking sure of it. You're probably capable of almost anything.'

Despite all his best efforts, Peter started to cry unashamedly.

'Oh, for fuck's sake grow up! You might be a poof, but you're still a bloke. Grow a pair of balls and take it like a man. You must have known this was coming!'

Deep down, Peter knew Des was right. They'd never got along and it was only a matter of time before Des found a good enough reason to sack him, but it still hurt and angered him. Seeing the group of them together in the photo had answered a lot of questions for Peter, but he wanted to hear it from Des's mouth.

'Why are you so horrible to me?'

'Because I don't like you, in fact, I fucking hate you and your sort.'

'But *why*?'

'Change the record Pete, we've been through all this before.' He rubbed his hand over the stubble on his chin. 'Look, you're a faggot, a fudge packer and I don't want that type of person working for me. Then you become prime suspect for killing Tony, who was not only my supervisor but also my friend…'

'I didn't kill him,' Peter broke in. 'You've got to believe me.'

'I don't *have* to believe you! In fact, I *don't* believe you. I know you're lying because your fucking lips are moving. People like you wouldn't know the truth if it hit you with a sledgehammer.'

His anger was bubbling to the surface, replacing his feelings of self-pity and Peter could feel himself about to react violently, to hurt Des like he so badly wanted, but that was something he really couldn't afford to do… not yet.

'You're a prick, Thayer, aren't you?'

'At least I know where to stick mine!'

Peter couldn't resist one last insult; this might be his last chance.

'You quite sure you're not gay yourself, Des? You know what they say – those who shout loudest about their hatred for gays are just repressing their own true feelings. You'd make quite a cute woman.' He pursed his lips as if blowing Des a kiss across the desk.

Des could barely control himself.

'Just get out.'

'Okay, I'll go, but I want paying up-to-date, plus a week in lieu of notice.'

'Your money's already been made up. It's with Caroline in the office. It's all there, including your week's notice.'

Leaning threateningly over Des's desk, Peter fixed him with narrowed eyes.

'I'll get even with you, Thayer, you just see if I don't.'

For a moment, Des felt a shiver of unease; if Peter really was a killer and all the evidence indicated he was, he could easily have meant what he'd just said. On the other hand, Des had a reputation as a hard man and he wasn't about to back down.

'Yeah? Bring it on, you don't frighten me.'

Peter turned his back on Des and moved to the door. Before he closed it, he turned around one last time.

'Watch your back, Des. Tony didn't and look what happened to him.'

Jumping to his feet, Des pointed threateningly at Peter.

'Watch your fucking mouth, he was my mate!'

Leaving the door open, Peter made his way through the open plan office.

'Bye girls, been nice knowing you.'

With a wave of his arm, he was gone.

Back in the workshop, he announced the outcome of the meeting to his colleagues.

'I've just been sacked!'

He walked up to Bill and held out a hand. After looking nervously at the others, Bill extended his arm and shook hands with him.

'No need to worry, Bill, I'm not a double murderer. That DCI has got it in for me because she's clearly as homophobic as Waters was.'

Bill nodded his understanding but still looked a little uncertain. Peter moved across to Vince and shook hands with him in silence.

Finally, he walked towards Andy, stopping a yard away from him. He stared at him for several seconds, recalling what he'd seen on the photograph only minutes earlier and when he spoke his voice was cold.

'It's been nice knowing you, Andy. You take care, you take very good care indeed.'

Andy sneered. 'Oooh, am I supposed to be scared? Just fuck off. If I never see you again it'll be too soon.'

Holding his gaze steadily for a few more seconds, Peter turned on his heel and walked away. After collecting his things, he left through the sliding door without a backward glance. For the umpteenth time he was being forced to move on in his life, away from what he knew and felt comfortable with, towards a completely new beginning.

FORTY-SIX

November drifted into December; not a great time to be searching for employment as a mechanic, something Peter was finding to his cost. His sacking ten days previously still rankled. He'd heard nothing from anyone at the garage, which was probably to be expected, but he'd also heard nothing from either murder investigation, which felt like very good news indeed.

His weekend at the flat had passed without incident and this time he was fairly certain he hadn't been followed. On Saturday night he'd stayed at Archie's place and rather than sex, they'd enjoyed good food, drink and music. Their feelings for each other were deepening. Peter came clean about what he'd done to James Pincent, which meant he was now trusting Archie with details of both murders. He also told him about finding the photograph of the KBS gathering and his feelings of hatred towards Des and Andy. In return, Archie tried to reassure Peter that he would support him however he could and that all would be fine.

It was now Thursday evening and Peter was feeling particularly miserable. He'd been informed earlier in the day that his application for employment at a garage in Tonbridge had been unsuccessful, it had been a position that seemed perfect for him and which he'd been convinced he would get. His self-indulgent moping was interrupted by his phone ringing.

'Hello?'

'Hi Pete, it's Bill.'

Apart from speaking occasionally to Archie and a couple of visits to the shops, Peter had been lonely during the week and was pleased to have someone to speak to.

'Hello, Bill, wasn't expecting to hear from you. What's this in aid of?'

'I'm in your village pub having a drink with Vince. Fancy joining us?'

The pub was in the centre of the village, a two-minute drive or fifteen-minute walk from Peter's cottage.

'Yeah, sounds great. I could do with a walk. I'll be about fifteen minutes.'

'Great. See you when you get here.'

Swiftly getting changed, Peter set off on foot.

A quarter of an hour later, he pushed open the door of the busy pub, quickly spotting Bill and Vince sitting at a table for four. He made his way through the drinkers and warmly shook hands with them both.

'Thanks for inviting me, lads. What are you drinking?'

Bill held up his pint glass with a tiny amount of beer at the bottom, drank it down and handed it to Peter.

'Pint of Larkins please, mate.'

'Vince?'

Vince's pint glass was still half full. He handed it to Peter.

'Half of Larkins in there, please.'

Peter didn't take the glass from Vince.

'Tell you what, I'll pay for a pint and leave it in the pipe. You can collect it whenever you're ready.'

Vince raised his glass.

'Cheers, you're a gentleman.'

Standing at the bar having ordered three pints of Larkins, Peter found himself wondering why they'd suddenly asked him to come for a drink in a pub after ten days of silence.

Do they want to ask me about the murders? Are the police using them to befriend me and gain my confidence, hoping I'll let something slip? Can I trust them?

Clasping the drinks for himself and Bill in his enormous hands, he took them to the table, and sat down, smiling.

'I must say this is a nice surprise. How are things at work?'

After an enquiring glance at Vince, Bill received a nod.

'To be honest mate, it's all getting a bit weird.'

Peter frowned. 'Weird? In what way?'

Bill took a sip from his pint and looked thoughtfully at Peter.

'Vince and me aren't getting overtime anymore, even with the garage being two short now. Des and Andy have suddenly become best of mates, so any overtime goes to Andy. Sometimes Des works on the tools in the workshop with him, he'd rather do that than give me or Vince any extra. I even saw them having a drink in The Bullfinch the other night.'

Placing his pint on the table, Peter leaned back on his chair. He had to be very careful how he handled this, unsure whether he could totally trust them.

'Tell me more.'

'Yesterday, Des called us into his office and spent ten minutes lecturing us about what an evil bastard you were. He's convinced you killed Tony and that copper, so is Andy, and they can't understand why we refuse to believe it.'

Peter was genuinely touched by their support. Their words sounded genuine and he doubted they were good enough actors to be faking it.

'I didn't kill either of them, you have my word on

that.'

Vince smiled, 'We know you didn't.'

Peter was intrigued by the strength of his conviction.

'How do you *know* I didn't?'

'Because you've taken crap from everyone since you arrived. You could easily have turned violent at any time, but you didn't, you ignored it. It doesn't make sense that you'd suddenly turn into a murderer.'

Nodding his appreciation, Peter said, 'Thanks, Vince.'

'And anyway,' Vince continued, 'even if you had killed Tony, why would you suddenly kill a copper who'd never done anything to upset you? It doesn't make sense.'

Peter grinned.

'You don't fancy being my brief, do you? You'd be fucking brilliant!'

They all laughed then Bill became serious.

'Come on then, Pete, spill the beans. We're on your side, but we haven't heard your version of events yet.'

Although increasingly inclined to trust the two men, Peter knew he must stick closely to his story.

'There's not much to tell really. I swear that I didn't kill either of them. I'm not sure how I'm supposed to explain any better than that. It's like trying to prove that God doesn't exist.'

Bill was downing his pint and eyeing Peter over the rim of his glass. Swallowing a large gulp of beer, he persisted.

'We know what the police are saying you did, but what did you actually do on those two days? You were in the same area on both occasions, so you can see why they've got you in their sights.'

Peter could see that he would have to tell them enough to satisfy their curiosity.

'When Tony died, I was out clubbing. I'd picked up

234

a guy called Robert and I wanted to take him back to my flat. Unfortunately, he wanted to wait until he knew me better, said he didn't do sex on a first date so, after leaving the club, we said goodbye in Greek Street and he went home. I returned to my flat and went to bed. I came to work on Monday morning expecting a normal day at work and got arrested for Tony's murder, solely because we don't get on and he was in that area of London at around the same time.'

They both nodded, then Vince had a question of his own.

'But Andy and Andrea from the office both told the police they'd heard you threaten Tony in the past.'

'That's right, but I didn't threaten him with violence. I just told him to stop picking on me or he'd regret it, it was just words. I was going to report him to the union for discrimination in the workplace. It wouldn't have pleased Des much and it would have caused Tony serious bother.'

Vince and Bill looked at each other and exchanged nods, his explanation apparently having satisfied them.

'And anyway, he was killed just down the road, at a time when they know I was in my flat, otherwise, I would have been spotted on CCTV somewhere.'

'Sounds fair enough,' said Vince, 'but what about the copper who was killed?'

'I've no idea. He was okay with me, a bit aggressive during interviews maybe, but nothing extreme. They were playing the classic good cop/bad cop routine and he was the bad one. I spotted him following me in Soho and approached him for a laugh. He was well embarrassed that I'd sussed him.'

'What happened then?' asked Bill.

'Nothing. I walked back to my flat and went to bed.'

'Des said there was a hotel near your flat. That's

where he was killed wasn't it?'

'Yes, and once again the police assumed it was me, even though the cameras showed me going home and not leaving again until the following morning. He was murdered during the early hours.'

Bill leaned forward and placed a reassuring hand on Peter's shoulder.

'I believe you, mate. I've only known you for three or four months but I don't see any way you'd be capable of killing someone. What do you reckon Vince?'

'I agree.' He raised his eyebrows at Bill. 'I reckon we should tell him about that detective's meetings with Des and Andy.'

Peter's ears immediately pricked up.

'What detective?'

Deep down, he already knew the answer.

'The woman leading the investigation into Tony's murder, I think her name's Neider. She's popped in to see Des twice since you left and both times Andy was asked to join them.'

Taking a long draught of his drink, Peter thought carefully. This didn't sound good.

'What were the meetings about?'

They both shrugged and Vince said, 'No idea, mate. Thing is, neither Andy nor Des will give us any details of what's going on.'

'We thought you might have some idea?' asked Bill.

'No… I haven't got a clue. Seems odd though, doesn't it?'

Bill and Vince nodded, but nobody spoke for several seconds. Then Bill suddenly banged his glass down hard.

'I think they're trying to fit you up.'

Peter looked surprised at this outburst.

'That's one hell of an allegation. What makes you say that?'

Bill exchanged looks with Vince, who looked as puzzled as Peter.

'I overheard Des and Andy talking as they walked past the toilets, they couldn't have known I was in there. I heard Des say, "I've had another call from Natalie, she's come up with an idea."'

Peter was transfixed, 'Then what?'

'That's all I heard, they'd walked out of range.'

'Fucking hell,' said Vince. 'You didn't tell me that.'

'Sorry, mate, it was earlier today. I've been stewing about it all afternoon. That's why I wanted a beer here tonight, so Pete could come and join us. I thought he should hear it first.'

Vince nodded then looked at Peter.

'Anything we can do to help?'

'Yes, keep your ears open and call me whenever they have another meeting with her.'

'Anything else?' asked Bill.

Peter pondered for a moment.

'Let me know if you find out they're arranging to be alone at the garage together. They'll be more relaxed without the two of you there. I might be able to do a little nosing around and find out what they're up to.'

Back in his cottage an hour later, Peter made himself a hot drink and turned on the TV. Matters were developing and he needed a little thinking time before bed.

FORTY-SEVEN

The Conference Room on the 2nd floor of Vine Street Police Station was small, cramped and packed with around twenty officers. It was eleven on the morning of Friday 9th December and this was the first joint meeting of officers from Sevenoaks and Vine Street. They had joined forces and linked their respective investigations, following failures by both teams to find the vital piece of direct evidence that would conclusively link Peter Hardy to either of their crimes.

DCI Neider and DI Jameson had travelled up by train as representatives from the Kent team. They watched with interest as DI Bernie Tanner confidently entered the room and closed the door. Natalie hadn't seen him like this before. He was dressed in a crisply pressed blue suit, white shirt and grey tie, his hair neatly combed and his shiny black shoes sounded like they had old-fashioned 'Blakeys' inserted into the heels, as he made his way across the floor.

'Good morning everyone and thank you for coming. I'd especially like to thank DCI Neider and DI Jameson, who will be assisting us from the Kent Police.' He indicated them to his colleagues. 'Welcome.'

People were packed tightly into the room, all of them seated, except Bernie Tanner.

'We're so close, ladies and gents, so close. Hardy is an arrogant bastard and he's confident he has literally got away with murder… twice.'

He looked at Natalie and Carolyn.

'My officers have viewed the video evidence gathered by DI Jameson and her team. It must have been incredibly annoying, being able to almost put Hardy and Waters together, but not quite.'

'It was, yes,' said Carolyn with a wry smile.

'Well, we may have solved that for you.'

He nodded at a short, slim officer named Will, a man with a permanent fixed smile on his face who clearly enjoyed his job. He stood up, turned on the TV at one end of the room and pushed a video cassette into the player underneath. As the screen lit up, both Carolyn and Natalie could see that the image showed a crowded street at night.

'This was recovered from the patisserie shop Maison Bertaux between the junctions of Romilly Street and Old Compton Street. The image you are looking at is pointing up Greek Street.'

Carolyn looked confused.

'But my officers checked all along there. They didn't find any cameras outside that bakery.'

'No, you're right, there are none, but there was a camera *inside* the bakery. My officers missed it too at first but luckily one of them couldn't resist a chocolate éclair and popped inside.'

'Why would they have a camera inside the premises looking out? Doesn't make any sense.'

'You're right, Carolyn. Normally the camera points inside towards the counter area, but they'd had windows broken on two occasions over the previous three weekends, so the manager decided to turn the camera around in an attempt to identify the culprit.'

Carolyn and Natalie looked at each other, impressed. Bernie grinned at his skinny colleague.

'Play the tape, Will.'

The image burst into life and Natalie leaned forward

in her chair, desperate to see anything that could mean she finally had conclusive proof Hardy *had* met Waters that night.

She watched as Hardy and Robert came into view in Old Compton Street at the left-hand side of the screen, turned away from the camera into Greek Street and continued walking up the left-hand pavement. They were now at the top left-hand corner of the image and a long way off, at least fifty yards from where the camera was situated.

'Now watch this,' said Bernie.

Hardy and Robert came to a halt, just as they were about to move out of shot at the top of the screen. A man had crossed the road and appeared to be blocking their path, he stood facing them on the pavement. The image was blurry, but there was no doubt in anyone's mind that they were looking at Tony Waters. He was wearing black shoes, very dark blue or black trousers, a light-coloured shirt and a three-quarter length navy blue or black overcoat.

The figures were small on the screen and very slightly fuzzy due to the camera looking through the shop's window, but it was more than clear enough for Natalie. She spoke with a raised voice, pointing at the screen.

'That's Tony Waters, I'm sure of it! And the clothing, that's what he was wearing when he was found in the stream.'

'I thought you'd be pleased,' said Bernie, looking slightly smug.

Natalie smiled widely as she said, 'We knew they must have met somewhere around that location. Hardy has denied meeting him throughout this investigation. That'll be enough to nail the bastard, I'm sure of it.'

Bernie turned his attention away from Natalie, told

Will to turn off the TV and addressed the whole room again.

'Something interesting has also come to light regarding our investigation into the murder of DS Pincent.'

He held up a photo showing the front of La Belle Homme Café in Wardour Street.

'An off-duty officer who, for reasons best known to himself has only just come forward, spotted one of our SOCO's, Archie Cowper, in what he described as "intimate conversation" with a well-built white male tucked away at a rear table of the café. They were there from around noon until 12.40 on the afternoon after the murder of James Pincent. From his description, I strongly believe that this man was Peter Hardy.'

His assertion brought small but audible gasps and shakes of the head from officers who'd worked closely with Archie in the past.

'Cowper is being arrested as we speak and will be brought here for interview by myself and DC Wilson. If indeed he is in some form of relationship with Hardy, it gives us plenty of justification for re-examining Hardy's flat, in which case we will be applying for another search warrant, and this time we'll tear the place apart. DCI Neider has told me that at one stage Cowper appeared to find something of interest, but when challenged said it was nothing important. It's entirely possible he was covering for Hardy.

'Things are moving along nicely and it's only a matter of time before we gather sufficient evidence, when that happens, Peter Hardy will be charged and sent to court. Hopefully, he'll be convicted and sent down for a very long time.' A murmur of appreciation rippled around the room. Bernie smiled at Natalie, who returned his smile with a discreet wink.

FORTY-EIGHT

While the meeting in Vine Street was taking place, Archie Cowper was sitting at his desk two miles away in Lancaster House, Belgravia, where one of the Metropolitan Police forensic sections was based. He was busy completing paperwork regarding a string of high-end burglaries on roads around Curzon Street in Mayfair.

Two young, uniformed officers were waiting alongside a separate desk five yards away. They had been sent there by a DI to collect urgent statements from another SOCO, statements that were required for a court hearing taking place at Southwark Crown Court. They were chatting idly about nothing in particular, when Archie overheard the words "the DS from Kent."

He stopped concentrating on his paperwork and strained to listen in. The female officer was now speaking and Archie could hear her voice clearly.

'Steve told me they've found CCTV of Hardy meeting the bloke found dead in Kent; they're bringing him in this afternoon.'

One of the officers nodded whilst taking a huge bite out of a sausage roll, then spoke with his mouth full, liberally sprinkling crumbs on the floor as he spoke.

'That's brilliant. I heard a whisper from the Clowns* that they've found something on the DS's murder too. Sounds like Hardy's fucked.'

*Short for Clowns in Disguise, a derogatory term used by officers in uniform for the CID, to avenge their use of the label "wooden-tops."

Their words slammed into Archie's brain like a hammer. Peter, his friend, his lover, would shortly be arrested and charged with two murders. In an instant, he'd made up his mind to do something about it and grabbed the receiver of the desk phone.

In Underriver, Peter was making a drink in the kitchen when he heard the phone ring in the lounge. He walked through and lifted the receiver.

'Hello?'

As Archie was about to speak, out of the corner of his eye he saw two DC's he knew to be working on Pincent's murder enter the room. They both looked around the room before their gaze settled on him, their expressions convincing him without a shadow of doubt that that they were coming for him. Just before they reached him, he managed to shout out, 'Peter, they've got enough on you for both jobs! They know about me and you! Get out of there... now!'

As Peter took in Archie's words in horror, he could hear raised voices at the other end and what sounded like Archie's receiver being dropped on the desk. Then he heard the words of one of the DC's.

'Archie Cowper, I'm arresting you for assisting an offender and perverting the course of justice. You do not have to say anything, but it may harm your defence if...'

The sounds of a struggle and Archie screaming interrupted the officer's caution and he could hear the officers shouting 'Calm down! Stop struggling!'

Then he heard Archie's voice, for the last time.

'Run, Peter, for God's sake run!'

Peter slammed the receiver down and stood breathing heavily, his legs like jelly. Not only had his own world come crashing down around his ears, the man who he had come to think of as more than just a fling, the first person he had seen as possibly a long-term partner,

with whom he realised he was falling in love, had
effectively thrown away any chance of saving his own
career and freedom to save him. Now he was feeling
rage, not only for himself but on behalf of Archie and he
was damned if his sacrifice would be in vain. His mission
was far from complete.

FORTY-NINE

Within minutes, Peter had a plan. He knew that he would soon be one of the most wanted men in the country and if caught, he would be spending the next two or three decades behind bars. He needed to run, to find somewhere nobody would find him. He'd done it many times before: started life from scratch somewhere new, somewhere where nobody knew his face, his name, or his sexuality.

There were things he needed to do, untidy fragments of his life that needed straightening out, but they would all have to wait. Escaping the clutches of the police, and in particular that bitch, Neider, were now uppermost in his thoughts. The officers had heard Archie screaming for him to run and they would have passed that on to Tanner without delay. A message would have been sent straight to Sevenoaks Police for his arrest, so he had to move quickly.

The weather was bitterly cold and he packed accordingly. Throwing as much warm clothing and food as he could into a large rucksack, he pulled on light grey tracksuit bottoms, black over-trousers, a thin black t-shirt, a light black jumper, a waterproof navy-blue triple-layered overcoat, and a black woolly hat.

Peter had always been a keen camper and walker, usually making trips out into the Kent countryside on his own. He swiftly packed all his camping gear: tightly rolled green ground mat, small and compact one-man tent, small burner-stove, tin mug and bowl, Swiss-army knife, spoon, sleeping bag, binoculars, a lighter, and his Camelback containing three litres of water. The only other items he needed were his wallet and passport. It was extremely unlikely he would be able to escape and leave the country, but he wanted to keep his options open.

As he rummaged through a drawer in search of the passport, he came across several polaroid photographs of a particularly memorable sexual encounter. The background was unmistakable: an opulent bedroom with a super king-size bed on which a naked man lay sprawled, his hands bound securely to the brass bars of the headboard. He smiled as he remembered the man to be Thomas, the guy with the flash home and pool house.

Just as he was about to shove the photographs back in the drawer, a photo frame in the corner of the shot caught his eye; the face in it was slightly out of focus, but clear enough for Peter to recognise it. The shock was like electricity surging through his body as he stared into the distinctive green eyes of his nemesis; Natalie Neider!

This changed – and clarified – everything. Stuffing the photos along with his passport and wallet into his rucksack, he was about to leave when the house phone rang. He considered leaving it unanswered, figuring it might be the police and answering would alert them to his whereabouts. But conversely, something told him they wouldn't want to alert him to danger in the first place, so he lifted the receiver and quietly said, 'Hello?'

'It's Bill, have you got a minute?'

'Hi, mate. Look, I'm in a bit of a hurry, but fire away.'

'I heard Des and Andy chatting again in the car park, they knew I could hear but it didn't seem to bother them. Des said that Neider had phoned him and that she had important information. She really needed to see them but was busy today, so she asked to meet with them both at one o'clock tomorrow.'

'And they agreed to meet her?'

'Yep. Des said it was ideal because he'd got paperwork to catch up on and there was overtime working on his sister's Land Rover from eight till one if Andy wanted it.'

Peter smiled to himself. 'I'll bet Andy snapped his hand off.'

'Off course he did, the greedy bastard. None for me and Vince, though.'

'Bill, I hugely appreciate the call and I don't want to appear rude but I've really got to run.'

'That's fine mate. You get going, we'll catch up soon.'

'Thanks again, Bill. I won't forget this, you've been a good friend. Bye.'

Slightly puzzled by the emotion in Peter's voice, Bill simply said, 'Bye' and hung up.

Peter's adrenaline was through the roof; he needed to get out of his cottage – fast. Messages were possibly going out to police cars in the area that very moment. Giving the rooms a final check, he left the cottage locking the door behind him, raced to the car, threw the rucksack into the boot, and climbed into the driver's seat. He had no idea if the police would come for him in seconds, minutes, or within the next hour, all he knew was that he needed to get away from the cottage as quickly as possible.

He drove as quickly as he dared, to the nearby village of Shipbourne, less than three miles away along quiet country lanes, then pulled up in front of the village church. Its parking area was hidden from the main road and he parked close to the churchyard entrance, ensuring his Astra was parked behind three other vehicles, one of which was a large white van, conveniently obscuring it from any police vehicles that happened to be passing on the main road. He leapt from his car, lifted out the rucksack, walked through the beautiful old lychgate, and entered the cool, shady churchyard.

He made his way swiftly along the footpath which snaked around the right side of the church under ancient trees to the back of the building, then headed straight for the far left-hand corner of the churchyard, where there was a small, wooded overgrown area. It was often used for the storage of cut branches from the trees and bushes in the churchyard and had a carpet of ivy covering much of the ground.

Picking his way respectfully between the tightly packed gravestones, he trampled through the ivy and hid his rucksack behind the wide trunk of a fir tree, reckoning that on a cold and miserable Friday afternoon in early December, there was no likelihood of anyone finding it in the couple of hours before he returned to collect it.

It was shortly after noon when Peter emerged from the churchyard. He headed to the main road that cut through the village, crossed the road then stood patiently waiting inside the bus shelter opposite the village pub for the bus into Tonbridge. He was well concealed inside the old wooden structure and felt confident that the police would be searching for his car and not looking too closely at people waiting for buses.

Peter knew the area around the village well and also knew that the bus into town ran every half an hour or so. The chance of any police officer bothering to check that particular bus stop was remote, to say the least; it was much safer than taking his car into the town centre, where he reckoned officers would have been given full details of his vehicle, meaning he would almost certainly have been spotted.

He'd only been waiting seven or eight minutes when the bus arrived. Climbing aboard, he glanced into the downstairs section of the double decker, which was deserted except for two elderly ladies, one seated each side of the aisle.

'Return to Tonbridge, please.'

Without speaking, the sour-faced driver handed him his ticket and tapped her finger twice on the price stamped across it. Peter paid the fare, took his ticket and made his way upstairs. The top deck was deserted apart from a mother with her two small toddlers sitting in the front seats. As the bus pulled away, both children pretended they were driving the bus themselves, and the mother was too preoccupied trying to keep them in their seats to notice Peter. He moved halfway down the bus, then took a seat by the aisle to keep his face well away from the windows, clear of anyone walking on pavements, or inside passing cars, who might happen to be looking up into the bus.

As the bus pulled up in the High Street, Peter stepped onto the pavement and walked back the way he had come, keeping his head down and moving quickly, drawing out a substantial wad of cash on his way. His first port of call was Milletts, where he bought a small can of *Campingaz*, then he entered a small camera and gadget shop. Minutes later, he left with a pair of *Trijicon* night-sight binoculars and crossed the road to the line of bus stops close to the river, where he waited at the stop for the bus back to Shipbourne.

That's Part 1 of the plan completed.

Peter knew they would come looking for him at the cottage and he knew they would be turning the place inside out, searching for anything that might prove he was involved in one, or both, of the murders. In the ultimate "hunter becoming the hunted" twist he intended to be on the scene but invisible while the search was taking place, watching and waiting, all night if necessary.

Twenty-five minutes later, he jumped from the bus right outside the village pub and made his way back to his car, which was still perfectly hidden behind the van. He'd considered leaving a false trail for his pursuers by dumping his car in the carpark of one of the major local train stations, thinking they would assume he'd left the area by train and would have to waste time and resources spreading the net looking for him. In the end, though, he thought they might have had the stations covered within minutes of Archie warning him and it just wasn't worth the risk of an early capture.

He knew of a nearby country lane, with a dirt track leading to a cleared area which allowed parking for up to five cars. A small lake in the nearby woodland was popular with both daytime and night-time anglers; courting couples would also sometimes park up there, away from prying eyes. It was the perfect place to leave his car, a place where it would almost certainly be ignored by others using the area and, more importantly, was unlikely to be found by the police for at least a couple of days, allowing him ample time to carry out his plan.

He was at the parking area within a couple of minutes and squeezed his car into a gap between a red Seat Ibiza and a white Mercedes estate. Nobody was about, so he climbed out, closed his car door, and jogged quickly down a footpath into the woods. It was a footpath he knew well and in less than twenty minutes it would lead him across a muddy field and through the back gate into Shipbourne Churchyard, where he would collect his rucksack and begin phase two of his plan.

FIFTY

Detective Constable William Lilliwhite (known to everyone as Lilly) and Trainee Detective Constable Daniel Froome pulled SOCO Archie Cowper from his desk. They'd heard his screamed warning to Peter Hardy down the telephone as they approached and then grabbed him, he struggled violently, flailing his arms and dropping the phone onto the desk with a clatter. They pushed the top half of his body down across the desktop and yanked an arm each behind his back. Lilly managed to get one cuff onto his right wrist and as he did so, Archie had shouted his final words of warning to his friend. Moments later, the second handcuff was secured, allowing Lilly to finally complete the arrest and finish cautioning him.

Danny Froome lifted the telephone receiver.

'Hello… Mr Hardy… are you there?'

He looked at Lilly and shook his head. They roughly pulled Archie upright.

'That was rather stupid, wasn't it?' said Lilly.

'No idea what you're talking about,' replied Archie, a broad grin on his face.

Lilly shook his head and turned to Danny.

'Call for a van. We need to get this arsehole back to Vine Street.'

***

DI Tanner pressed the red button on the tape machine in

the Interview Room. As well as himself, there were three other people listening in to several seconds of loud buzzing: DCI Natalie Neider, Archie Cowper, and his solicitor, Malcolm O'Neill. When the buzzing stopped, everyone introduced themselves for the taped interview and Bernie began.

'Why did you do it, Archie?'

'No comment.'

'You had a good job, promising career, yet you helped someone you knew was a murderer. Why?'

'Because he was a better man that you'll ever be, better than any of you.'

O'Neill frowned at Archie and signalled for him to be quiet.

'How was he better?'

'No comment.'

'Did you know him before you were involved in the forensic search of his flat?'

'No, I didn't.'

'Are you sure?'

'What sort of question is that? Of course I'm sure.'

Bernie glanced at Natalie and she nodded an apparent instruction to him.

'We've recovered a curtain from Peter Hardy's flat with a stain on it. We're having it tested now and I think that test will show it to be Tony Waters' blood.'

He leaned forward in his chair, fixing Archie with an accusatory stare.

'You saw that stain, didn't you? You knew it was blood but told DCI Neider it was "nothing of interest", convincing her it was just a food stain. Now why would you do that?'

Archie turned to his solicitor, who shook his head and mouthed "No comment" to him, but Archie ignored his silent advice; he had something that needed saying.

'Because he didn't deserve to go to prison for striking a blow against bigotry, homophobia, and intolerance.'

'And because of your belief in his motivation, you were happy to cover up the murder of an innocent man?'

'He wasn't innocent!'

'Why do you say that?'

Archie shuffled uncomfortably and remained silent. A silence that engulfed the room for several seconds, until the weight of it finally forced a sullen reply.

'No comment.'

Bernie absent-mindedly searched through the pile of papers in front of him, then lifted his gaze and stared at Archie.

'I want to hear about your relationship with Peter Hardy. How close were you to him? Were you lovers?'

Archie looked exasperated, glanced towards his solicitor, then back to Bernie Tanner.

'Look, I know I'm going to be charged at the end of this, so why don't you just get on with it? I'm not going to answer any more questions. I want to go back to my cell.'

'Sorry, Archie, you're not in charge around here, I am, and there are plenty more questions I have for you.'

He stared intimidatingly at Archie, but he didn't engage, leaning back in his chair and closing his eyes tight shut. Bernie continued questioning him regardless.

'When did you make the arrangement to meet at La Belle Homme Café?'

'No comment.'

'We know you met him there at noon on Saturday, a few hours after DS Pincent had been murdered. What was the meeting about?'

'No comment.'

'Did you know at that stage he'd killed James

253

Pincent only hours before?'

'No comment.'

Bernie Tanner stuck to his task for a further forty minutes but so did Archie, responding to every question with a quiet "No comment." Eventually, he was satisfied he'd given Archie every opportunity to explain his actions. More importantly, he'd asked every question he could think of regarding Archie's activities and relationship with Hardy, derailing any chance his defence counsel would have at court for claiming his client hadn't been given the opportunity to answer a particular question. When he terminated the interview, Bernie wasn't too bothered about Archie's non-compliance, there was more than enough evidence to charge him.

Archie and his solicitor remained in the room after the interview at his solicitor's request for a ten-minute private consultation, before returning to the custody suite, where Archie was spoken to briefly by the custody sergeant before being returned to his cell.

As the door slammed on cell number three, the very same cell his lover Peter had been incarcerated in less than two weeks previously, Archie stood impassively staring at the cold wooden bench. He'd made his choices regarding Peter Hardy and was both satisfied with his decisions and proud he'd supported him. He accepted that he would now have to pay the penalty for making those decisions and it was likely to be an extremely harsh penalty, but one he was willing to pay.

FIFTY-ONE

Collecting his rucksack from behind the tree, Peter hoisted it onto his back, returned to the small car park between the church and the main road, then checked his appearance in the reflection of a car's window. He was pleased with what he saw: a young man who looked just like one of many other hardened walkers who passed through that area through all seasons of the year, some of them camping out for the night, just as Peter intended to do.

Satisfied with how the day had gone, he headed back through the churchyard with his senses on full alert, aware of every tiny bird that flitted from branch to branch, hearing with alarming clarity the crunch of each footstep on the path. He passed through the old gate in the wall at the far end of the churchyard, turned right through the hedge and stepped out along the footpath into the fields. This was one of his favourite walks and he knew every twist and turn.

A family of two adults and two small children were walking towards him along the enclosed track, cloying mud sucking at their wellington boots, the whole group looking tired. Peter politely moved to one side, allowing them to pass freely without breaking step.

'Thank you,' said the father.

'No problem, enjoy your walk.'

The mother and children smiled warmly as they passed, reminding Peter that the normal world carried on its business, and that it was mainly filled with kind and decent people. Striding out almost carefree, he made sure he chose the route which skirted Ightham Mote, a 14th Century Manor House which welcomed thousands of visitors all year round. It was twenty minutes since he left the churchyard and as he neared the property, the number of walkers he was passing increased. Normally he would have stopped to admire the grand house but not today, instead quickly crossing the huge car park to a footpath on the far side. Soon he was dropping down away from the car park, before climbing up onto the North Downs where, in less than forty-five minutes, he would have a perfect view of the valley floor from the top of the ridge, including a view of his cottage.

Everything he'd done up to this point was intended to lure the police away from Underriver, figuring that if they were stupid enough to have failed to produce sufficient evidence to convict him so far, they were just as likely to believe he'd done a runner and was attempting to get as far away from Underriver as possible. He was convinced they would fall for his deception, hook line and sinker.

He knew they'd soon be searching all nearby town centres, checking train stations, bus stations, and taxi firms to see if someone of his description had left the area that day. They'd have every available unit scouring the station and town centre car parks for his Astra, which would at least give them a starting point for the search. But one of the last places they'd be likely to search would be hundreds of yards down a small dirt track on the outskirts of Shipbourne.

The new police technology enabling them to automatically recognise his car number plate would undoubtedly be used in the hope of finding his vehicle, but they would draw a blank. His bank account would be swiftly checked and they would find he had purchased something to the value of £279.99 from a shop called *Vision*, and withdrawn money from a cashpoint in Tonbridge High Street just after 12.40. Once that was done, they needed to find out where he'd gone from there.

Peter knew that completing these enquiries and gathering CCTV footage along the High Street, would take at least a day. They might get a result regarding the binoculars later today and the thought of that made him smile, thinking about the alarm that would cause. Even if they did discover he'd taken a bus heading north out of Tonbridge, how would they know where he'd got off? The bus went all the way to Borough Green and buses didn't have CCTV on board.

Having reached his chosen location, Peter dropped down the steep hillside through the woods, until he was thirty yards off the footpath, forcing his way downhill through thick brambles and areas of gorse to finally reach an area of thick rhododendron bushes, where he was certain he couldn't be seen by anyone passing on the footpath above. More importantly, because of the difficulty gaining access to that area, it was highly improbable that anyone would bother him there.

He'd been carrying out recces on that area of the footpath ever since his initial arrest, just in case it all went belly-up and he needed to go on the run. He was glad he had. Peter was in position by mid-afternoon and on the bitterly cold and dismal December day, light was fading fast.

Perfect.

Dumping his rucksack on the ground underneath the canopy of a particularly large, dense rhododendron bush, he managed to find an area where he could just about erect his one-man tent. It was an ideal spot: dry, well hidden, out of the wind and away from prying eyes.

There would be no ambient light from street lights, vehicles or houses and nobody would be using the footpath once darkness had fallen so, once it was completely dark, he could safely light his stove for warmth and food, confident any smoke would be invisible.

He rummaged through the rucksack for his daytime binoculars, removed the dust caps covering the lenses then, crawling carefully to the outer edge of the branches, he parted the branches to reveal, just as he thought, a perfect view of his cottage and the nearby farmyard from a distance of about 150 yards.

He trained the binoculars on the cottage, adjusted the viewfinders to his eyes and stared in shock at the scene before him. He'd expected a police car or two and a few officers to come looking for him at the cottage, but nothing like this: a police van, two panda cars, a 'Forensic Investigation' van and three unmarked cars, which he assumed belonged to detectives. The front door of the cottage was open and the small patio area outside a hive of activity. By tweaking the focus, Peter could just about make out individuals. Three uniformed officers climbed into the van; two officers in full forensic gear were comparing notes while engaged in deep conversation and at the rear of the van, Peter could just make out the back of a male in plain-clothes. By his body language, he appeared to be in conversation with others, out of sight.

Lowering his binoculars, Peter stared into space, asking himself why he'd been so desperate to observe what was happening back at the cottage. No matter how hard he tried, he really couldn't explain it to himself; all he knew was he simply had to be there to witness it... it just felt right. The bonus was that he was now in the very last area they would consider searching for him, practically on his own doorstep.

Once everything had died down at the cottage, he would rest where he was for a couple of nights, before making his way across the fields to Hildenborough train station. He would have to take the chance that police had stopped watching train stations by then. Where should he go? He wasn't sure just yet; maybe Suffolk, he'd always liked Suffolk. Staying under the radar wouldn't be easy though; his size alone marked him out, but he could grow a beard and crop his hair, and being in a different county would certainly help.

Raising the binoculars to his eyes again, he was just in time to see the police van pulling forward, so the rear doors of the van were now alongside the front door, presumably to make it less of a journey for officers removing items after searching the house. It also revealed who the unknown male in plain-clothes had been... it was Mark Dawes. The people he had been in conversation with were now in plain view, Natalie Neider, Bernie Tanner, and Graham Carter.

Officers were carrying out armfuls of Peter's belongings, including many of his dresses and other women's clothing. Boxes that must have contained more of his personal possessions were also being carried out. He was intrigued as to what items they might have found interesting, but had no idea what those items might be; there was certainly nothing relevant to either of the murders. Nevertheless, it felt strange and unnerving to see his life being dismantled and taken away in a police van before his very eyes.

Darkness fell quickly and Peter changed over to the night-sight binoculars, which weren't as powerful as his daytime ones, but still allowed him a reasonable view of his home. Over the next couple of hours, activity around the cottage started to diminish. One by one, the police vehicles moved off, until just Natalie Neider and Matt

Dawes remained.

He watched with a sinking heart as he realised he could never again return to his dear little cottage, somewhere he'd felt safe and happy. Neider and Dawes climbed into her Saab and drove off after closing the front door of the cottage, light drizzle illuminated clearly in the car's headlights, perfectly matching his mood.

Putting on his head torch, Peter switched it on. He was beginning to feel cramp from kneeling on the cold ground, but the small area underneath the branches of the rhododendron meant that he couldn't stand upright. In fact, he could only just kneel, but he didn't care, he was pleased with his choice of hiding place and settled down inside the concealing branches which were keeping out the vast majority of the drizzle, as well as the biting wind.

He quickly pitched his tiny one-man tent, lit his burner stove and cooked himself a tin of oxtail soup, into which he dunked his two slices of bread, followed by an apple and banana for pudding. It wasn't a great meal, but it brought him some comfort; he felt safe in his hiding place and knew he'd chosen well. As he sipped on a mug of coffee, he tried to think about what tomorrow would bring, then found his thoughts drifting to events of the day and two moments which dominated.

He could still hear Archie's frantic screams down the phone, intended to give him a chance to get away, but at the same time condemning his lover to inevitable arrest. A wave of guilt overwhelmed him, leaving him exhausted and depressed. Then his mind returned to the moment he had seen the face in a photo within a photo, the face of a woman he had come to hate so much and whose hatred of him he could now understand – but never forgive.

FIFTY-TWO

At 7.30 the following morning, Natalie stretched as she woke up in the very bed where, unbeknown to her, her husband had shared some of the best sex of his life with Peter Hardy only three months previously. She pulled on her dressing gown after slipping from the bed and walked silently across the thick carpet on her way to the en-suite bathroom.

The previous evening, Graham Carter had been urgently required back at Vine Street regarding a separate case; Bernie told him to take the car, saying he would stay to help Natalie and would find a hotel for the night before travelling back to Vine Street in the morning.

At Sevenoaks Police Station, once the forensic teams had completed their paperwork and while Natalie's investigation team were busily logging and recording everything that had been seized from Hardy's home, she'd turned to Bernie.

'Look, don't bother getting a hotel room. My place has plenty of spare beds. I'll even rustle you up a meal and we can chat about the cases over dinner.'

Bernie nodded appreciatively. 'Thanks, that would be great.'

The evening had passed pleasantly, although when they arrived at Natalie's home, she found herself too shattered by the day's events to want to cook and they'd ordered a Chinese takeaway, accompanied by a bottle of wine.

Natalie found herself wondering what it would be

like if she suggested they take their drinks upstairs; it had been a long time since she had shared her home – or her bed – with anyone and the wine was going to her head. She was on the point of saying something when Bernie, as if sensing her intention, put his glass down on the coffee table and, smiling gently, said, 'I think we'd both better turn in and get a good night's sleep. It's been a great evening and perhaps, when this whole thing is over, we can do it again.'

He leaned over the table and squeezed her hand before standing and making his way to one of the guest bedrooms. Next morning, he was already awake, dressed and in the kitchen making a coffee when Natalie eventually made her way downstairs.

FIFTY-THREE

A couple of hours earlier, while it was still dark, Peter had woken at six, just as he had done for years, and ate a bread roll followed by a handful of nuts and raisins for breakfast. Not bothering to turn on the burner and make himself a hot drink, he washed his breakfast down with several long gulps of water. It wasn't the most substantial breakfast to start the day, but he reasoned he would be surviving on adrenalin anyway.

Settling down into his sleeping bag the previous evening, Peter was reconciled to the thought of staying put for a couple of days, then going on the run; he knew it would be incredibly difficult to evade capture, but intended giving himself the best chance possible to restart his life somewhere else. He eventually drifted off to sleep with that basic plan in his mind. But during the night he'd struggled sleeping, the life-altering events of the past three weeks playing over and over in his mind, and when he awoke his intentions had changed.

By running away, he wouldn't be making a stand for other victims of abuse, people who, like him, had suffered years of taunting, abuse and ridicule at the hands of bullies like Waters and Pincent. If he ran away and hid, his personal suffering would have stopped but animals like Des Thayer and Andy Clark would feel they had won. That was something he simply couldn't allow to happen. His mind went back to the day he had committed to his mission; he couldn't back down now. What's more, he felt he owed a debt to Archie who had so bravely put his own freedom on the line to protect his. So he'd come to a decision, a decision requiring drastic action, but before worrying about Thayer and Clark, he needed to teach Natalie Neider a lesson she'd never forget.

He reckoned that she would be leaving her house early; she was, after all, heading up a murder enquiry that had just cranked up a few notches. His plan wasn't to hurt her, that simply wasn't something he was prepared to consider. No matter how much he hated her, it went against everything he believed in to physically harm a woman. But he needed to strike back against her somehow and he knew the perfect way.

He'd been to her house before and reckoned it was less than three miles from where he was currently hiding out; his mind was made up, that's where he intended to head for. He would leave the photos in plain view, get well clear, then call the police reporting a burglary taking place now. Her colleagues would find the pictures of him and her husband and her reputation would be destroyed.

But walking along the main roads would put him at risk of capture, he needed to stay concealed on minor footpaths in the woods, which made his route far more challenging and time-consuming.

By 6.30, Peter was on his way, having given the area under the rhododendron bush one final check to make sure he'd left no rubbish and shortly after eight, he was close to his destination. He walked quickly along Forest Rise, to the dramatic row of huge leylandii bushes marking out the boundary of Natalie's home, the home where he'd spent a memorable afternoon with her husband, Thomas. He pulled out the photographs from his rucksack and secured them in an inside pocket

Forcing a way through the closely packed bushes, he scanned the house carefully before peering through the branches towards the house. He was disappointed to see Natalie's Saab still on the drive. Peter knew it was her car because he'd seen her drive away from his cottage in it the previous evening. Could this mean she hadn't left for work yet? If so, that would completely scupper his plan.

Through his binoculars, he scanned the windows of the ground floor and soon spotted Natalie through the kitchen window, tucking into a bowl of cereal. Then a man walked into view and as he turned to lift something from a cupboard, Peter got a good look at his face. Detective Inspector Bernie Tanner!

Fucking hell! What are they playing at? They must be shagging! But why are they still here?

This left him with a problem and he needed to think, quickly: did he abandon his plan to shame her among her friends and colleagues and get the fuck out of there? Or did he wait it out and hope they left for work sooner rather than later? He took another look through the binoculars. Both were now eating their breakfasts; they didn't look like they were in any kind of hurry, or leaving anytime soon. Decision made.

Packing the binoculars into his right-hand coat pocket, he forced his way out of the bushes to the road where he turned right, walking quickly towards his next destination: the place where he would surrender himself to the authorities, the place where his life as he knew it would be over, the place where he had once hoped he would find happiness.

At the very moment he was packing his binoculars away, Natalie glanced up at the digital clock on her kitchen wall.

'Shit, it's ten past and the traffic will be a nightmare. Come on, Bernie, we need to get moving.'

Standing up, Bernie started to rinse his bowl out in the sink.

'Leave it,' she said. 'I'll load the dishwasher when I get home.'

Two minutes later they climbed into her distinctive convertible and Natalie drove down the drive to the large wooden electronic gates which opened automatically as she approached. She wondered how much longer she'd be allowed to live there unhindered by her husband; he would surely either buy her out and move back in himself, or put the house up for sale so they could split the equity. Whatever he decided, it was likely to happen sooner rather than later.

She turned right, intending to use back roads as much as possible to avoid the traffic on their journey to the police station.

FIFTY-FOUR

As he reached the far end of Forest Rise, Peter heard the sound of a car engine revving as it pulled out of a driveway some distance behind him. Being a private road that very few vehicles passed along, he instinctively turned around to see where the car was coming from and was horrified as he saw Natalie's car heading straight towards him; they would be upon him in seconds.

Turning right on the main road, Peter thought he would jog to the next driveway and duck behind a hedge or maybe behind a car. But fate wasn't being kind to him that morning; in this neighbourhood of large properties, the next driveway was over fifty yards away and just before he reached it, Natalie's car passed him. To his right in the driveway, a young mother was leaving the front door of the house with what looking like twin daughters. They walked towards a black BMW 525 parked on the drive.

For some reason that he would never be able to fathom, Peter looked towards the road to check they'd gone past without seeing him. Inside the car, Bernie had been curious about the large man with a huge rucksack in a posh area so early in the morning, and was looking back over his right shoulder through the rear window. To his horror, Peter saw Bernie Tanner staring straight back at him.

Despite the black woolly hat pulled down low on his forehead, he was still clearly recognisable and Bernie shouted, 'That's him! Stop the car!'

Natalie slammed on the brakes.

'What are you talking about?'

He turned and pointed at the large man they had just passed, who by now was running into the driveway of the house.

'That's Hardy! Back up, back up! He's getting away!'

Natalie checked her rear-view mirror, looked over her left shoulder then slammed the vehicle into reverse. Gunning the accelerator, the car flew backwards.

Having just seen Bernie looking at him and registering the recognition and astonishment on his face, Peter knew he was in trouble, deep, deep trouble. He had to do something, quickly. On autopilot, he ran onto the driveway where the woman was now opening the car door for her children.

'Come on, girls, in you get. Jessica, stop dawdling!'

Both girls moved on their mother's instructions towards the open car door. Peter ran at the woman with wild eyes. He must have looked terrifying to a young mother and she let out a long piercing scream that startled her daughters, causing them to scream too.

'Give me your fucking car key!' he yelled.

The woman pulled her girls toward her protectively, and screamed out a plea to Peter as she held out her the key to him.

'Take it, just don't hurt my children!'

Snatching the key, Peter ran round the car to the driver's side, opened the door, threw his rucksack across onto the passenger seat and climbed in; he turned the key in the ignition and the engine roared into life.

At the same time, Natalie's car screeched to a halt on the opposite side of the road. Bernie was out of the passenger door like a greyhound leaving the trap, using his right hand to balance himself on the car's bonnet as he flew around the front of the car and raced towards the drive.

Inside the BMW, which still had the rear near-side door open, Peter selected first gear, depressed the accelerator and flew out of the drive without bothering to check whether any vehicles were coming along the road. The open rear door smashed into the gatepost, denting it badly and slamming it shut. Suddenly, Bernie Tanner was right in front of him and before Peter could react, the front off-side wing of the BMW caught him a vicious blow on his right thigh. He was tossed into the road, where a startled looking Natalie had just climbed from the driver's door of her car. Seeing what had happened, she ran over to Bernie, who was crying out in pain and frustration.

Peter's heart was hammering inside his ribcage and he was breathing heavily.

What the fuck am I doing?

But his brain had no answers. Everything was going wrong and he was simply responding to the latest bucket of shit that had been thrown at him. He'd set out that morning with a clear and achievable plan in his head, a plan that had gone swiftly to the dogs. He was no longer being proactive, he was being reactive and for the time being, there was nothing he could do about it; he was simply going with the flow. He was beginning to wish he'd stuck with his plan of going on the run.

Turning left and heading away from the town, he drove like a maniac through country lanes and villages until eventually abandoning the BMW in a quiet residential road on the outskirts of Kemsing. It was an area he knew well. In the distance he could hear police sirens screaming through the cold stillness of the day. Abandoning the car, he left his rucksack on the front passenger seat; it had served its purpose and would be of no use to him from now on.

Peter quickly left the road, following narrow footpaths up through the fields to double back on the route he had just taken in the car, always keeping sufficient cover between himself and the roadway so he couldn't be seen. When a perpetrator is fleeing the scene of a crime, they usually either go to ground, or keep moving in the same direction they start running in. He was gambling on the police sticking with that logic; it was unlikely they would start checking back in the direction he'd just fled from. Everyone knows that villains anecdotally revisit the scene of the crime, but that usually occurs days later, not just after the offence happened!

Within fifteen minutes, he had reached a popular local footpath he knew well, tightly enclosed by hedges and trees that ran for over half a mile emerging opposite the very school he'd attended not so many years ago.

Despite the bitterly cold day, events of the morning had Peter sweating profusely. Once inside the relative safety of the path, he removed his woolly hat and coat, holding his hat in his right hand and tying his coat around his waist. The path was a hugely popular cut-through and at nine that morning it was busy with dog walkers and people out for an early morning stroll.

He followed the path to its end, coming out directly opposite the familiar buildings of his old secondary school, the school where the abuse had turned really nasty as he entered his teens. He smiled; in a funny way it completed the circle for him and seemed the perfect place to end up. This was where most of his problems had started and it was only right he was back there again, shortly before his problems ended forever.

In the far distance, towards Kemsing, the sounds of sirens intensified. Then, along the main road he was now standing on, flashing blue lights were approaching fast, heading in his direction. He dived into the telephone box

Evan Baldock

where the path joined the road, picked up the receiver to make it look like he was making a call, then turned his back towards the road and waited until the police car flashed past.

The police would have found the BMW by now and were almost certainly sealing off the village, convinced he'd gone to ground somewhere nearby. Within a couple of hours, they would realise the trail had gone cold and begin widening the search area, so he had to work quickly. Keeping well clear of as many main roads as he could, Peter used his knowledge of the road and footpath network in the area to make his way towards his final destination – Duke's Garage.

FIFTY-FIVE

Peter's route to the garage took him through quiet residential streets, alleyways, footpaths, and at one point, a small allotment, invisible to his pursuers. Once there, he found himself a vantage point behind a wall underneath a large bush, almost directly opposite the garage frontage.

Pulling his binoculars from his pocket, he lifted them to his eyes and directed his gaze at the window of Des's office. The office window afforded his boss a decent view of anyone browsing through the vehicles on the lot but also gave Peter a clear line of sight of Thayer himself. He soon had the lenses perfectly focused and could see Thayer doing what he did best, sitting at his desk with the phone clamped to one ear. He was, as usual, animated and appeared to be shouting at someone on the other end of the phone.

Nothing new there then... tosser.

Moving his binoculars to the right, he scanned the windows in the main office. Caroline and Wendy were seated at their desks, Caroline presumably waiting patiently for a customer interested in buying a car, Wendy busily catching up on admin. Peter returned his gaze to Des Thayer and stared intently at him.

You wanker, think you're such a big man, don't you? I'm about to show you just how insignificant you are.

Moving the image slowly across the rear yard, he made a tiny adjustment to the focus and found himself looking at the sliding door of the workshop, where Bill had informed him Andy would be working alone, earning overtime denied to both his colleagues. Doubts began to creep into his mind.

Am I doing the right thing? It's not too late to hand myself in... or just make a run for it.

But Peter knew his mind was made up and he glanced at his watch; it was just after ten. According to Bill, they would be there until one, when they had a meeting planned with Natalie, although Peter very much doubted whether the meeting would now go ahead, considering the unexpected events of the morning. He had plenty of time, so no need to rush and make mistakes; instead, he settled down with his back against the wall, to wait until the right moment. He was desperately thirsty, but had nothing to drink so he would just have to put up with it.

At 10.35 two cars pulled into the customer car park within a minute of each other, a man and a woman in each car. The respective couples walked onto the car lot and began browsing separately through the vehicles on display. Within a few minutes, Caroline and Des descended on a couple each, but the couple Des had approached seemed unimpressed with his sales patter and soon walked back to their car and drove off. The other couple stayed happily chatting and asking questions of Caroline, while Des stomped morosely back to his office.

After twenty minutes on the car lot, during which time they looked to have set their heart on a blue Audi 80, Caroline lured them inside, presumably to discuss a sale or finance terms. During their discussions, Peter knew Caroline would be offering a test drive and that would be the perfect time for him to strike.

Sure enough, at 11.10 Caroline led the enthusiastic young couple out to the Audi and handed the keys to the man, who in turn handed them to his partner. The woman shared a joke with Caroline about her faux-pas before climbing into the driver's seat while the man got into the back. Moments later, the car pulled out into the flow of traffic, turning right towards the village of Riverhead. Peter knew from experience they would be out for around fifteen to twenty minutes, no more; the time for contemplation was over, it was time for action.

Checking what Des was doing, Peter saw he was off the phone and had settled down to deal with paperwork spread across his desk. Peter climbed over the low wall and onto the grass verge alongside the road; his coat and black woolly hat were back in place, which was just as well because he was now shivering, uncertain whether that was down to the cold, or as a result of an attack of nerves.

A gap in the traffic on the busy road was the spur he needed. He ran swiftly onto the lot and crouched down behind a classic Volkswagen Beetle, checking all the while to make sure Des hadn't seen him. He knew his behaviour must have looked extremely suspicious to passing motorists and their passengers, but he really wasn't bothered; by the time the police got there, he hoped to have completed his task.

Running to the side of the building, he felt he could breathe a little easier since Des now definitely couldn't see him from his office. He made his way cautiously around to the far side of the building, ran across the staff car park and stood panting outside the partially opened sliding door into the workshop, his heart thumping with a mixture of excitement and fear. He wasn't fazed at seeing the workshop door partially opened. Even on a bitterly cold day like today, once the workshop's gigantic heater-blowers had cranked into gear, it made little difference if the door was open or closed.

Just for a moment he stood, frozen. His hands were

274

clammy and his vision blurred and he almost felt as if he was having a panic attack, so he closed his eyes momentarily and forced himself to take some slow deep breaths. When he opened them again, his vision, and his mind, were clear.

FIFTY-SIX

Creeping in through the gap in the door, the first thing he noticed was mess everywhere along one end of the workshop. The old workbench had been ripped out and it looked like builders were in the process of replacing it, gleaming new timbers making up the thick wooden framework of the new bench already in evidence. Tools were liberally scattered on the floor, giving the workshop an unusually untidy appearance.

Looking further inside, he could see Andy bent double, working inside the engine compartment of an old Datsun Sunny, which surprised him, because Bill had said he'd be working on Des's sister's Land Rover.

The radio was blaring out *I Would Do Anything for Love* by Meatloaf, a song that Andy was tunelessly singing along to, unaware of Peter's presence. Lifting a roll of duct tape from a nearby shelf, Peter crept up to Andy until he was standing right behind him. Andy had his head under the bonnet with his right arm reaching a long way down to the bottom of the engine, completely at Peter's mercy, which was just how he wanted him.

Using his huge left hand and enormous strength, Peter grabbed the back of Andy's neck and forced his face onto the top of the engine, pinning him in position, unable to move.

'What the fuck… who's that… I can't breathe!'

'Hello Andy, it's your old colleague. Have you missed me?'

On hearing his voice, a voice he knew so very well,

Andy almost wet himself; he'd been brutal in his abuse of Peter since Tony's death and correctly guessed that there was only one reason Peter would run the risk of returning to the garage... revenge. Peter was dangerous, very dangerous, and Andy needed to quickly think of a way to talk him round.

Andy knew that Natalie had phoned Des the previous afternoon with information that they now had sufficient evidence to charge Peter on both counts of murder. She'd also told Des he'd done a runner and that anyone receiving contact from him should notify the police immediately.

'Why so quiet, Andy, aren't you pleased to see me?'

Peter released the pressure very slightly on the back of his neck so that Andy could reply. He sounded breathless and in pain as he spoke.

'Pete... mate... what the fuck are you doing here?'

'Mate! Don't give me that shit, you fucking slug. I'm doing something I should have done a long, long time ago.'

Paralysed with fear and hearing the venom in Peter's voice, Andy desperately tried to reason with him but Peter was thoroughly enjoying himself, the sheer terror in Andy's voice sending warm ripples of pleasure through his body.

'Tell you what, Pete, let's go into Des's office, have a nice cup of tea and a chat.'

'No thanks, that's not what I'm here for.'

'Can I stand up please, mate? It's really hurting.'

'I'm here because I want you and Des to understand how much you've hurt *me* over the past few months. I wanted you both to feel a fraction of the pain I've gone through.'

'Come on, mate, it was only banter. I didn't mean any of it, nor did Des. I'm sorry if we upset you.'

On hearing Andy's words, Peter released his grip.

'Thank you, that's all I was hoping for. I just wanted to hear apologies from you both.'

Pulling himself upright, Andy turned to face Peter, grease and oil smeared across his cheeks where his face had been rammed onto the engine housing, but his skin was still ashen with fear underneath the grime. The tremor in his voice was at odds with his outward display of confidence.

'It's a pleasure, mate. You're an okay bloke in my book and I'm sorry if we pushed it a bit far at times.'

Peter smiled and nodded at his old work colleague… then in a flash, smashed his right fist into his face, connecting with a sickening crunch on his nose and left cheekbone. Blood sprayed from his nose as his head flew backwards, connecting with the lip of the open bonnet and splitting open. He crumpled to the floor where he lay on his back in an untidy heap, his face a blood and snot covered mess, looking upwards through misty eyes at Peter towering over him. He was still conscious, but only just, his vision blurred, the injuries on his head causing a blizzard of pain.

Peter acted swiftly while Andy was in no state to defend himself. Crouching down beside him on one knee, he lifted Andy's head and wound the duct tape around it several times, sealing his mouth closed. He then grabbed some tissue from the workbench, returned to Andy, who was now struggling to breathe and firmly wiped his nose, causing him to flinch in pain.

Peter then securely taped Andy's right wrist to the right side of the bumper then did the same with his left wrist on the other side, forming the upper part of his body into the top half of a crucifix, and leaving Andy completely helpless, incapable of defending himself. Peter knelt and moved close to his face. Andy was struggling to breathe again as more blood poured from his nose, so once again, Peter wiped the blood and told him to blow his nose, which he did eagerly.

'Time to pay the penalty for your actions, Andy. I've been looking forward to this for a very long time.'

Walking to a corner of the workshop, Peter picked up a five-gallon jerry can which was about half full of petrol, then went to the rest area, where there was always the odd box of matches lying around, for those that fancied popping outside for a quick smoke.

Andy's eyes widened in horror as he realised Peter's plan; he started struggling against his bonds and tried to climb to his knees, but he was unable to manage it, the tape held firm.

'You know, whenever you think about death, Andy… do you think about it sometimes? I know I do. Well, the thing that scares me the most is the thought of being burned alive. I mean, can you imagine the terror and the excruciating pain?'

Peter looked deeply into Andy's terrified eyes and shook his head.

'It must be truly unimaginable.'

Tears poured down Andy's cheeks; he was struggling to breathe again through all the mucus.

'Sorry, *mate*,' said Peter in a sympathetic tone. 'Here, let me help you.'

Grabbing a Stanley knife, he did the same as he'd done for Tony Waters, gently cutting a slit into the tape around Andy's mouth, taking care not to cut his lips. Andy was weak through lack of oxygen and greedily gulped in the air.

'I wouldn't have wanted you to miss the main event.'

Standing up, he clicked open the catch on the jerry can and sloshed petrol all over Andy, who was making as much noise as he could through the tape, kicking out at

Peter's legs, bucking and writhing as he fought against the bonds. After emptying about half of the can's contents, Peter calmly placed the can outside the sliding door and walked back to stand in front of Andy, who could do nothing but stare up at him, pleading with his eyes.

'I feel cold,' said Peter. 'Do you feel cold?'

Andy shook his head.

'Well, I think we need something to warm us up!'

Lifting the matchbox, he pulled out a match, lit it, and without ceremony threw it onto Andy, who was immediately engulfed in flames. He fought like a wild animal to be released from the pain he was now suffering, but it was too late for him... far too late.

As he fought, he emitted high pitched screams, despite the tape around his mouth. His skin started to bubble, the blood boiling in his veins and his hair turned into a torch, far more intense than the rest of his clothing and body. Peter stood, motionless, watching his suffering with intense pleasure and a degree of fascination for a few seconds, feeling a strange sense of release. Then he turned, picked up a nail gun the builders had left lying on the floor and collected the jerry can as he left the workshop.

FIFTY-SEVEN

Peter had worked quickly. The whole thing, from leaving his hiding place across the road, to walking back out of the workshop leaving Andy behind, writhing in agony, had taken just eight minutes. Time was running out though; Caroline and her prospective buyers would be back soon so there was no time to lose.

On an adrenaline high, Peter strode confidently across the staff car park, up the three short steps to the sales entrance and pushed open the door into the main office. Wendy looked up and almost jumped out of her skin. Peter raised a finger to his lips. Looking through the glass panels separating Des's office from his staff, he could see his ex-boss on the telephone, standing with his back to the main office looking out at the car lot.

'Hi Wendy,' he said, 'how are you?'

Wendy's eyes widened with fear. Peter had been the talk of the office; the girls had been warned by the police that he was a homicidal maniac, a dangerous double killer who could strike again at any time. She replied in a hoarse whisper, 'I'm f…fine. Please Pete, please don't hurt me. My kids… they…'

Peter raised his hand, cutting her off.

'Wendy, I've never hurt a woman in my life and I don't plan to start now. Perhaps it's best if you leave.'

He pointed towards the door, once again placing his left index finger onto his lips, reminding her to keep quiet. She didn't need asking twice; jumping from behind her desk, she was out of the door in a matter of seconds.

The nail gun that Peter had collected from the workshop floor was a Phoenix SP47, a gas fired gun, capable of firing 60 nails a minute at a speed of around 200 feet per second. He had used a similar nail gun when helping Suzanna at her flat and knew exactly how it worked. He released the safety catch and was pleased to see it contained 4" flat headed nails, perfect for what he intended. He placed the jerry can down outside the door to Thayer's office then flung the door open with such force that the glass in the door shattered against the side wall.

Des, who was still on the phone, span round with a startled expression on his face, a look that changed to one of fury when he saw Peter standing in front of him.

'You prick! Look what you've done to my door! You'll fucking pay for that!'

Peter didn't speak. Instead, he responded by raising the nail gun and Des's face underwent another change. Drained of all colour, the anger had given way to sheer terror. Approaching to within a couple of yards of Des, Peter aimed the gun at his crotch and firing twice in rapid succession.

Pain exploded between Des's legs. He let out an ear-piercing shriek, dropped the phone and crashed to the floor by the side of his desk holding his groin, groaning and writhing in pain. Peter walked round behind him and aimed a brutal kick at his spine, making Des arch backwards, a movement that only accentuated the pain down below.

At that moment, a loud explosion rocked the building, causing the windows to vibrate alarmingly. Looking over to the workshop, Peter could see that much of the building was now alight. He guessed that either the fuel tank of the Datsun had just ignited, or another jerry can of fuel had exploded.

'I think the owner of that Datsun Andy was working on might want his money back,' joked Peter.

Des was in no mood to laugh; struggling to breathe, the kick had badly winded him, his body now weak with pain. Lying on his left side, he looked up at Peter with a mixture of fear and loathing.

Peter stepped forward, yanked Des's right hand away from his groin, stood on his forearm with the palm facing upwards, and fired two quick nails, one into his hand and one into his wrist, securing that arm to the wooden floor.

Des howled in agony, his face a pitiful mockery of the strong and proud man he'd always been.

After stamping on Des's right ankle, then his right knee, weakening them both, Peter pulled his right leg out straight and stood with all his weight on Des's right shinbone, causing indescribable levels of pain and making him scream out in agony. He then fired three nails, one through his foot and two through his ankle, smashing bones and flesh on their way through, while tightly securing his right leg to the floor.

Des was in so much pain, he'd gone into shock. He was no longer crying out, only giving a muffled and quiet whimpering sound at each explosion of agony inflicted on him. Lying on his back facing up at his tormentor, he knew he was utterly helpless.

A minute later, Peter had repeated the process on his left arm and leg and stood over his prey like a lion over a badly wounded gazelle. Another loud explosion made Peter jump and the distant sound of approaching sirens reminded him that time was running out. After checking that there was no chance Des could move, he threw the nail gun to the floor, retrieved the jerry can and poured the remainder of the contents over Des, making sure to cover his face and mouth. Then, almost as an afterthought, he said casually, 'See ya!' before lighting a match and dropping it onto his face.

Des's face, body, and clothing erupted with a loud *whoomp* and the flame leapt towards Peter, making him jump backwards. Suddenly, Des found his voice again, as the level of pain increased several more notches. He howled and screamed at the top of his voice for mercy, but Peter only watched his suffering impassively, before turning and walking out.

Peter left by the office's only entrance and as he was walking down the three small steps, he passed a fire engine racing into the car park. He saw the firemen leap from the vehicle and run out hoses, then he calmly crossed the road and sat on the opposite verge. The workshop was now entirely engulfed in flames and the far end of the office, where Des's room was situated, was also starting to burn fiercely. Peter sat on the damp grass with his knees folded to his chest and wrapped his forearms around his legs, like a child, watching the flames impassively, waiting for the inevitable to happen.

FIFTY-EIGHT

The woman whose car had been stolen had phoned 999 shortly after Peter's departure and within minutes an ambulance and several police cars had arrived. Natalie had remained with Bernie until he was taken off to hospital with a suspected broken femur, then she returned to base. It wasn't long before the police located the BMW and officers were drafted in from surrounding areas as a huge search began.

Back at Sevenoaks Police Station, Natalie was briefing her investigating team on the turn of events the morning had thrown up when suddenly, at 11.30, reports came over the radio of a disturbance and fire at Duke's Garage, which was only about 500 yards towards Riverhead from the police station.

With a deep sense of foreboding, Natalie sprinted to her car in the rear yard and together with two Panda cars drove quickly to the scene. When she pulled up outside the garage, she couldn't believe the scene that greeted her. There was Peter Hardy, sitting as cool as a cucumber on the grass verge, while just yards away was a raging inferno where the garage had once been. She shouted at the uniformed officers climbing out of their cars.

'With me… over here. Now!'

Two officers ran to join her and the others started closing the road to traffic. Just then, a police van and motorcyclist also arrived.

She walked up to Peter, her heart racing. She gasped out the inevitable words.

'Peter Hardy, I am arresting you for the murders of Tony Waters and James Pincent. You do not have to say anything, but it may harm your defence if you fail to mention, when questioned, something which you later rely on in court. Anything you do say may be given in evidence. Do you understand?'

Peter didn't look at her and didn't respond, just sat nodding his head. He was roughly hauled to his feet by the two uniformed officers and handcuffed behind his back. Looking across at the burning buildings, Peter spoke almost absent-mindedly.

'You might want to add a couple more murders to those charges, sweetheart'

Natalie frowned, struggling at first to comprehend what he meant, then she too looked across the road at the mayhem. Peter nodded at the garage, the workshop still well ablaze, but the fire in Des's office now under control.

'Two more of the *Keep Britain Straight* anti-gay brigade have been well and truly fried. Shame really, I liked working there.'

Natalie stared at him incredulously.

'You sick fuck!'

'Oh, and by the way, it won't be long before your colleagues are looking at some interesting photographs.'

She looked confused.

'What photographs?'

'Some snapshots of me and your husband making love… on your bed… in your house.' He smiled, as if enjoying the memory.

The two officers holding his arms exchanged a glance.

'You're lying. Thomas wouldn't have done that to me.'

'Oh wouldn't he? You can see your wallpaper and

bedside cabinet clearly in the pictures, even the photos on the cabinet.' He winked. 'There's plenty of choice. There's one where he's looking round at the camera and one where I've just…'

Natalie cut him short, quaking with anger.

'Take this piece of shit out of my sight and get him back to the station. Tell the custody officer I'll be there shortly!'

As he was dragged away, she could still hear him shouting.

'He fucking loved it, couldn't get enough!'

Peter was thrown into the van, which quickly moved off towards the police station.

Natalie stood on the grass verge, shaking with fury. She'd got her man, but he may well have got her too.

Meanwhile, in the police van, Peter looked through the bars of the cage as they pulled into the now familiar rear yard of Sevenoaks Police Station. He was now the killer of four men; did that make him a serial killer? He wasn't sure. Either way, he realised he didn't care.

They were four horrible bastards who were small-minded bullies and bigots. Four men who wouldn't be able to torment anyone else, ever again. They deserved to die.

He had run away from hatred, abuse, and bullying his whole life, but he wasn't running anymore. He was standing up for himself and for everyone like him and it felt great. In the custody suite, the part of the plan he'd been waiting for had finally arrived. This was an unusual event for the police in Sevenoaks; a multiple killer was in their custody and a large audience of officers from the station's various offices had arrived in the custody suite to see the infamous cop-killer.

After one of the uniformed officers had given evidence of arrest, the sour faced custody sergeant Bert Davies growled at Peter, 'Empty your pockets on the counter, remove your belt, and take off any jewellery.'

'Certainly, Sergeant, I've been looking forward to this.'

He carefully and deliberately removed every one of his possessions from his person, until with a final flourish he lifted the photographs from his pocket and theatrically dropped them onto the counter.

'There you go Sergeant, that's the lot.'

Davies and the two uniformed officers who'd taken him to the station, began picking up the pictures and there was an audible intake of breath.

'These are fucking disgusting,' said one of the officers, dropping one of the pictures as if frightened of contamination.

'Really? I think they are quite artistic myself. I'm rather proud of them.'

Davies peered more closely at the photo he was holding and frowned.

'I'm certain I know the face of the pervert you're with. I've seen him somewhere before.'

Peter smiled.

'Probably at a police event, Sergeant.'

'What do you mean?'

'His name's Thomas Neider, DCI Neider's husband.'

His words caused a stir, a wave of murmuring and expressions of surprise amongst the assembled officers, several more of whom stepped forward to scrutinise the pictures. It would appear that many of them had indeed seen him, or spoken to him, at social events.

'That's enough!' bellowed Davies, realising the delicate nature of the situation. 'If you're not directly responsible for a prisoner, I want you out... now!'

Half a dozen officers sheepishly replaced the photographs onto the counter and moved towards the door, which had just opened. As DCI Neider stepped into the room, a blanket of silence fell on the custody suite; nobody moved, nobody spoke, everyone except Peter looked uncomfortable.

Looking at the officers' faces and the pile of photographs on the counter, Natalie's face went white. She looked at Peter Hardy and knew he'd had the last laugh; her reputation was in tatters.

Seeing the expression on her face, Peter's heart soared; revenge on his tormentors was now complete. Looking forward to a lifetime in prison didn't faze him in the slightest. For the first time in his life, he felt truly free.

ACKNOWLEDGEMENTS

I'm grateful to SRL Publishing for their continued support in publishing Trans Mission. Like any author, I'm delighted to finally see it in print. The subject matter required extensive research and advice from many people, I thank them all from the bottom of my heart.

I'm indebted to Jamie, a neighbour of mine who was the inspiration for the story. He knew he'd been born into the wrong body from the age of 8. He explained to me in heart breaking detail the senseless prejudice that Peter/Petra in the story would have suffered.

My wonderful editor Gail Williams has once again turned my ramblings into a readable book, an impressive achievement! Thank you, Gail, you're amazing!

Many people kindly read largely unedited versions of Trans Mission and their feedback was greatly appreciated.

Yet again, my wife Virginia had to put up with me endlessly writing, something she suffers without complaint. Thank you darling, you're the best.

Finally, thank you to each and every one of you for reading this book. It means the world to me.